SON of the
FATHER

SON of the FATHER

Andrew Stone

AMBASSADOR INTERNATIONAL
GREENVILLE, SOUTH CAROLINA & BELFAST, NORTHERN IRELAND

www.ambassador-international.com

Son of the Father

ISBN: 978-1-62020-866-3
eISBN: 978-1-62020-887-8

Cover Design and Page Layout by Hannah Nichols
eBook Conversion by Anna Riebe Raats

Scripture taken from the Holy Bible, New International Version®, NIV® Copyright ©1973, 1978, 1984, 2011 by Biblica, Inc.® Used by permission. All rights reserved worldwide.

AMBASSADOR INTERNATIONAL
Emerald House
411 University Ridge, Suite B14
Greenville, SC 29601, USA
www.ambassador-international.com

AMBASSADOR BOOKS
The Mount
2 Woodstock Link
Belfast, BT6 8DD, Northern Ireland, UK
www.ambassadormedia.co.uk

The colophon is a trademark of Ambassador, a Christian publishing company.

With love and thanks to Alison for all your encouragement and belief.

He taught them many things by parables.

—Mark 4:2a

PROLOGUE

There are not many people who can say that a party ruined their life.
But I can.

It was harvest time on our farm and I was walking home from a tough day in the fields. As I approached home I saw far more lamps shining from the windows than normal. The sound of excited chatter, punctuated with raucous laughter, rose progressively louder and my nostrils were tantalised by the aroma of roast beef wafting out from the house before dissolving into the calm, still evening air.

I racked my brains trying to work out what was going on. My parents hadn't mentioned anything about a party that morning. In fact, my parents hadn't thrown a party for years – they weren't the type, particularly since my brother had turned the family on its head and my mother had become sick. They had mentioned something about a small celebration once the harvest was finished – but that was still at least a week away and the sight, sounds and smells that were assaulting my tired, aching body would never have been described as a small celebration.

I was not impressed at the prospect of having to face a house full of people. Twelve hours in the fields had left my twenty-one-year-old body aching and I was feeling far from in a party mood. I wanted to lie down and relax. Having left the fields pleased to have done a good day's work, however tiring it may have been, I could feel my mood changing at the prospect of a house full of people. I was shattered, and I wondered what had persuaded my parents to break a habit of a lifetime and throw a party that sounded as if most of the village were attending. Admittedly my two cousins Dan and Josh had been with me in the field but they were about as much help as their mother, and she had been dead for years.

As I wearily trudged on, puzzling over this unexpected turn of events, I heard the distinctive sound of my mother laughing.

I stopped dead in my tracks, utterly shocked. I wondered whether I had been mistaken, but then I heard it again. My mother was laughing, a sound I hadn't heard since she first became sick. I didn't know what was wrong with her. If I asked I only got an embarrassed 'women's problems' in reply and I reckoned that was all I needed to know. But whatever her problems were, I did know that the doctors' fees had eaten into our family's already diminished resources and left my mother the outcast of society.

Perhaps that was why my parents didn't throw parties.

But they were throwing one that evening, and my mother was laughing. There was only one explanation as far as I was concerned – my mother had been healed! By some miracle, one of the doctors must have actually justified their fee and brought her back to good health!

I was elated. This was good news, and God knew we were due some after the hardships of the past couple of years. Despite my aching limbs and painful back, I felt a new vitality surge through my body. I started to run towards home.

I should have known better.

As I approached the house I encountered one of our last remaining servants, Zacchaeus. He was young, about my age but physically he was a small lad and weak whereas I was tall, well-built and as strong as an ox. That's why I was working out in the fields rather than our servant. But Zacchaeus was cheap to employ which is why he had remained with us.

I'll never forget the smile on his face even though he was struggling to carry armfuls of food from one of the warehouses. I slowed my pace. Obviously, my parents were planning on the party going on for many more hours, so I had time to catch my breath and perhaps even rest a bit before I joined them all.

I paused to speak to the servant. 'That's quite some celebration my parents are holding,' I said between pants.

Zacchaeus beamed back at me.

'Yes, your brother's come back home.'

My fist connected with Zacchaeus' beaming smile. The armfuls of food he held dropped to the floor as his own hands instinctively flew up to his mouth and nose which were pumping out blood. Another blow, this time to his stomach, brought him to his knees, crushing and ruining the precious food as he collapsed on top of it. Even though I had spent days harvesting, I could not have cared less that some of it was going to waste. My fury was still not abated, and Zacchaeus quickly found himself prostrate amongst the pulp and mud as my foot contacted with his head leaving him stunned and trying to use his hands to defend himself from my blows.

I paused for breath, shocked at the way my temper had flared up. I was shaking, and I think it was in fear of the way my rage had consumed me. As I stood there I became aware of a soft whimpering coming from the servant. I didn't know how to react to what I had done, but I knew it wasn't his fault that my brother had returned or that my parents had thrown a party for him. The bile rose in my throat and I turned my head and threw up.

'Son?'

My father usually spoke with authority and even some harshness – particularly towards me – but the softness of his voice at that moment cut right through me. I looked up and saw him, just a few yards away, staring at me and the crumpled figure on the floor.

'What have you done, boy?' the authority had returned to his voice.

Without waiting for me to reply, my father walked over to Zacchaeus and bent down and touched his face. Zacchaeus murmured, and Father quickly drew his hand away.

'Thank God he's still alive.' He seemed to be genuinely concerned for his servant's welfare. 'Well, at least at the moment. He needs attention and soon. Help me carry him back into the house.'

'I'm not going in there!' I shocked myself with the force of my response. 'What are you doing throwing a . . . ' I stumbled over my words as I tried to keep my temper. 'What are you doing throwing a party for my pig of a brother? There's no way I'm going into the house if he's in there.'

'If you don't help me with this lad right now you'll be executed for murder.'

'I wish I was dead anyway!'

Without thinking about what I was doing, I turned and ran. My anger had given me a new burst of energy and I ran until I came into a field with an old, large sycamore tree in one corner. I sat behind the tree and wept. It was the first time I had cried since I had been a young boy. Through my tears I tried to think why my brother had returned. Surely, he had already done enough damage to the family already. And why had my parents accepted him back? They must remember what he had done – and the pain it had caused. They had never thrown me a party and yet I had been the one who had stayed with them, shown them loyalty, been the better child. Then my mind turned to Zacchaeus. Was he really so badly hurt? Could he die? What would happen to me if he did?

In the distance I noticed the sounds of the party had come to an abrupt end. Had a death brought the celebrations to a crushing end? I wondered what I should do next. It was getting cold and staying in the field all night was not an option, but I stayed where I was. I'm not sure how much time had passed, but the cold had reached through my sweat-drenched clothes and into my bones. I heard footsteps approaching. I looked round to see my father carefully finding his footing in the dark of the night as he made his way across the harvested field. In the darkness our eyes met, and Father made his way over to the tree and slowly sat down on one of the tree roots which had forced itself up out of the ground.

'Zacchaeus's going to be all right . . . eventually. But he'll not be any use for the rest of this harvest.'

I found it hard to understand why my father was so concerned about the health of a servant rather than the fact he had upset me by accepting my brother back into the family. There was no way Zacchaeus' life was ever in danger – he'd beaten up and hurt, but not anywhere near fatally. It didn't make any sense.

Without any notion of the confusion he was causing me, Father continued, 'Fortunately for you, your brother's spoken to him and convinced him to say he slipped and fell – not that anybody believes him, but they'll not make a fuss. You've a lot to thank Izzy for.'

I don't know if it was the use of my brother's pet name or the fact that Father thought I should be grateful to him that spurred me into leaping up from my perch and grabbing the old man by the front of his outfit.

'Are you stupid?' My face was just inches from his. I had raised him off the ground and was shaking him ferociously. 'I should be grateful to that scumbag after all he's done? What about you being grateful to me? What about you appreciating all I have done. The way I've worked my fingers to the bone for you and stayed with you after my brother betrayed us all? You've never even allowed me to have one of my mates round for a meal. But Izzy comes back home and the whole village is invited round to celebrate his return.'

The abject fear in Father's face was enough to cause me to let go of him. He stumbled but managed to find his footing. His composure returned as I tried to regain control of myself.

'Everything I own is yours, no one can take it away from you,' he replied. 'Isn't that appreciating what you've done? I know better than anyone the pain this family's been through. But for the past two years it's been as if your brother was dead. His coming home is like Izzy coming back from the dead. Your mother and I had to celebrate, don't you see that?'

'I don't know, I'm not sure about anything anymore.'

'I understand that it's hard for you. I'm going back to the house now. Think about what you're going to do and when you're ready, come home. You don't even have to see your brother tonight if you don't want to, but you need to understand that he's staying and you're going to have to work out how to deal with that fact.'

My father gingerly stepped over the harvested field as he carefully made his way back to the house. After he had walked just a few yards he stopped and turned around to face me.

'And Barabbas . . .'

'Yes?'

'However, you decide to handle it and whatever you decide to do, I'll understand.'

My father turned back and continued his walk. Later that night I followed in his footsteps and also went home. Once I was there I killed him.

PART ONE
JUDEA 28 AD

CHAPTER ONE

OF COURSE, THERE WERE DAYS I regretted killing my father, things had not gone great since then. But, almost ten years on, I was certain that things were going to get better again. For the first time that I could remember, I had a spring in my step and a smile on my face. At last I could finally imagine my long-held dream coming true. But there were risks attached to fulfilling that dream. If what I had planned went wrong, the consequences didn't bear thinking about.

But I had to take those risks after all that had happened since Father's death. In the days immediately afterwards, I convinced myself that he deserved it for his sheer stupidity in the way he treated my younger brother. I was always brought up with a firm hand, regularly beaten and punished normally, I always thought, more severely than my misdemeanours ever warranted. Izzy, however, could always get away with murder. Although, in fairness, it was me who had literally got away with murder on the night Izzy was allowed home after walking out on us two years earlier.

On that night, as I watched my father walk back towards the house, hatred rose up within me and took over my entire being. I hated Izzy for leaving us. I thought that, instead of throwing that party, Father should have thrown him back out onto the streets to rot. In that cold evening air as he walked away from me, I knew that was what our father should have done and so I hated him because he had welcomed Izzy back with open arms.

But more than anything else I hated myself. I had spent too many years allowing the rest of my family to walk all over me. Too many beatings had been accepted, too many slurs and slights. I was not the second-rate member of the family my parents treated me as. I was a man in my own right, hardworking, loyal and bright enough to see the way Izzy was taking advantage of all of us. At that moment I realised that everything had to change, and I had to take charge and put the situation right. The only way for that to happen was for me to become the head of the family and that meant Father had to die – and if the family was to be saved, he had to die that night.

I left the field and walked back towards the house and waited for my opportunity. Once the last light had been extinguished I silently crept through the door. My father and mother had slept separately ever since she had become ill and so there was no one near enough to hear my father's panicked, muffled cries as I smothered him with a pillow. He tried to fight back, to save himself, but he was old and weak and no match for the strong young man I was then. It probably helped that he had also consumed a lot of wine celebrating Izzy's return. Without a hint of remorse or sorrow for what I had done, I went to bed that night looking forward to being accepted as the head of the house which would mean my brother's return home would prove to be a very brief stay.

The next morning when the body was discovered it was assumed the excitement of Izzy's return had been too much for my father's old heart and that it had given up on him as he slept. Everyone accepted this version of events, everyone that is except my mother. As I got up that morning and found her weeping she gave me a look which told me she knew what had happened. My heart froze as I waited for the accusation. I doubted how well I could lie over something so important. But no accusation came. Instead she looked away and turned to Izzy for support and comfort. Father was buried the same day, and the word murder was never mentioned. But I never really got away with it because my punishment came in ways I had not anticipated.

My plans to head the family certainly never came to fruition. Although, as the eldest son, the position as the head of the family was mine by right, it was mother who took on the mantle. In a way I've known no other woman to ever do, particularly one who was ill, she dominated the whole household. I wanted to fight back, to claim the role which was rightfully mine, but, deep down, I knew I did not have the moral authority to do so.

That was when the regret started as it became obvious that Mother had no idea how to run a farm and I began to worry that the whole business would collapse. Mother made decisions that made no sense at all. She failed to understand the natural rhythms of the earth and crops began to fail under her stewardship. She also failed to understand the need to keep good staff on board. I was amazed when, one by one, she appeared content to let a number of workers who had been with us for as long as I could remember leave our employment.

As she tried desperately to find ways to save the farm, Mother began to develop the roles played by my cousins Dan and Josh. They had grown up with me and Izzy because their mother, my aunt, had died while they were still young children. I'm not sure what happened to their father, but I can only think that both of their parents had been mentally challenged because to call my cousins 'thick' would have been an understatement.

The farm continued to struggle. When Izzy had left the family two years earlier, he had taken a third of our fortune with him. As a result, the farm, which had been our family's business for generations, was already near financial ruin. As time passed after my father's death it became obvious that our suppliers and our customers were losing faith in our ability to keep going. One by one they slowly dropped us from their business plans and the farm, already weakened by Izzy's actions, finally fell into bankruptcy.

We had to leave and move into a small home in the village of Bethany, which, at best, could be described as a dung heap – or the part we lived in anyway.

I realised killing Father had been a pointless, evil thing to do. When I looked back I could not imagine how I had justified what I had done. I had deprived my own father, however flawed he may have been, of his life and I had no right to do that. I woke up each day weighed down with soul-consuming guilt. That guilt was only added to as I saw the long-term consequences of what I had done. The impact had been to destroy the standing of the family.

I decided I had to put matters right as far as I could. I couldn't bring Father back from the grave, but I could work to take us back to the farm. I worked all the hours I could to scrimp and save the funds to buy back the family's old small holding. I kept my eyes on the place. I was encouraged that nobody else came in and started to work the land that was once ours. The place went to rack and ruin which was immensely sad to see, but I knew it would mean that the value of the land would decline the more overgrown and under-cultivated it became and my dream was born.

I had worked years to try to get it back, but still I did not have anywhere near enough to buy it. I borrowed money from the usual sources to try to improve the situation, but the dream of owning the farm seemed to get more distant. The regrets I felt for killing my father grew with each passing day.

But not this day. Over the past few weeks I had gained some work with one of the newer patriarchs to the area. Reuben had moved to the outskirts of Bethany only in the past few months and although I had heard of his arrival our paths had never crossed until a month or so ago.

He had been looking to hire someone to carry out the heavier, manual work that needs doing in a household with wealth. Given that I am a good head and shoulders taller than most other men in the village and with a muscular physique that came from a lifetime of hard graft I wasn't too surprised when he approached me about the job.

He was a good boss. He expected me to work hard but he paid well, and he began to take an interest in me. He would ask about my background and, unusually for someone in his position, my aspirations. I was embarrassed to tell him about my dream for the farm, but he accepted it and wished me well in my efforts.

Then his good wishes turned to something more substantial. I had been working on the wall around his property. It was made of heavy stones which needed replacing from a quarry a mile and a half away. Over the past few weeks, I had been slogging my guts out dragging new stones to the wall to replace the old ones and now I was making the reverse journey, dragging the old stones to the quarry in part payment for the new ones that had been supplied.

With the sweat pouring down my back and my limbs crying out in exhaustion, I was surprised to hear footsteps coming up behind me.

'You've done well with that wall.'

I looked round, there was Reuben making his way towards me. He inspected my work and nodded appreciatively. I stopped what I was doing and wiped the sweat from my eyes and painfully straightened my back.

'I was thinking about your farm,' he said without taking his eyes from the stone work.

I stood still, my heart pounding, waiting to see where his thoughts about what he called 'my farm' had taken him.

'How much have you saved so far?'

'About enough to buy the path leading up to it,' I replied.

'What after nine years of hard work? I think you must have done a little better than that.'

'I don't know,' I said as I desperately tried to remember how much I had saved and work out where this conversation was going. 'Perhaps about a fifth of what it would cost to buy it.'

Reuben turned around to face me for the first time in the conversation. Taking his gaze away from the wall, he looked at me as if finally coming to some sort of judgement.

'I've been impressed by your work and I hope that you've felt that I have treated you in a proper way while you've been working here. So, I've come to make you an offer.'

He paused. I could hear my blood pulsing in my ears and feel my legs shaking. It was an eternity before he spoke again and put his offer to me.

'You give me the fifth that you have saved, and I will buy the farm with you. We'll be joint owners and you will pay me a third of what the farm makes until you have paid me back my initial outlay. Then you will pay me a fifth of the farm's profits for five years.'

The shake in my legs reached a point where they buckled under me. I reached out to grab the wall I had been working on to stop myself from falling over. After all those years of dreaming of buying the farm back it was finally within touching distance. We could be back in time to sow for next year's harvest. I opened my mouth but found that I couldn't utter a word. I stood there, leaning against the wall with my mouth open in disbelief.

'I take it we have a deal,' Reuben chuckled.

We did, and it was a deal that was going to change my life forever. But, at that point, I could not begin to imagine just how much.

CHAPTER TWO

THE SMOKE FROM THE FIRE inside the house really made my eyes smart.

I often wondered if it was because I had blue eyes that they were more sensitive. Anything from smoke to strong daylight bothered me more than anyone else. I was the only one who didn't have the dark eyes which normally go with our olive skin. I hated being different in that way. My mother told me that it was a throwback to a distant uncle on her side of the family. He was dead long before I was born so I grew up as the only kid in the area with freaky coloured eyes. Early in my childhood that had been a problem and left me at the mercy of older bullies. Fortunately for me, as I grew into my body and became as big, and then bigger than the kids who were older me, the bullying stopped as the others discovered I had a hard punch to go with my blue eyes.

But it didn't matter how big I got, my eyes were still more sensitive than anyone else I knew, and it was not long before tears were trickling down my face as I made my way into the room where Mother was cooking our evening meal. I have to admit though, that all the smoke in the world would not have wiped the smile off my face.

'You look very pleased with yourself.' Mother looked up from the pot she was tending to.

She was no great cook and the concoction she was creating that evening smelt no better than any of her other culinary efforts.

'I've had good news!' I exclaimed. I had intended not to say anything straight away, but it was impossible to stay silent. 'Reuben is going to provide the funding for us to buy back our farm.'

23

Mother gasped and the bowl she had just picked up to serve my dinner into was dropped into the cooking pot and sank to the bottom. Normally she would have been quick to salvage it but not now.

'Is this true?' she asked, her face a mixture of confusion and elation. 'How is he going to do that?'

'If we hand over a fifth of the price to him, he will buy the farm and allow us to work it, paying him back out of the profits.'

'You stupid boy,' a scowl shot across her face. 'We have to pay a fifth? How are we going to do that? We don't have enough money to come even close to that figure.'

She was right. My pride had made me inflate the level of resources I had available to me and when Reuben had made me the offer that same pride had stopped me from looking foolish and telling him the truth. But I wasn't going to admit that to my mother.

'I will get the money. I'll find some extra work. I'll borrow some more.'

'You'll saddle us further in debt?' Mother's voice began to rise. 'You'll do no such thing. This is where we belong now; this hovel is all we're good for and you might as well get used to that.'

I opened my mouth to reply but thought better of it. I knew I had taken risks in over inflating how much I told Reuben I had in savings and in being prepared to take on more debt. But I knew these risks were worth it if it meant getting back the farm. However, I also knew that my mother was a bitter, sick old woman with a tongue so vicious that there was no point in arguing with her. I turned around and walked out of the house before my tears from the smoke could be mistaken for the frustration and misery I was experiencing right then.

The worst part was, I knew she was right. The whole deal was terrible but reclaiming the farm had been my ambition since the day we were forced out and Reuben's offer had suddenly made the prospect of returning seem like more than just a pipedream. But could I borrow the funds I needed?

Over the next few days it became obvious how difficult it was going to be. In between my shifts at Reuben's I tried to get my finances into some form of order and discovered that I had less than half the money I needed.

I said nothing to my mother. I tried to avoid finding myself in a position where I was alone with her. Normally I found Izzy's and my cousins' company a chore, but during this time I was delighted to have them around as it meant that Mother was not able to say anything more to me about my plans. That suited me as I knew she would certainly not approve of what I had in mind and that she would see right through any lies I tried to tell her.

My plan was to go back to Benjamin, a money lender who had already extended us terms in the past that had enabled us to keep our heads above water when I was struggling to get regular work. He was a man who loved his money, but he was also a fair man and had a brain for enterprise. I approached him with my plans for the farm and explained the business proposition Reuben had put to me.

He was less than convinced. He said he could not see how I could repay the additional loan, plus what I already owed him while still keeping my obligations to Reuben. I pleaded with him and he told me to come back in three days so that he could think the proposition over.

They were a long three days. Reuben came to me on the second day and asked why I hadn't accepted his offer.

'I would have thought you would have bitten my hand off for it,' he said somewhat disappointedly. 'I was giving you a good deal and the opportunity to realise your dreams. Perhaps you're not the person I thought you were.'

He went to walk away. My heart was thudding in my chest. If he went now my hopes would be destroyed and I would probably lose my employment with him which had given me my most regular income for years.

'It's my brother,' I blurted out. 'He has a stake in the money, but he's been away and I've not had the chance to speak to him about it yet.'

'Really?' Reuben turned around to face me.

'Yes,' I lied as my mind raced to try to think about what I should say next. 'I'm sorry, I should have told you before now. Forgive me. But he's back now and I'll speak to him before I come into work tomorrow and then I'll speak to you again.'

Reuben shrugged his shoulders obviously not sure whether to believe me or not, but he said nothing as he turned around and walked away.

'Thank you!' I called after him. 'I do appreciate all that you are offering.'

I also appreciated the situation I now found myself in. I had to see Benjamin early the next morning and hope that would have given him long enough to make his decision. I could only pray – not something I did often – that he would agree to my request.

After a fitful night's sleep, I crept out of my home the next morning and made my way to Benjamin's house. I took the funds I had accumulated over the past nine years. It really amounted to very little for days of hard graft and going without and I was conscious that I only really had these funds because I had previously borrowed from Benjamin. In the past I had made some late payments, but I had always caught up in the end and I hoped that would count in my favour.

It was very early when I knocked on Benjamin's door. The look on his servant's face, and his dishevelled state, told me immediately that, in his opinion, it was too early for visitors, but he still let me in. I explained the reason for my visit and he told me that it was far too early to speak to his master when the door to room we were in flew open.

'What's all this noise down here?'

Benjamin, fresh from his bed by the look of him, stormed into the room.

'You!' he exclaimed when he saw me. 'What do you mean by disturbing my sleep and getting me out of bed at this hour of the morning?'

Even at the distance there was between us I could smell that awful breath of someone who hasn't drunk yet that day. I could also smell the stench of failure. I had panicked. I had lied unconvincingly to Reuben and put myself in a position where I had to have an answer for him before I went to work this morning. In my haste I had disturbed Benjamin's sleep and, in the process, ruined any chance of receiving his financial support. I was finished. My dream was over, and my employer would feel insulted because I would turn down his offer. I turned to leave, mumbling an apology on my way out.

'Wait.'

I stopped and turned back to face Benjamin who I saw had picked up a glass of wine which he was gulping down like a man dying of thirst. As he was obviously not going to speak again until he had finished his drink, I waited as instructed. I tried to think why he would want me to stay. Then I realised that, having angered him so much he was going to call in the loans I already had with him. My heart sank.

After he had drained the cup he placed it down on the table from where he had taken it and belched loudly. He wiped the back of his hand across his mouth before speaking again.

'You came to me with a business proposition,' he said. 'As you are here and as I am, much against my wishes, out of bed and here with you, I might as well give you my answer.'

'There's no need. I understand. I'm sorry to have bothered you.'

'I will give you the money.'

I wanted to ask him to repeat himself, but I knew that would be a mistake. Instead I stood there not knowing what to say or do.

'Well, what are you standing there for? I've made arrangement with my treasurer James who will provide the necessary funds when he starts work this morning. I suggest you go and see him to sort out the legal necessities.'

With that Benjamin walked out of the room. I looked at the servant who had opened the door to me. He said nothing but showed me out of the house. I walked into the fresh morning air in a state of amazement. I looked around me and everything seemed brighter, all the colours more vivid and the bird song more tuneful than I had ever heard before.

I stood still and savoured the moment. Finally, something in my life had gone right. The farm would be mine. I could atone for killing Father and destroying my family's life. This would be a new beginning of a better life. I realised that I was receiving some strange looks from the few people who were around at that time in the morning. It must have been unusual to see a grown man standing in the middle of the street grinning broadly to himself.

Then I realised. I had no idea who James was or where to find him.

CHAPTER THREE

REVENGE WAS THE FUEL THAT powered Zacchaeus' life and this time it was proving to be so sweet he wondered if it was possible for life to get any better.

It was what he deserved after all that had happened him. Whenever he looked back on his early life, evidence of his mistreatment at the hands of others was everywhere to be seen. And those others were primarily members of Barabbas' family.

Zacchaeus' first misfortune was that his entry into the world was shrouded in mystery. At no time could he remember knowing either of his parents. He understood that he was a child who never had a father. This was something he was happy to accept until his knowledge increased enough for him to realise that there had to be a man, and therefore a father, involved. From that point on and into his late teens the story about his father changed. Originally, he was told that he died, then that he had moved away until finally the story was that his mother was a loose woman who had no idea who his father was.

Zacchaeus never had the opportunity to discover the truth of any of these accounts from the woman who gave birth to him. His mother died shortly after he had made his first wailing appearance into the world.

This had left him at the mercy of charity and it had been Barabbas' parents who had, in public at least, done the decent thing and brought him up, although certainly not as one of their own. For as long as he could remember, Barabbas' mother, Elizabeth, had been brutal in her treatment of him. She was far harder with him than she was with any of the other servants. Every dirty, unpleasant or dangerous job was always given to him and if someone needed to be blamed for something then it was only a short matter of time before Elizabeth sought out Zacchaeus. It was amazing that he lasted as long as he did on the farm. Amazing that he didn't run away or that he wasn't dismissed, but that, he felt sure, had something to do with Barabbas' father.

Simon was a good man. While Elizabeth had treated Zacchaeus like dirt, Simon had treated him in a way a good master treated all his servants. There were even times when Zacchaeus was sure he detected Simon trying to make up for the mistreatment he received from Elizabeth. But that was probably just his imagination as he tried to find someone in the world who he might be able to consider was even remotely on his side.

What was not his imagination was Simon's treatment of Barabbas. Although the father's firmness with his eldest son was not on the same scale as the treatment Zacchaeus received from Elizabeth, Simon was sometimes so hard on Barabbas, and in front of the servants, that it took Zacchaeus' breath away.

But that was not all that took his breath away when it came to his master's son. Zacchaeus could not say when it was he realised he was in love with Barabbas. Growing up he had always been drawn to the lad who, because of his size and build, looked so much older than him when in reality only about a year separated their ages. By the time he was twelve Barabbas was head and shoulders above the rest of the household, including his parents, whereas Zacchaeus was smaller. There was nothing special about him, nothing to make him stand out in the crowd like Barabbas' blue eyes made him look distinctive and attractive at the same time.

Zacchaeus' small build meant that the hard graft of farm labouring left him exhausted often before lunchtime. But those tough days in the fields were worth every aching limb and blister as it allowed him to work alongside his idol and, as the heat increased, and Barabbas stripped down to the barest minimum of clothing, watch every rippling muscle and rivulet of sweat on his body.

The torment Zacchaeus went through at this time just added to his own feeling of the unfairness of life. The Scriptures made it clear that feeling the way he did towards Barabbas was not normal and wrong. But no amount of ritual cleaning could wash away the feelings he had, and the sense of confusion melted away to a sense of awe whenever he was in Barabbas' presence.

That was why the night Barabbas had attacked him, he left him not only with a broken nose but a broken heart as well. He thought Barabbas would have been pleased to have his brother home, but the rage and venom with which he attacked him demonstrated beyond doubt that Zacchaeus had seriously misjudged the situation and that he had also misjudged Barabbas. The guy was a bully, hard-hearted, and totally without any remorse for what he had done.

As that first fist thumped into his face, Zacchaeus' feeling went from those of adulation to hatred. It was only because Simon had promised him a none too small sum of money that Zacchaeus told a story releasing Barabbas from any blame for his battered appearance.

But then Simon died before he had given the money. Zacchaeus waited until after the funeral and approached Elizabeth about the matter. He was not optimistic of her giving him the promised sum. What he had not expected was that, instead of giving him the money, she gave him his marching orders. She told him to leave the farm and never return. As he left the property without a penny to his name Zacchaeus decided that was the last abuse he was going to take from that family or anyone else come to that. He had lived the first twenty years of his life miserably accepting his lot. Now, things were going to change. And life was going to change for the family who had mistreated him the worst.

The farm had struggled since Izzy had left a couple of years beforehand and Zacchaeus was determined to ruin the family for good. It amazed him how a well-placed word with the right person could set off a whole chain of events. He had found work with one of the farm's main trading partners. Of course, he hadn't got anywhere near to the master, but he did meet the head steward at the end of every day to receive his basic wage. After spending three days working out exactly what he should say, he hung around as the queue of men waiting to receive their money formed, ensuring he was the last to get paid. As he approached the bench, he suggested that his previous employer was struggling to meet all their current financial obligations, which was true, and that they were devising a plan to undercut his new employers, which was not true.

What Zacchaeus discovered that day was that a lie accompanied by a grain of truth was far more likely to be believed. After his new master had spent a couple of days looking into his trading partners' finances he believed the message his chief servant had passed on. All business with Barabbas' family farm ceased. Within a few months, no one else was willing to work with Barabbas' family and the farm went under.

For Zacchaeus, the opposite was true. He was rewarded for his action and rapidly made his way up the servant's pecking order. He continued to scheme and lie his way through life until eventually he had established enough contacts to start his own business in money lending and, materially at least, life became good. With his increasing wealth he moved to the more affluent city of Jericho, where he enjoyed a pampered, wealthy life as a money lender and tax collector.

But still Zacchaeus had unfinished business with Barabbas. He had deprived him of his farm, but that was not enough. He had wasted too many years idolising the brute. He wanted to destroy him. Zacchaeus could go days without thinking about Barabbas. But then he would wake in the middle of the night thinking about him and wanting him to suffer more. Sadly, he could never think of a way to achieve that until, one day, the man's cousins, Dan and Josh, visited Jericho and Zacchaeus saw them drinking outside a local tavern.

He had never understood why Barabbas had continued to take responsibility for them even though they were older than him. But while Zacchaeus remembered them it was clear they had no recollection of him at all. So, when he stopped to sit outside the tavern just along from where the two of them were sitting they ignored his presence and continued with their conversation.

'He's convinced he's going to do it one day,' said Josh.

'Never,' replied Dan. 'There's no way he could ever pull off something like that.'

'I don't know, you know what Barabbas is like when he gets an idea in his head.'

'But buy the old farm back? It's been years since we lost that place and he's no nearer having the money to buy it now than he did when he first mentioned it nine years ago.'

Josh said something in reply which Zacchaeus failed to hear as a group of women, chatting noisily walked past the tavern. The women's arrival was enough to distract Josh and Dan from their conversation as they watched the group make its way down the street.

Zacchaeus got up from his seat and walked in the other direction from the women. His brain was whirring with excitement. So, Barabbas had dreams of buying back the old family farm, did he?

He could almost taste the sweetness on his lips as he plotted his plan to wreak revenge on a man he had once adored.

CHAPTER FOUR

IT DID NOT TAKE ME long to find where James lived or to complete the necessary formalities for me to receive the money I needed to be able to hand Reuben a fifth of the value of the farm.

It was still early morning, but I felt as if I had already completed an entire day's work when I arrived at Reuben's. I was surprised to find that he wasn't there; one of his servants told me he had headed out early on business. It struck me as amusing that both of us had been up with the dawn looking to do deals, although I guessed that my concerns were small compared to someone like Reuben. However, I doubted if his business was as exciting to him as mine was to me.

Or as important.

It took no time at all for my amusement to be rapidly replaced by concern. Reuben knew I was coming over that morning with the money to complete my side of the deal. In fact, it was him who had demanded I should. So why was he not here to allow me to show my good faith in keeping my side of the bargain? As the morning dragged on and there was still no sign of my employer and potential business partner's return, more worrying thoughts filled my head. Had he decided to go ahead and buy the farm without me? Perhaps I had come across too keen to acquire the property and prompted him to purchase it for himself.

I kept telling myself that I was worrying for no good reason, but my agitation grew worse with every moment Reuben was away. Somewhere within me, I knew something had gone wrong and that my dreams would be shattered.

I had so fully convinced myself of this that, by the time Reuben appeared just after lunch, my stomach lurched. I stopped my work on the wall as he walked towards me. I tried to judge from his face whether all my hopes had been in vain. His face was a mask; it was almost as if he was trying not to show any emotion. That worried me. What was he trying to hide? It had to be bad news. I braced myself as he started to speak.

'Well, Barabbas, have you got the money?'

'Yes,' I said guardedly waiting to see what would come next.

'If you give it to me now, I'll go and do the necessary negotiations.'

'What?' I asked, a smile growing across my face. 'You mean we're going ahead as we agreed? I'll be able to move back to the farm?'

'If you give me the money.'

I had expected Reuben's excitement to match my own, but he almost seemed downcast about the entire enterprise. But my own excitement was enough for the two of us. I had kept the funds close to me right throughout the morning and I quickly bent down to hand them over to him, almost spilling the money in my haste.

'Thank you so much,' I said as I struggled to hand it over in full to him. 'You have no idea what this means to me.'

'I think I do,' he replied as he took hold of the money and turned around. He began walking away but then stopped and turned back to me. 'It could take the rest of the day to get this sorted out. You might as well go home now and come back tomorrow morning when we can make the necessary arrangements between ourselves.'

'Ok, if you're sure. And thanks again Reuben. This is fantastic.'

The two of us parted and I picked up my remaining stuff and began to walk home. Never again would I have to be a hired man. From the next day I was going to be running my family's farm again, restoring my family's fortunes and pride. I was going to atone for killing my father in the best way I could have possibly imagined.

I decided not to tell the others what was going on or why I had returned from work early. In her normal fashion, my mother decided I could only be home because I had been sacked. It made for a tense and unpleasant evening, but I was immune to it all. Life was going to be very different from tomorrow and mother would see how wrong she had been.

The morning, though, took a long time to come. I hardly slept at all and was up as soon as the first rays of the sun appeared. Since it was too early to see Reuben I decided to visit my new property. It took me a good couple of hours to walk over there but I barely noticed. The anticipation of all the day held and the excitement of knowing that I would be taking this route again later on in the day with my family as they also returned home meant the time sped past and I was at the farm before I knew it.

Before walking up to the farm house I paused and reflected on the evening when Izzy had returned, and I had killed my father. The guilt of my anger-fuelled actions could finally be washed away. Perhaps a return to her old home would even help my mother's health. She had been ill for so many years now. Of course, my father was no longer with us, but at least I had restored my family's fortunes and returned our home to us. I began to laugh. There was nothing funny about the situation, but I could not contain my joy.

'What are you doing here? This is private property.'

The man was a thug, obviously a hired heavy willing to take anyone on. He must have heard my laughing and come out to see what maniac was cackling uncontrollably outside the house he had evidently spent the night in. It made me laugh all the more when I saw him look at me and realise that I was bigger than he was. I guessed that was not something he was used to. It took him only a few moments to regain his composure.

'Get lost,' he said as he advanced towards me.

'This is my property.'

'Yours?' Confusion was etched over his face. 'You're not the person I'm working for here.'

Obviously, Reuben had hired someone to guard the place before I moved in. I was impressed with his efficiency.

'No, but I'm Reuben's business partner so you don't need to worry.'

The confusion remained on the man's face. Reuben's name clearly did not mean anything to him. My heart began to beat faster as the first hints of concern came into my mind.

'It was Reuben who hired you, wasn't it?' I asked.

The guy shifted his stance; he unconsciously ran his fingers through his hair. Obviously not very bright, he was contemplating how to deal with a situation.

'I don't know what his name was,' he replied. Everything about his body language and tone of voice told me he was lying. 'But I know I'm not to let anyone on this land. I suggest you go and get this Reuben and bring him here, so we can get this sorted out.'

I was suddenly aware that my breathing had sped up. I could feel the colour rising in my cheeks. Something was not right. The man was right, I needed to find Reuben but there was something I wanted to know first.

'Are you sure you can't remember the name of the guy who hired you?' I asked walking in what I hoped was a menacing way towards the hired muscle. I saw a trace of panic flicker across his eyes as I approached. I think it may have been the first time he had doubted his ability to win if it came to a fight.

'I dunno,' he said taking a barely noticeable step back. 'Something like . . . no, I'm not sure.' Clearly, he was worried that a wrong answer would not be good for his health. 'I don't worry much about the name as long as they pay me for my work.'

There was no point in pushing him any further. It was obvious that it was not Reuben who had hired him, but he was too scared to tell me who did. I decided wasting my time here was only delaying me finding Reuben, so I turned around and started my walk back towards Bethany and Reuben's property.

The walk back seemed much longer. I kept trying to convince myself that Reuben had asked one of his other workers to hire a guard for the property but all that long walk a nagging doubt shouted louder and louder at the back of my head. Eventually I reached my destination. I banged on the door desperate to speak to Reuben so that my mind could be put at rest. It may have just been my sense of urgency affecting my judgement, but it was a very long time before the door was finally answered. I was sorry to see Reuben's principle servant stood there rather than the man himself.

'Where's Reuben?' I demanded too uptight to worry about general niceties with a man I had met a few times while we had shared the same employer.

'The master has left,' his servant replied. 'There was a personal situation that arose, and we don't anticipate him returning in the near future. He instructed me to pass on his sincere apologies that he was not able to secure the farm for you.'

I wanted to cry. 'Why not?'

'I'm afraid I don't know that information. But I am to inform you that your services will no longer be required here.'

'My services!' I could feel my rage igniting inside me. 'Never mind about my services! What about my money?'

I noticed the merest hint of a smirk on the other man's face.

'I really wouldn't know,' he said, shutting the front door at the same time as he spoke.

In that moment my worst fears were confirmed. I had been conned. Reuben had never intended to buy the farm with me. He had just been after my money. I beat on the door repeatedly shouting incoherent curses and damnations until my fists bled. This was not right. Today was meant to be the day that I atoned for my past sins and all that had happened as a result to my family. Instead of which I had been robbed of the little I did have and the huge amount I had borrowed.

It took me much longer than normal to return from Reuben's house to my own. I spent much of the walk cursing myself for my own stupidity, for being so gullible. What an idiot. What was my mother going to say? I was in no hurry to arrive back home. I wanted to buy myself some drink hoping it might deaden the sense of hopelessness that had overcome me, but all my money was gone.

By the time I finally plucked up the courage to return home and face Mother it was lunchtime. My mother would not be in. Because of her ongoing illness she could only go to the well to gather water in the middle of the day. The other women in village went in the morning but she was barred from their company because her illness made her unclean and unable to enjoy other people's company.

I still had not decided how I was going explain what had happened to her, Izzy, or Josh and Dan for that matter, but at least I could be assured of some solitude with no one else at home.

As I turned the final corner in my journey home I realised that solitude was not going to be possible as I came face to face with Benjamin, the man who had lent me the money for the farm. My plan had been not to let him know about what had happened and just work to make the repayments as we had agreed. It was going to be difficult, but I couldn't think of any other alternative. I wondered why he was waiting outside the house and concluded the reason would not be good news for me.

He spotted me and walked down the street to meet me. His face was a picture of anger.

'Barabbas you lying scum bag!'

I opened my mouth but not a word came out.

'I've just spoken to a gentleman who told me your old farm was sold last night – but not to you. Therefore, I want the money I lent you to buy it returned immediately.'

'I haven't got it . . . ' My brain refused to keep up with what was going on. 'Why can't I just pay you back as we agreed?'

'Because I understand you never intended to buy the farm in the first place. The previous owner said he had no agreement with you. I don't like being lied to and so I want the money back.'

'But I haven't got it.'

'Well, you'd better have it by the end of tomorrow or else you will be in very serious trouble.'

With that Benjamin walked away leaving me standing outside my house with a head full of questions I had no answers for.

How could I explain that I thought the negotiations for the farm had been done through Reuben, a man who had now cleared off and left the area with the money I had given him without a legal contract between us?

Then I wondered who had told Benjamin about the sale of the farm? Other than my creditor and my mother, I had kept the whole plan to myself. If Reuben was planning on stealing the money why would he have told anyone else, surely, they would have stopped him?

But, the most important question of all was, how on earth was I going to get my hands on any money between now and tomorrow evening? I knew that if I didn't my life could be as good as over.

CHAPTER FIVE

DESPERATE TIMES CALL FOR DESPERATE measures and my situation certainly ranked high on the desperation stakes.

In just a few days my life had been ruined and I felt all the more miserable because of the hope I had experienced at the start of those days. I still could not work out how it had all gone so horribly wrong. How had I misjudged Reuben and trusted him with all of my money? How had Benjamin found out so quickly and why had he demanded his money back immediately when he would have known that I had no way to pay him?

I had spent a fair part of the previous day trying to find the farm's owner. It was well into the evening before I did. He had been out, celebrating the sale, and was worse the wear for drink. He had managed to sober up once I confronted him. It never ceases to amaze me how frightening some people find me! But he refused point blank to tell me who he had done business with, continually saying that he had been given extra money to keep his mouth shut. I could only surmise that whoever the purchaser was projected an even more frightening persona than me, although that knowledge was of no help to me whatsoever.

It was as if God was bringing about His final judgement on me for murdering my father and the result would be that I would be sold into slavery because of my debts, me and the rest of my family.

That is what had led me to the point where I had been hiding for hours in the rocks along the Jericho road with the sun beating down and with the heat unbearable even in the shade. It was now midday and I was hot and uncomfortable, and my tongue was sticking to the roof of my mouth. I needed a drink, but I had already drunk every drop of water I had brought with me. I looked across the road to where I knew Josh and Dan were hiding.

'Have you got anything left to drink?' I asked.

'No, it's all gone,' came back the reply although I wasn't sure which of my cousins answered. The voice continued. 'This is a waste of time Barabbas. Why don't we go home and see how many purses we can steal tomorrow when it's market day. There's always a crowd of people about then.'

I was sorely tempted to go along with the suggestion. We had been staking out the road, looking for someone to rob since the morning but without encountering a single potential victim. Groups had travelled past, too large to be threatened by three bandits, but not a single individual.

I could hardly say I was surprised. The road was well known for its dangers. Robbers had a multitude of hiding places from which to spring out and relieve travellers of their wealth — and sometimes their lives. People knew that if the road had to be used it was best to travel in large groups. Only the foolish or a stranger made their way from Jericho to Jerusalem by this route.

Trying to steal purses on market day probably did make more sense but I didn't have the luxury of waiting until tomorrow. Benjamin had made it clear that he wanted his money back that evening and, not being a criminal mastermind, this was the best idea I could come up with for getting my hands on the money.

I was not keen on resorting to theft in this way but what else could I do? The consequences of not having the money by the end of the day did not bear thinking about although, as I sat there in the small recess of one of the large roadside rocks, I constantly wondered if I would have the nerve to actually carry out my plan. A part of me was secretly relieved that nobody had been dumb enough to travel the road alone. However, Josh and Dan did not appear to share my reluctance. When I had privately taken them to one side at the start of the day and told them my plan they had been keen to come with me. In their simple-minded way they appeared to see it as some sort of adventure.

I was just about to end the adventure when my cousin's voice cut through my thoughts.

'There's someone coming.'

'What? Where?'

'Are you blind? Up from Jerusalem. He's on his own.'

I looked down the road and saw him. It was a man making his way unsuspectingly towards us. My breathing became shallow and I could feel my heart racing. It was now or never. Could I attack this man? Could I steal whatever he had on him? If I did would I ever be the same person again? I tried to work out what sort of a man he was.

As far as I could see he was not exactly poor, but neither was he flouting any sort of wealth. He looked worried, nervously glancing around him, obviously aware of the risks he was taking travelling this road alone. I picked up a large stone I had found earlier in the day, ready to use as a weapon against whoever I selected as my victim. As the man came within a few hundred yards of where I was hiding I started to doubt if I could go through with the attack. This man was just trying to make his way in the world the same as me, what right did I have to rob him of what he had? My situation was desperate, that was what had got me to this point, but the nearer the man got the less certain I became of my ability to go through with my plan.

Just as he was drawing level with me I decided that I was going to let him pass. Then I saw Dan and Josh leap out from their hiding places on the other side of the road. The man stopped dead in his tracks letting out a startled cry. He looked at my two cousins who looked back at him, all three seemed uncertain of what should happen next. Then the man darted away from them. Josh lunged after him, grabbing his tunic, but the man was able to shake him off and head further towards my side of the road. He began scrambling around in his bag as he moved. I was sure he was looking for a weapon to use against Dan and Josh and in a moment of sheer impulse I sprang from my hiding place with a roar. The man looked up in shock and horror as I leapt towards him and, with the fist that was still wrapped around the stone, smashed him in the face. He didn't stand a chance. He immediately fell backwards and clattered to the ground, hitting his head on a small rock.

I yelled with pain and dropped the stone wondering if I had managed to break a bone or two in my own hand. I looked at it, but it was covered in my victim's blood. When I looked down at him my blood ran cold. I thought he was dead. He was lying still with a steady trickle of blood coming from the back of his head.

As if reading my mind, Dan dropped down on one knee and felt for a pulse.

'He's alive.'

I thought I was going to be sick. I had hesitated over attacking the man, I certainly did not want another murder on my conscience.

'Should I look to see what's in his bag?' Dan asked.

I nodded my head.

Dan picked up the cloth bag and peered inside. He looked up at me as he turned the bag upside down and allowed the content to fall out onto the dusty road. The content consisted of a hammer — which undoubtedly would have been the weapon he had been reaching for — a chisel, and an assortment of other stone masonry tools. Worth a fortune in the hands of their owner who could earn a living from his craftsmanship, but worthless to me and the other two.

I sank to my knees in despair. The man was half dead and yet we had gained nothing from the attack. I still had no way of paying back my creditors. My plan had failed, just as every idea I had failed. Suddenly the hand I had hit the guy with began to throb.

'What do we do now?'

It was Josh who broke the silence. It was a fair question but one I did not know the answer to. My plan had been to attack, rob, and then clear off with the plunder. I had never given any consideration about what would happen to our victim once we had relieved him of the wealth. My plan certainly did not envisage us robbing someone who had nothing worth stealing and whose life hung in the balance as a result of our attack.

I stood up and looked at the scene. The man was still bleeding, and his breathing looked to me as if it had become shallower. I shook my head, trying to focus my thoughts. Josh and Dan stood where they were, not moving a muscle.

I was about to ask them what they thought we should do when some movement further down the road caught my attention. We had taken our eyes off the road and now a group of people travelled towards us from Jericho and up towards Jerusalem.

I looked down at the man I was convinced was dying before looking back at the group heading our way. We were going to have to act quickly if we weren't going to find ourselves accused of murder and facing execution. The next few moments could shape the rest of our lives — and decide whether they were going to last beyond the next few days.

CHAPTER SIX

'QUICK! THERE ARE PEOPLE COMING!'

My words acted like a crack of a whip on the other two. They took their
eyes off the man and looked down the road to where my eyes were focused.
Instinctively they scurried across the road to a hiding place further back than
their original one. It was only a matter of seconds before I joined them. I
looked back down the road. There were three, no four, people. I cursed my
over-sensitive blue eyes as I squinted in the sunlight to try to determine how
the group was made up and the threat they posed to us.

As the group got nearer I realised that two of them were travelling at the
front of the party, another was following just behind them, and then the
fourth was a few yards behind again.

As the group neared I understood the reason for the travelling order. The
two at the front were holy men. One of them was certainly a priest, the other
one was a Levite. Two important and wealthy individuals. I could not believe
that I had picked a poor workman to attack on the road. The priest and his
high-ranking friend were probably on their way to the temple in the city.
Just behind them was one of the temple lads, probably the priest's servant.
He was carrying a lot of bags for his master that would have contained a fair
amount of wealth, but the servant looked strong and certainly a match for me,
particularly with my painful hand.

The last member of the party was probably a Samaritan judging by his
outfit. He had with him an old donkey which carried a considerable load on its
back. I could not believe that this was another prime target that I had missed
out on. The priest and Levite would have hated travelling with the Samaritan

because they would have considered him beyond contempt — there was no love lost between a Jew and a Samaritan. But, when it came to travelling the Jericho to Jerusalem road, there was safety in numbers and the higher the number, the greater the safety. Having a fourth member of the party, even if he did have to walk a few yards behind, made enough sense to overlook the undesirability of that person.

As they approached our victim the party's pace slowed down noticeably. I was too far away to see their faces, but I could imagine the look of initial concern turning into one of fear as the four realised they were approaching the scene of a crime. This was a dangerous time for us. The priest and the Levy were holy men, but they also upheld the law and if they decided to send their servant and the Samaritan to search for the outlaws their testimony would be enough to convict all three of us and sentence us to our deaths.

I was certain that neither Dan nor Josh would have the nerve to resist a priest. They certainly didn't follow every one of our Jewish customs, but they would never consider disobeying such a revered person. No, if the priest decided to investigate what had gone on I knew that we were done for.

I held my breath as I watched the priest and the Levite stop, forcing those in their wake to do likewise. They were evidently in discussion over what they should do next. Would they investigate the scene? Would they help their fellow countryman?

Of course, they did not know who we were. Not every bandit on this road would have the same scruples as my cousins. Potentially hanging around the scene of the attack could put the travelling party in danger. I realised that they might decide to get away from the area as soon as possible.

Of course, if they were heading to the temple then they would not want to go near the body at all. For all they knew, the man might already be dead and, according to their religious rules, touching a corpse would prevent them from carrying out their holy duties for a week. I started to hope that they would move on and leave the scene entirely.

But I still held my breath, waiting to see what they would do. Their indecision seemed to last a lifetime. I was aware that Josh and Dan, hiding next me, were also barely breathing as they too waited to see the outcome.

Then the priest and the Levite turned, said something to the other two in hushed tones and promptly walked around the man on the ground giving him as wide a birth as possible. Their fellow companions followed suit.

I finally let out my breath. We may have missed potentially rich victims, but at least we were not longer in danger of arrest. Then the Samaritan stopped and looked back. He stopped walking and appeared to stare at the helpless man on the road. The other three initially continued their journey, unaware that one of the party was not with them. Then the priest looked around. He stumbled and almost fell in surprise at his companion's actions. He called out, telling the Samaritan to keep going, but his instructions were met with a shake of the head. By this time the other two had also stopped to see what was happening. The trio looked at each other and with an exaggerated shrug of their shoulders turned and continued their walk, leaving the Samaritan to whatever fate had in store for him.

'We could overpower him if he's on his own,' Josh whispered excitedly. 'With that donkey and whatever it's carrying we'd get a load of money from him.'

'Not yet,' I hissed back, throwing out an arm to stop Josh from charging back down onto the road. I knew he was right, but there was something wrong with what I was seeing. Samaritans didn't help Jews, this man with his donkey was up to something and before I committed myself to action I wanted to see what it was.

The Samaritan gingerly approached the injured man on the ground. He was obviously worried he may be walking into a trap. He examined the man while constantly glancing all around him, aware that a group of bandits could jump out of hiding at any time.

'We're not going to get you yet my friend,' I mumbled to myself, still uncertain of what I was witnessing.

The Samaritan sat the other man up and appeared to start rifling through his clothes. At that I wondered if I was watching another criminal, an opportune thief who wanted to see if the victim had given up all of his valuables. But my opinion changed as I watched the Samaritan fiddle with the injured man's clothing and expose his naked flesh.

'He's a pervert!' I hissed.

I had seen enough and went to push myself up to attack. But the effort sent my hand into a new level of agony and stopped me from making any progress. Then I realised I had been wrong about my assessment of what I was watching. Almost as quickly as the Samaritan had exposed the mason's body he covered it up again. I realised he had been checking for other injuries. The Samaritan went to his donkey and brought out some oil and cloths. As he sat the other man up, he began to treat his head injuries.

'This is our chance.' Josh looked at me, waiting for the order to attack.

But I shook my head. I could barely believe what I was seeing. This man was helping a complete stranger and endangering his own life in the process. It didn't make any sense. But what made even less sense was what happened next. The Samaritan helped the other man to his feet and placed him on his already over-burdened donkey. Once he had made sure the patient was securely mounted on the uncomplaining animal, he restarted his journey towards the city.

I was stunned. In all my thirty-one years I had never witnessed anything like it. Why would someone behave like that and help a complete stranger from a country which hated his own?

'Why didn't we attack him?' asked Dan, who I think was equally as confused but his confusion was that we had allowed the Samaritan to get away. Dan appeared oblivious to the act of kindness which had so stunned me.

'Yeah,' spat Josh. 'We've missed out on a fortune there, you moron. You owe us big time.'

'I owe *you?*'

Josh's words beggared belief. I turned to face my cousins.

'I have kept you for years, you ungrateful gits.' As I spoke I moved towards them, making sure I kept my bad hand out of harm's way.

I had had enough of these two. I knew that they had lost their place on the farm because of me but I had done everything I could to try and look after them and make sure they had a roof over their heads. I couldn't believe they were now saying that I owed them. How dare they! They owed everything they had in life to me and I was only too ready to remind them of that fact.

Josh and Dan, though, were not interested in being reminded. They ran out from their hiding place, away from the road, and into the wilderness which ran alongside it.

'See you later, Barabbas!' one of them shouted.

I was worried they would be seen by the Samaritan as he made his way towards Jerusalem, but he was preoccupied by his patient.

I watched Josh and Dan run, and then looked back at the blood stains my victim had left on the road. As I watched the blood dry in the heat I tried to understand why I had failed to attack the Samaritan when he was at my mercy. I had attacked the stone mason only a few moments beforehand, so why hadn't I taken advantage of a situation that in all likelihood would have provided the solution to my debt problems? The man undoubtedly was wealthy and, with three of us to attack him, would have been easy to overpower.

I cursed my inaction. Why had I shown any mercy when my situation was so desperate? But what I had seen had amazed me. I struggled to comprehend why a man would endanger himself and help a total stranger. Shamefully, I knew I would not do it, but perhaps that was the difference between the rich and the poor. The poor have to grab every opportunity they can to improve their lot. But if that was the case, why had I failed to do that?

'Forget it,' I said to myself, clenching my fists in frustration.

As I did, my hand reminded me of the pain the attack on the stone mason had caused and warned me that, because of my failure to steal anything of worth on the road, I could expect more pain and misery when Benjamin took action over the money I owed him.

I was certain he wouldn't be as merciful as that Samaritan.

CHAPTER SEVEN

I TOOK MY TIME MAKING my way home. I was in no hurry to encounter Benjamin, or his thugs — and I was in no hurry to tell my mother that I had landed myself, and the family, in such dreadful debt that all of our futures were in danger. Truth to tell, I dreaded Mother more than I dreaded Benjamin in many ways.

I knew my life was never going to be the same again by the end of the day. What I didn't know at that point was just how much my life was going to change. By the time the sun had set everything about my life, even my understanding of who I was, was going to be in tatters. However, nervous as I was entering into the family home, I had absolutely no idea of that as my eyes began to water again as the smoke from the fire enveloped itself around me as soon as I opened the door.

Through that smoke I immediately made out the figures of Dan and Josh. They instinctively turned their heads away from me and I knew they had told their aunt all that had happened early in the day.

'What a mess! What were you thinking of?'

I had taken only a couple of more steps into the house before the torrent of abuse started from my mother. 'I don't know what you were thinking of taking to that road like common criminals, I didn't realise we had sunk so far! But as you were there, you should have at least taken the money off that Samaritan fella. God in Heaven knows they're the scum of the earth.'

I was about to reply, but then realised that she still had more she intended to say.

'The only mercy is the mason you attack has died. What were you thinking of letting him be taken away like that when he could have identified you or your cousins.'

My legs suddenly buckled under me. I had to grab hold of the table in the middle of the room to stop myself collapsing to the floor. The stone mason was dead! I had been trying for ten years to atone for the murder of my father. I had failed to do that and killed someone else in the progress.

'Oh, you didn't know that?' my mother asked before continuing. 'Yes, Josh and Dan discovered that the Samaritan had taken him to the Gate Inn and asked the inn keeper to look after him; but he died shortly after he had left.

'So, the good news for you is you'll never be identified. But you'll have to find a way of making some honest money tomorrow as we're due to make a repayment. But, in the name of all that is sacred, you don't have to become a common thief to get the money, why aren't you working at Reuben's anymore?'

I was still trying to come to terms with the fact that I had killed yet another man. I was struggling to think straight, and I responded to Mother's question before I thought through what I should say to her.

'He's gone, and he's robbed us of everything,' I blurted out before realising what I had said.

'What do you mean?' my mother shot back. 'How can he have robbed us? I said not to go through with buying . . .'

Her voice trailed away as she realised I had pressed on with my plan even though she had warned me off. But she still made me tell her every detail, every part of the story.

'So, we're finished,' I concluded. 'Benjamin wants his money back this evening and I haven't got it for him. I'll be sold into slavery.'

'Could we be sold?'

Dan's alarmed voice broke through. Josh shifted uncomfortably as if considering whether or not to make a run for it then and there.

'No,' I reassured my two nervous cousins. 'Family can be sold to help meet a debt but only family on the father's side and as we're related through Mother you'll be fine. The same can't be said for Izzy, though.'

The sound of my brother's name and peril she now realised he was in, stung my mother into action.

'Get out! Get out!' she screamed at her two nephews as she ran towards them grabbing them by their garments and pushing them towards the door. Startled, they put up no opposition and left the house, my mother slamming the door behind them. Breathless, she turned around to speak to me, but she managed only nine words before the door behind her flew open again.

Through it stormed four huge men, followed by Dan and Josh who were bemused and alarmed in equal measure by all that was going on. I knew I stood no chance against all four of them, but I'd had to be a fighter all my adult life and I was ready for this one. I surprised myself how rationally I reasoned that it might be better, and quicker, to be killed in a fist fight rather than face whatever consequences lay ahead for failing to repay my debt.

My four opponents stopped to assess the scene in the house and, through the smoke-filled room, work what they had burst in on. In the split-second advantage that gave me, I spun around and put the fire that was in the centre of the room between me and the men. But my movement alerted them to my location and they moved towards me.

I overturned the cooking pot, propelling its contents towards them. It may have been weak broth, but it was boiling hot. One of the men shouted as he was burnt by the liquid. His colleagues instinctively took a step back, literally putting them on the back foot.

Josh then reacted quickest to the situation. He leapt forward towards the man hurt by the broth. But even with boiling hot liquid over him, Josh was no match against the man he threw himself at. He found himself thrown off and, as he hit the floor, his midriff became the focus of attention of the feet of the other thugs.

But while Josh's actions may not have had the effect he was hoping for, they did buy me some vital seconds. As the mismatched scuffle unfolded in front of me, I made a dash towards the window. It was a risky strategy because the only window in the house was behind their position, on the other side of the room. My bid for freedom was successful. I jumped through the window hoping I would land well enough to hit the ground and run. But as I brought my arms up ready to protect my head from the landing, I felt myself being yanked back by a strong pair of hands wrapped around my ankles.

As I landed on the floor I knew I had run out of places to run. Not for the first time that day the pain soared through the hand I had hurt when I attacked the stone mason. The pain was so bad that it was a few moments before I registered that my forehead was also throbbing and that the vision in my right eye was being obscured by what I could only assume was blood pouring from whatever wound had opened up.

With nowhere to run, my only option was to fight — however futile that battle would prove to be. With as much energy as I could manage I leapt to my feet, blindly thrashing my arms around. I knew it was a waste of time, but I was not going to be captured without a struggle, until the fight went out of me as what felt like a solid block of stone smashed into my stomach. I bent double and saw a fist retract itself from my midriff before seeing my assailant's knee come up and smash me in the face knocking me to the floor in one swift blow.

Before I had time to think about what was happening, I was aware of being hauled onto my feet.

'Barabbas, I take it.' There was a sarcastic tone to the scalded man's voice. 'You're due to give my boss some money.'

'Your boss is a disgrace,' I heard my mother say.

I looked up, trying to blink the blood out of my eyes. The sound of my mother's voice had shocked me. After those shattering words she had said just moments before the four men had burst into the house, I was surprised she had spoken in my favour. Well, I reflected, if not in my favour, certainly in defiance of my opponent.

'I can't believe people working for Benjamin would behave in this sort of way with one of your own kinsmen,' she continued.

'Benjamin?' The man who was obviously in charge looked genuinely puzzled. 'I don't work for any Benjamin. Barabbas' debt is to Zacchaeus of Jericho.'

I couldn't help myself. I groaned loudly and if it wasn't for the two men holding me by my arms I would have collapsed to the ground again. I had never met Jericho Zac, but I knew him by reputation. He was one of the most hated and feared men in the area — a tax collector, a collaborator with the occupying Roman forces. A man renowned for his love of money and his ruthlessness in its pursuit.

I knew that if I had to give an account of an unpaid debt to Jericho Zac that my life would be over before the day was out. And it would not be a pleasant or quick death.

'Oh no, not him,' my mother whispered.

It was at that point that the words she had spoken to me just moments before the door had flown open came back to me. I was a grown man, but I found myself crying like a little boy.

CHAPTER EIGHT

AS I WAS LED THROUGH Jericho Zac's rooms, my mind struggled to take on board everything that had happened. Why had Reuben run off with my money when he had seemed so genuine in wanting to work as a partner on the farm? How was it I now owed the main man in Jericho money when I had borrowed money from Benjamin? How had I managed to kill yet another man? And how had what my mother said made any sense at all?

Before I could dwell on any of these things I found myself taken into a room where Zac was standing at the far end of a raised platform. I guessed that was to disguise his lack of height. We had never met before, but his reputation for being a small man was well known in the area. However, as I was manhandled by his thugs towards him, I thought I recognised his face, though I struggled to think how we could have met before that day.

He looked at me and hesitated before saying, 'You owe me money. I require it now.'

It was brief and to the point. Zac did not mess around when it came to claim back any money that was his. Some people paid the debt they owed him with their lives. The tax collector's links with the Roman authorities meant that for years he had gotten away with murder. But it had come at a cost, the man was more hated in Jericho than any other collaborator and more than some of the Romans themselves.

But fear always outranks hatred. Nobody came out of any encounter with Jericho Zac without the man having had the upper hand. Not only could he calculate how to demand the money he wanted from those whose taxes he collected, but the money grabber could always calculate the way to most frighten and hurt his victims.

'So, where's my money?'

I could see the remains of his lunch stuck to his teeth. But that didn't mask the hard edge to his voice. I remained silent until a firm fist hammered me between my legs causing me to double over with a loud bellow that resonated from the pit of my stomach. Before I had time to react any further, my face exploded in pain as a knee connected with my nose again.

'Again? Again?' yelled Zac. 'Another pathetic pauper trying to rob me of my money!'

His spit sprayed all over me as the little man became overwhelmed with rage. As I looked up I saw pure hatred in the man's eyes. I decided I wanted this to be over quickly. Despite the agony in my face and groin I found myself able to think surprisingly clearly. I needed to find a way to provoke Zac further. I wanted to make him lose his temper more, so he would kill me there and then without having to suffer too much. I was surprised how calm I felt about my fate, but I reckoned I probably deserved death at the hands of someone like Jericho Zac.

I decided to ignore my pain and to go for it and push the creep as far and as hard as I could.

'I don't owe you anything,' I said through a mouth of blood and loose teeth as I tried to stand upright. 'My debt is to Benjamin, I didn't authorise him to pass it on to you. You won't get a copper coin out of me. I don't even know who you are.'

That was it. Zac leapt at me with a blood-curdling scream. He caught me off balance, and we fell to the floor together. He was flaying about with his fists and feet. There was no fight left in me. This was where it was going to end. Beaten to death on the marble floor of a Roman collaborator. I closed my eyes and waited for the end to come. My only hope at that moment was that death would come quickly.

Suddenly I was aware that the pounding had stopped. I opened my eyes to see Zac being restrained by one of his hired thugs.

'Not like this boss, it's too easy for him.'

'You're right. If he can't pay me with cash I'll make him pay with pain, and I will enjoy that. Then he'll remember exactly who I am.'

As I heard his words, I groaned inwardly. The quick end I had hoped for had been denied. As I started to get to my feet again a swift kick to the back of my legs sent me sprawling back to the floor. Before I could react, a strong hand grabbed my feet and I was dragged face-down across the floor towards the door. The dragging did nothing to help the pain in my face or between my legs. In fact, it added to the agony. The vomit started to rise in my throat and my head began to swim. Then it all went black.

* * * * * *

When I came around I thought night had fallen. Then I realised that the room I was in had no window or any form of light. It may well have been night, but the hour would make no difference in that room. I had no idea how long it had been since my encounter with Jericho Zac or how long it would be before the two of us met again. I reckoned it would be as long as it took for the money man to work out how he was going to torture and kill me.

In the darkness I tried to assess the severity of my injuries. I tentatively felt my body and realised I had been stripped naked. For some reason that concerned me more than my physical injuries, but I still checked my body from head to toe and all areas in between. There was nothing that would not heal given time, although I doubted I would be given the time needed for that to happen. Even the touch of my own hand was agony to some parts of my body and the hand that did the touching still hurt from when I had attacked the stone mason on the Jerusalem road.

That already felt like a life-time ago. I found myself sympathising with my victim as I gingerly touched my own face. My nose was undoubtedly broken, and my dry mouth confirmed that breathing through my blood-clotted nostrils had proved to be almost impossible. My whole body ached. Whatever my captor had in mind for me I doubted my body could realistically take much more.

I wished I could put some clothes on. It was stupid, this discomfort at being naked. I knew no one could see me in the darkness and judging by the wetness on the floor, if I had clothes on I would have wet them. But I felt more vulnerable in my nakedness, which was ridiculous really. I was going to die whether I was clothed or not. What should have concerned me more was the manner my death was going to take.

Any further reflections were stopped as the door to the room swung open. I instinctively raised my hands to my eyes to protect them from the light I expected to burst through the opened door way. But no light came. I had been out cold for only a short while or had I laid here for an entire day? I had no way of knowing.

One of the thugs who had dragged me away from my home entered the room holding a light in one hand. I moved my hands from my face to my groin in anticipation for the next solidly placed kick. But no blow came. Instead the man threw my clothes at me.

'Finally, with us?' he sneered. 'You've been unconscious so long I thought the boss must have killed you yesterday. Get dressed. He'll see you now.'

With that he turned his back and walked out of the door.

I was amazed. I had evidently been left naked in this room for an entire day and now I was being given privacy to dress? Surely Zac had something in mind for me when he had me stripped of my clothes. Had something changed? It did not make any sense. He never relented. I could only assume that he was trying to give me false hope in order to make me suffer more later. I could not afford to hope for any improvement in my situation. There is no place for hope in a hopeless situation. But I still hurried to put my clothes on, even though it was a struggle in the dark.

Then I sat and waited to be taken again to the impressive room where I had encountered the tax man. When the door opened I stood waiting to be taken to whatever part of the mansion I was going to. But I was roughly shoved to the floor.

'On your knees in front of the boss.'

I almost gasped out loud when I saw Zac step around from behind his thug. This was something unusual, Jericho Zac would never make his way to see one of his debtors. They always came to him. It terrified me as I considered what it could mean.

'So,' he sneered, 'you have no way of paying me back my money, is that right?'

'I can't repay you.'

'Then you are in trouble, because nobody defaults on me.'

I said nothing. There was nothing left to say. My life was over, I just hoped it would not be slow and painful. But I knew the odds against that were as short as the man standing in front of me. Then he bent down and whispered in my ear.

'Beg me to forgive you your debt.'

I was stunned and struggled to know what to do. I knew begging would be useless, and I certainly did not want to die begging for mercy like some pathetic wretch. However, not following Zac's instructions would only make matters worse. As if to confirm the point he gave me a well-aimed kick to my ribs.

'I said beg me to forgive you.'

'Please . . . pl . . .' I was unable to speak. Here I was on my hands and knees in front of one of the smallest men in the district. I was hurting from almost every area of my body. I felt as if I was losing all sensibility as I was sure I could hear Zac laughing.

'What's the matter, can't you speak you poor thing.'

I shall never forget the feeling of that man's hand gently caressing my face in the gloom of that room. At that point I so wanted to knock his head off, but I was too weak. Was this going to be my final humiliation — touched in the dark, knowing that all that was to follow was my own death?

'Try again . . . beg.'

'Please, I can't pay you . . . I'm sorry . . .'

'Well, if you're sorry let's just forget about it shall we?'

Zac moved his hand away from my face and took a step back. I did not know how to respond. It was clear to me there was no way he was going to forget about any money owed to him, let alone a debt the size of mine. I decided to say nothing, to wait and see what came next. Perhaps if I failed to play along with Zac's games the little man would grow annoyed and kill me quickly in a fit of temper and frustration.

'Well, what are you waiting for? You've begged me to forgive you your debt and I've agreed. Now go to my kitchens, get something to eat, and get out before I change my mind.'

I slowly got to my feet. I was still waiting for whatever Zac had up his sleeve, but I was going to face it on my feet, towering over my captor, rather than as a snivelling wreck on the floor. As I stood, though, my creditor turned and walked towards the door. Could it be real? Could it be that I was going to be allowed to leave with the debt cancelled?

'Why?' With my throat closing up completely my question came out as a whisper.

'It's been pointed out to me that we've not had a year of Jubilee for quite some time, so I've put that right by writing off your debt.'

Now I was even more confused. There was an ancient tradition that meant that all debts were written off every seven years, but that aspect of Jewish Law had been dropped generations ago. Why would a money grabber want to reintroduce the custom? For the life of me, I could not imagine what the real reason was for this sudden change of heart. I followed the tax collector out of the door into the evening air of a courtyard. The cool air stung the wounds on my face and I winced.

'The servants in the kitchen will see to your wounds. It's just through that entrance way.'

I was too dazed to respond. I walked past Jericho Zac to go through the way indicated by the little man, and I managed a slight nod of my head. It was a meagre acknowledgment for what the man had done, and its brevity provoked a stinging reaction. With a cry of sheer fury, the little man launched himself at me slamming my back against the cold stone wall. I wanted to scream out in new pain but the dried blood and spittle in my mouth stopped me from making any sound except a grunt.

Zac had somehow managed to pull himself up on my clothes so that his face was level with the mine, just inches away.

'And you can be grateful, you worthless peasant, that you have friends in high places,' he hissed. He released his grip on my clothes, turned, and stormed away in the opposite direction without looking back and without uttering a single word.

CHAPTER NINE

FOR A FEW MOMENTS I was at a loss as to what to do. The couple of thugs who had accompanied Jericho Zac also turned without saying a word and followed their boss. As I stood there I was puzzled about what had been said about friends in high places. I barely had anyone who I would call a friend, and the only people I did know were so low no one ever noticed them or would take any account of what they said.

It was yet another mystery which I might have been able to work out if the inside of my head stopped pounding in agony. Although the truth would probably have evaded me even without the pain. So, I walked down the passageway that led to the kitchen and was greeted with the rare smell of cooking meat.

'Cor, they said you were big, mister.'

The young lad stared at me as if he was looking at Goliath himself. The boy was only about ten years old, but he was the only servant in the kitchen.

'Cook said you could have some wine and bread.'

That was typical of my luck, allowed into a kitchen that was roasting meat but only allowed some dried bread to eat. Then I stopped myself. What right did I have to complain? I should have been going through a long and painful death right now.

I grunted my acknowledgement to the boy and almost fell into the only seat in the kitchen. I was exhausted, both physically and mentally. The boy brought over the bread and a large cup of wine. Instinctively, I snatched both from him and began to gulp down the drink. My mouth still hurt and the relief of having some liquid in it was tempered only by the pain swallowing brought.

'Your face looks a right mess, mister,' continued the boy. 'I've got some rags I can wash it with if you like.'

I nodded my agreement and the boy turned and grabbed a large, dirty piece of cloth. He wetted it with some more wine and gently touched my injured face with it. But even the gentlest of touches was agony. I terrified the poor boy as I bellowed in pain and pushed him roughly away.

'Hey, I was only trying to help. I suppose you'll have a doctor look at you once you've ridden back to Jerusalem.'

'Ridden back to Jerusalem?' The wine, for all the pain swallowing it had brought, had at least loosened my tongue a little. It had been years since I had last been to Jerusalem; I asked the boy what he meant.

'I never meant nothing. I just reckoned you'd ride back like your friend did earlier today.'

A couple of days ago life had been simple. I was a poor man struggling to support a family. Now it appeared that the man I had always believed I had been was a lie. I was a double-murderer, had friends in high enough places to clear my debts and ride horses, and then there had been my mother's shocking revelation. My head hurt far too much to be able to take it all in, instead, I decided to concentrate on finding out about my newly acquired friend.

'Who was my friend?' I asked.

'I dunno but he came galloping over from Jerusalem this morning. He looked dead important and he insisted on seeing the boss straight away. After he had spoken to him he went riding off again and the boss said to Cook that you could have some food before you left.'

This made no sense at all. I had never been the type of man to have a saviour on a horse who could influence someone as powerful as Jericho Zac. There must have been a mistake and when he discovered it there would be trouble. With that thought in mind, I decided the time had come to speedily leave my current host. I grabbed the rag from the boy and wiped my face.

It was still agony to have even the lightest touch on my face but walking out into a Jericho evening looking like someone who had lost a fight would have been a mistake. It would have left me vulnerable to muggings from opportunistic thieves who would see me as an easy target — even though I had nothing on me worth stealing. I gulped down the rest of the wine.

'How do I get out of here?' I demanded from the boy who had never got up from the floor.

The lad pointed to a door, deciding that it might not do him any favours to say very much more. With that, I got up from my chair, picked up the remains of my bread, and strode towards the door which meant freedom. On the way to it, I passed the meat that was roasting over a fire. I reached out and tore off a chunk before barging my way through the door to the outside. It burnt my hand like the fires of hell, but it had been weeks, perhaps months, since I had last tasted meat and the pain was just one more to add to my collection, but this time it had a reward.

* * * * * *

Jericho was only a medium-sized city. It had one inn where travellers of my ilk would stay, but I knew staying the night there was impossible because I had no money. I might be able to find someone willing to travel with me back to Bethany. There were plenty of traders who moved between Jericho and Jerusalem, and Bethany was only a few miles outside the capital city. I knew only too well that travelling alone would be dangerous. I hoped one of the traders might have a spare mule I could ride. I was unsure I was up to walking the whole way home.

As I approached the inn I saw two travellers chatting outside, standing by some donkeys. I hoped that they were the owners of the animals.

'Good evening, gents, are you going to Jerusalem?'

'We may be . . . hey, what happened to your face?'

The man who spoke instinctively took a step back as if my injuries could be contagious. I had known my face was agony and that it must look a mess, but this reaction told me it was even worse than I had imagined. Thinking quickly, I decided that this could be used to my advantage.

'Robbers. They attacked me on the way here. Took everything I had and left me half dead. It's a miracle I'm still here. I just need to get back to my family, but I don't fancy making the journey back on my own.'

'We're heading back to Jerusalem in the morning. You're welcome to join us.'

'Are these your animals? I'm not sure I'm strong enough to walk all the way.'

A heavy silence hung between the three of us. It was one thing to offer company on the road, it was another thing for that company to then ask for a lift on a stranger's animal. Especially when the man claiming to be injured would easily be big enough to overcome both of his newly found companions if he turned out to be far fitter than he claimed. I could see the two men weighing up the situation. After a few moments it was the second, older man who spoke.

'It'll cost you a denarius.'

To say I was taken aback would be an understatement. Here were two Jews demanding an entire day's wage for me, a fellow Jew, to ride their donkey to Jerusalem. It made me think again about the Samaritan I'd seen helping the Jew I had attacked. That Samaritan had not asked for any money off the stone mason.

'I don't have it,' I replied. 'I told you robbers took everything I had. What if I paid you when we arrived, and I can get to my money?'

The older man laughed. 'Yeah, that sounds like such a good deal for us I don't think. If you want a ride, then you pay us this evening, or you sling your hook. Now, what's it to be?'

I knew there was no point in arguing. I needed money and I needed it now. If only I'd reacted yesterday and attacked the Samaritan on the road I would never have been in this mess. I cursed bitterly and turned away from the two men who laughed at my situation. My rage roared up inside me, but I checked myself. I knew that, battered and bruised as I was, I would only lose any confrontation against two men. I trudged wearily away, the cold night air penetrating my skin and chilling me to the bone.

Then, as I rounded the corner I saw him. He was not anyone I knew, but he was someone who looked like just the person I needed at that moment. He was middle aged, small, slightly built, and just entering what I hoped was his home. Acting purely on instinct and without thinking through what I was doing, I darted over to him and, before he had the chance to shut the door behind him, barged through knocking him to the ground. It was extremely risky. I was taking the chance that this was the man's empty home and that he did not have a couple of burly sons inside.

I leapt on the back of the bag on bones on the floor slamming the door shut behind me with my foot. The wind was knocked out of the man without him uttering a sound. Quickly, I had one hand across his mouth and the other around a clump of his hair as I pulled his head backwards. If there was someone else in the house I had a hostage. I looked around the hovel of a home and saw no one else was in.

'Stay silent and I'll let you live,' I hissed in the man's ear. 'I need money right now and you're going to give it to me.'

Slowly, I got off the man's back. As I stood I pulled him to his feet. I could feel the man panting in fear, and my adrenaline reduced fear began to rise in me. What was I doing? I was attacking yet another innocent victim. But it was not my fault this time. If those two men outside the inn had helped me as they should, I would not have been in this position now. I tried to calm myself with this thought, I needed to stay calm and stay in charge of this situation.

'Slowly walk towards where you keep your money.'

Keeping a firm grip on the man's mouth with one hand and the other around his throat we edged slowly towards the furthest and darkest corner of the house. It crossed my mind that this might be a trick to lure me towards a concealed weapon with which my victim could attack me. But then I smelt the fear emanating from him, and I was confident it was only the money we were heading towards. As we reached the corner the man managed a curt nod of his head towards the floor. Carefully I bent forward to allow the man to kneel down and rummage behind some old sacks lying there.

I was almost overcome with panic for a fleeting moment as I convinced myself he would spin around with a sharp blade in his hand. But I managed to keep my emotions in check and was soon rewarded with him pulling out nothing more dangerous than a small cloth bag accompanied by the clink of whatever coins were inside. As I snatched the bag from him I pushed the man forwards to the floor. I had been careful to always stay on top or behind him so that he never saw my face clearly. I intended to turn and leave quickly enough that if he looked around he would see only the back of my head.

But before I could move one pace away from him the door to the house opened.

'Dad?'

I spun around and came face to face with the lad I had met in Zac's kitchen. I froze. What was I to do? Surely, I wouldn't have to kill these two as well now?

'Timothy, keep out of this.'

Seeing his son had clearly given my victim a new lease of life. Regardless of the pain I must have inflicted on him, the man rose to his feet. My head was whirling as Timothy's father took charge of the situation.

'I owed this man some money and I'm just repaying him. Now he'll be on his way. Isn't that right?'

I was stunned. This man was more interested in protecting his son than he was about getting his money back. I wondered if my own father would have done the same. Then I remembered again what my mother had said and, immobilised by confusion, I stood in the middle of that stranger's house rooted to the spot.

'So, you'll be on your way.'

The presence of his son had given the man new found bravado and his stern voice cut through the swirl of thoughts and emotions I was experiencing, stinging me into action.

'Yeah, on my way.'

I pushed past Timothy and strode out of the door. I quickly turned the corner and made my way to the inn. As I looked in the money bag I discovered I had enough for the journey home, a bed for the night, and a few drinks before I got there.

I decided that what I really needed was to drink myself into a stupor. I reckoned it was as good a way as any of getting through my life's current difficulties.

CHAPTER TEN

'YOU AND YOUR BROTHER DON'T have the same father.'

My mother's words kept repeating themselves over and over again in my head. The sudden interruption of Jericho Zac's men meant there was no time for any further information. So, who was my father? Was it the man who had brought me up? Had his rough treatment of me been a result of him having to bring up another man's son or was his expectation of me higher than Izzy because I was from his lineage?

Then there was the question of the new light this shone on Mother. What sort of woman had she been that she had slept with someone other than her husband? Or was either me or Izzy secretly adopted and neither of the parents who raised us our birth parents? Did Izzy know about this? Was this only a secret kept from me?

The more I drank that evening the more intense the questions that raced through my head became. There was so much I didn't know and the more I drank the more convinced I became that everyone else must know. I became increasingly angrier with each mouthful of wine.

It was not long before my anger was redirected in other directions: towards the scum-bag Reuben who had run off with my money and my dreams of buying the farm and atoning for killing my father — if he was my father, that is. Then I was angry with the mason for not having the strength to live and to leave me guilty of another murder; then there was the treatment I'd received from Zac. Finally, in my intoxicated state, I decided I was angry with the mysterious horseman who galloped in to save the day. What right did a total stranger have to interfere in my business? All this I tried to tell the inn keeper as he manoeuvred me into my room where I passed out on the bed.

* * * * * *

I was woken abruptly the next morning by two pairs of rough hands hauling me off my bedding. Startled, I opened my eyes to see two of Zac's thugs who had brought me from Bethany to Jericho. I tried to wake myself up enough to make some sort of sense of what was happening, but the booze I'd had the previous evening was not helping.

'What? Your boss said that it was all over. I don't need to pay him.'

I tried to decide whether the searing pain in my head was a result of the injuries I had sustained over the last few days or the wine of last night. As the vomit rose up from my stomach I realised that it must be the wine taking affect. I tried to push the two men away, but they just held me tighter. They soon let go, though, when I proceeded to vomit over them.

'Hey!' the bigger one yelled as he pushed me away in disgust and onto the floor.

I knelt on my hands and knees as I emptied the contents of my stomach. Despite its putrid stench, I stayed close to the steaming pool of sick as I reckoned that the men would not risk being vomited on again. Staying where I was actually put some distance between me and my assailants.

I tried to work out what was happening. Through the fog of my hangover I attempted to make sense of this latest development. These men worked for Zac who had written off my debt yesterday. After giving me my freedom like that why would he now be sending out his thugs to get me again? It made no sense, but it was just another item to add to the list of nonsense that I'd been assembling over the past few days.

Although I had my back to them, I heard one of the men move, I presumed, towards me. I forced myself to retch loudly again, and I heard the footstep move back. Good, this was definitely giving me some time to think. But I had done nothing but think for the last forty-eight hours. I'd spent the evening using the wine in an attempt to stop all the confusion that was rushing around in my head. Who was my father? Why had I failed to attack the Samaritan? But the alcohol had solved none of the mysteries which now engulfed my life and now these two heavies had presented me with yet another riddle.

'I told you, your boss said that I didn't owe him anything when I saw him yesterday.'

'Oh no, you owed him, but he decided to let you off. There's a difference.'

I struggled to understand what was happening.

'He let me off then. So why are you here now?'

'I'm sure he'll tell you that when you see him. And he's *very* keen to see you now.'

'I'm not well. Tell him that I'll see him tomorrow.'

It was a calculated gamble. Normally a response like that would have been met with a swift, hard kick to somewhere on my body. But not today. It appeared these two tough guys could not cope with a vomiting victim. They were still keeping their distance.

'There must be a mistake, anyway,' I said, trying to think if not on my feet then on my hands and knees. 'Like you said, he let me off. You wouldn't want to waste his time . . .'

This time I had taken things too far. Without having time to react to the sound of the men moving, I felt a hand on the back of my head that shoved me, face first, into the pool of sick on the floor. Despite my hangover and injuries, I instinctively sprung up to my feet with a speed not even I realised I had. It took my two opponents by surprise. Before they had a chance to react, I smashed their two heads together with as much force as I could muster. I saw the bigger man's eyes roll as he lost consciousness. The other man, who was slightly smaller than me, stood still, temporarily dazed by the bang to his head. I took my chance and kicked his groin with so much force it hurt my foot. The heavy man screamed out with pain and collapsed to the floor on his knees. Without missing a beat, buoyed up by adrenalin and fear, I went around behind him and grabbed his throat.

'Now tell me why you were sent to get me.'

But my grip was too tight. The man could do no more than utter an unidentifiable croak. Looking across the floor I could see that the other man was starting to regain consciousness, I had to act quickly. Despite the injuries I had and the hangover I was suffering, I found myself able to tighten the grip on the throat in my hands.

I clenched tighter and tighter. Despite his injuries, the man started to thrash around, trying to get away, trying to get some air. I watched as his partner slowly started to come to and it encouraged me to tighten my grip on the other man's throat. One part of my mind told me I only had to wait for him to pass out, but another part — one I hadn't heard since the night I had killed my father — screamed at me to finish him off.

I kept my hands over his windpipe until his body had gone completely limp. Then, just as I saw comprehension dawn in the eyes of the other man I threw myself at him, and I sat on his chest, using my knees to pin him to the floor before he had time to react.

He kept grimacing and squeezing his eyes shut. He was obviously in acute pain and was trying to clear the fog of concussion from his head. A trickle of blood ran through the thug's hair from where he had collided heads with his colleague.

'Now tell me, what are you doing here?' I demanded.

'The boy, Timothy, in the kitchen. He told me how you'd taken the money his father owed you last night. I told Zac and he told me to bring you in. He was furious, said he was going to make you pay.'

So that was it. Zac had obviously believed the son's story and thought that I was collecting a debt even though I had been let off mine. I could understand the tax collector's fury, but I knew that the truth that I had been robbing the boy's father would not help my cause. I had to get away.

'Why is life never simple?' I heard myself asking out loud. The man below me looked at me in confusion. 'Oh, not your life,' I told him. 'Your life is very uncomplicated. You're going back to sleep now.'

Pulling on the front of his clothing, I raised the man's head nine inches above the floor. Then I lowered my own head so that it came level with my opponent, as if to look him in the eye before saying something. Instead, without a word, I tilted my head back and thrust it violently forward to head-butt the other man between the eyes. The pain that returned to my own head made me roar in agony. The other man, however, said nothing but his eyes rolled again as he rediscovered the world of unconsciousness.

As I was unsure how long he would be out for, I quickly got off him, gathered up the money I had stolen the day before and left the room. I went in search of the two men I had paid last night to go back to Bethany with. As I walked out of the front door I saw them just about to head off.

'Hey!' I called to them, 'Don't forget I'm coming with you.'

'What, when you're wanted by Jericho Zac and covered in puke? I don't think so,' one of them replied.

I had forgotten about my vomit, but in the fresh air its smell suddenly hit me, along with every ache and pain the last couple of days had brought. Without warning, my body began to give way and I had to cling to the door frame for support as I watched the ride I had paid for leave without me.

'But I paid you . . . ' was all I could despairingly call after them.

'Yeah, but if you've got Jericho Zac after you we're not keen on your company, or your puke's company either!'

Then they were gone. I knew I had to get out of that place. I didn't know whether I had actually killed a man that morning, but whether he proved to be dead or alive, Zac would not take kindly to me roughing up his hired muscle. It was not safe to stay in Jericho and the sooner I left the better it would be for me.

But at that precise moment all I could do was sink to my knees in misery, pain, and despair.

CHAPTER ELEVEN

AT THE HOTTEST PART OF the day Bethany stank of dirt, sweat, and animal dung. But to me, as I entered the village, it was the sweetest smell I had ever experienced. My whole body, from the bottom of my feet to the top of my head hurt after hours of walking. The only good thing about my dishevelled state was that I looked so wretched that any bandits on the road had left me alone, presumably assuming that I had already fallen victim to a mugging and was not worth attacking again. And so, after a sleepless day and night of walking, I had arrived in my home village. Not that it would be my home for much longer.

I was clueless about whether I had killed Zac's henchman. Even if he was still alive, Jericho Zac would not be impressed with the state I had left the man in nor that I had not turned up at his house as summoned. What frightened me was that he knew where I lived. He would want retribution as well as full payment of my debt. I knew I had to get out of town, and quickly. Or at least as soon as I had got my strength back after the trek home.

But first I needed to see Mother again. I was determined to discover who my father was. The long walk back to Bethany had given me time to think a lot of things over. First of all, I had come to see the significance of my name. Barabbas was usually a second name meaning son of his father. But I had been given it as a first name — son of my father, whomever that may be. I came to see my name as a beacon of the mystery of who I was. I had convinced myself that I was not the son of my mother's husband, the man I had always thought of as my father. His rough treatment of me, I decided, was proof of it. The mystery of who I was consumed me; and it was a mystery I was determined to confront my mother about and solve. But not straightaway. Mother could wait until I had rested. I was going to need all the strength I had if I was to successfully confront her.

Finding somewhere to rest was going to be a challenge. In a place as small as Bethany there were very few places to hide. It was also a typical village. Everyone knew everyone else's business. The news that I had been taken to Jericho would be common knowledge and so the uncommon sight of anyone returning from such a situation would be around the few houses in a flash. My other problem was that, much as I needed to rest and get my strength back, who knew how long it would be before some of Zac's other hired thugs would come looking for me. I knew I was still ahead of them as no group of heavies had passed me on the road. I guessed they had probably spent most of yesterday looking for me around Jericho. Once they failed to find me there I knew the search party would be sent on to Bethany. I had to be out of the village by sun down at the latest. But a couple of hours' sleep would have to come first.

'Barabbas!'

I was startled by the shout and for a moment the terrifying thought went through my head that somehow the thugs had got to Bethany first. But as I spun around I saw Josh in the doorway of a nearby house. Judging by the look on his already stupid face, Josh was having trouble trying to work through how I was walking through their home village when I had been taken off to a certain death three days earlier.

'Josh,' I acknowledged my cousin and cautiously made my way towards him.

'What happened to you? You look like death. What's going on?'

I opened my mouth to answer but found myself unable to speak. My mouth was so dry, my throat so sore, and the pain in my body so overwhelming that instead of speaking I sank to my knees and prayed that I would die. Putting one foot in front of the other in order to get home I had ignored my physical condition, but now that I was here the pain engulfed me and I just wanted it all to end if only God would let it happen. But God was evidently not listening. Instead of dying I became aware of a man following Josh out of the house. He was a young man and in my exhausted state I could not remember his name. But the man evidently knew me as he carefully helped me to my feet and into his home.

'Come with me Barabbas, let's get you sorted out. My sisters will look after you.'

He called out the names Martha and Mary, and two young women immediately entered the room. One went straight to the cooking area while the other one helped her brother ease me to the floor. As the man left the house with Josh, his sister began to softly tend to my wounds. She was an attractive girl and if I had been in better shape her attentions would undoubtedly have pleased me. But there was no life in any of me at that moment and so I contented myself by enjoying her soothing of my pains. The other woman came over and handed me some wine. She hesitated. In the end her other chores, or my obvious incapacity, convinced her to leave the two of us alone as she bustled out of the room.

'I'm Mary,' the younger woman whispered. 'I know who you are. I've always been afraid of you, so if I'm helping you now you'll have to leave me alone when you're better. And Martha and Lazarus as well.'

Of course, that was whose house I was in. It came back to me that the man was Lazarus and his two sisters Martha and Mary. All three of them were comparatively young but their parents had died in the last year.

They must have really kept together and kept to themselves. I was fairly certain that if I had spotted Mary just a few days ago, I would certainly have noticed her. But now I was helpless and in her debt. I laid back and allowed myself to be nursed by this young woman. It was a new sensation for me, I couldn't ever remember my mother looking after me like this.

'Barabbas, what happened to you? How come you're back here?'

Normally Izzy's voice would set my nerves on edge as being in his company normally only ever wound me up. But today I was pleased to see my brother, my half-brother as I now knew him to be, walk through the door and into the room. He stopped stock-still when he saw the state I was in.

'What happened to you?'

'Your brother's not well,' Mary answered for me and I was rather pleased to hear a sound of protection within her voice. 'Don't go bothering him now, he'll need to rest once I've sorted out his wounds.'

'It's all right Mary.' I took another sip of my drink hoping it would eventually stop my tongue from sticking to the roof of my mouth and allow me to speak more easily. 'There are important things I need to speak to my brother about. You can come back and sort out the rest of my wounds later on. I need to be alone with Izzy.'

Mary had been brought up well. She knew better than to argue with an instruction given by a man. But her face gave away how incensed she was at my snub. She left the room, following the direction her sister had taken just a few moments earlier. I struggled to sit up, leaning back against the rough wall of the house as I drained my cup. Izzy silently waited for me to spit a mixture of phlegm and blood onto the floor. I'd never known him to be so attentive to what I had to say.

'Zac cancelled my debt and let me go.'

'Why? Jericho Zac never does anything like that? And if he did, how come you're such a mess now?'

'It's complicated. His thugs beat me up before he cancelled the debt and then again later after he changed his mind.'

'If he changed his mind and you still owe him how come you're here now?'

'His thugs came back for me when I was staying in an inn in Jericho, but I decided not to go with them.'

'What happened?'

'I left them in a state where they couldn't make me do anything.'

I stopped short of saying that I thought I had killed one of them. Partly because I was not sure that I had and partly because I could not admit to myself, let alone Izzy, that I had killed two men in just a few short days.

'So, you're on the run from Zac and still owe him money?'

'That's about the size of it,' I agreed.

'Then what are you doing back here? He'll have his men here again before you know it.'

'Because I wanted to see our mother. Do you know where she is?

'I haven't seen Mother since the evening you were taken away.'

I was surprised. Izzy's reaction was one of bemusement. He clearly had no idea why I would want to risk my life to see our mother, so I knew he had not been told about our different fathers.

'Where have you been then?' I asked.

'Me? I've been nowhere. After you left the house Mother went straight out. She didn't say a word to me, but I think she headed off in the direction of Jerusalem.'

Now I went from being bemused to being stunned. Because of her sickness, mother never left Bethany. I tried hard to remember the last time she had gone anywhere outside of the village, but it was impossible to do.

'But that was three days ago. Where's she been since then?'

'I don't know,' my brother replied, and I got the impression he didn't care either, but then he always had been self-absorbed. With the arrival of Zac's men imminent, I decided I had to learn some of that selfishness myself. If my mother had left after telling me the family secret, then I had to go as well. However, if Izzy was unaware of our paternal differences then he could still end up being taken by Zac's men as part payment. He had to come with me, repellent as that thought was.

I didn't know how to bridge the subject with him, but it turned out I didn't have to.

'Where are you going to go now?' Izzy asked.

'I hadn't given it much consideration,' I confessed. 'Up north, I guess.'

'Then travel with us.'

'Us?'

'Yes, I know a group of people who are setting off to Galilee later today. We could travel with them.'

I was taken aback. I was amazed to find that Izzy had no guilt about leaving the family home again and absolutely no concerns about what had happened to our mother. Plus, Galilee was much further than I had thought of going although it did make a lot of sense. It came under a different jurisdiction to Bethany which would make it difficult for Zac to pursue me there, well, through legal channels anyway. Galilee had a lot going for it, but there was still one issue that needed to be clarified. I still had one concern that I could not shake.

'What about Mother?' I asked.

'What about her? It looks to me like she's abandoned us. Let her look out for herself.'

I was struggling to be so off hand about the woman who had given birth to us and I was frustrated that so many of the questions I had for her would go unanswered. But I had to get moving, there was no other option.

'Okay, but what's this group we'll be travelling with?'

'There's been a guy in the area called John. He's been criticising the Romans and baptising people.'

'Oh great, a religious nutter who's got it in for the Romans. He'll really be a safe companion on the road.'

'No, it's not him. It's some other guy called Jesus. He got baptised by John but he's now more popular than him. Jesus comes from Galilee and he's heading back there with a group of people I've got to know over the last few days. I think they'll let us travel with them.'

I groaned. It was so like Izzy to impetuously start following the latest fad or personality. He was so easily convinced by anyone who had the gift of the gab. A religious freak was not my ideal travelling companion, but right now it was the only option available to me.

'Right, well let me rest here for a bit longer. Tell me when you're heading off.'

I laid back down and within moments I was asleep. But my dreams were disturbed by images of dead men, including one with no face who called himself Father.

CHAPTER TWELVE

ZACCHAEUS WAS BOTH INFURIATED AND intrigued.

He had come so close to utterly destroying Barabbas, but then had been frustrated by events that were outside of his control and some were outside of his comprehension. The worst thing was that he had spent a lot of his money on this particular project without seeing any return on his outlay. That was not something he was used to. He always realised his ambitions, it was that drive and success that had got him to the position of power he was in now.

But Barabbas had slipped through his fingers, or more correctly, through the fingers of his hired muscle. They had returned battered and bruised from their encounter with the man, but if they had hoped they would find sympathy and understanding from their boss they soon discovered their mistake. Zacchaeus had flown into an uncontrollable rage, physically attacking them even though they were at least twice his size. He spat and scratched and thumped them like a man possessed before ordering more of his hired muscle to throw them out of his home.

As he stood, bent double trying to catch his breath and bring himself back under control, his mind set to work. If he was going to go after Barabbas again he had to try to make sense of all that had happened and work out how he could avoid the problems he had encountered this time.

He sat down, alone, shut his eyes and went through the plan he had spent so much time and money on in an attempt to understand why it had failed so spectacularly.

It had taken so much time to set up the situation with Reuben. The man seemed to have genuinely liked Barabbas and was initially reluctant to be involved in a scheme that robbed him of his money. But in the end every man has his price and the option of making so much money was too good for Reuben to turn down and so he had played along and let Barabbas think there was a deal to be done that would enable him to buy back his family's farm. Zacchaeus wondered where Reuben had gone. For his sake he hoped that it was somewhere he would never encounter Barabbas.

Benjamin had been much easier to convince. Being paid a handsome commission to front the loan to Barabbas that, all along, had come from Zacchaeus was enough for that money-grabbing crook. To be fair, both accomplices had played their part well and Zacchaeus had thought his moment had come when he had Barabbas in front of him.

He had been surprised and somewhat disappointed that the oaf had not recognised him, that would have made having him at his mercy all the more satisfying, but that was only a minor point in the scheme of things. However, it was after he had Barabbas led away, stripped and left to wonder what the future held, that things had started to go wrong.

From nowhere an official from Jerusalem had appeared on horseback insisting that he see Zacchaeus immediately. The official told him that, if he wanted to continue with his tax collecting and money-lending business, he should release Barabbas and cancel the debt. Zacchaeus was infuriated and screamed at the official that his business was his affair only and there was no one in Jerusalem who could possible tell him how he should carry it out or threaten to take it away from him.

When the official explained who had sent him, Zacchaeus realised that there was one person who could extend their authority all the way from Jerusalem to Jericho and that he had no choice but to do as he was told. Reluctantly, he signed the document the official had brought with him and made arrangements for Barabbas to be released.

That morning, speaking to Barabbas and telling him he was free to go was one of the hardest things Zacchaeus had ever done. He wanted to kill the man on the spot but knew that he would be ruined within just a couple of days if he did.

The elation he had known that evening when he heard of Barabbas' encounter with one of his servant's family members was impossible to describe. He had no doubt that the man did not owe Barabbas a penny; but the account of him supposedly demanding the repayment of a loan when Barabbas had just been cleared of all his debts gave him the perfect reason to bring Barabbas back into his custody. Surely that ingratitude made it acceptable for Barabbas' loan to be reinstated. Zacchaeus was not completely confident, but he felt that the argument could hold sway with those in Jerusalem who were intent on sticking their noses into his business.

However, as he waited for his men to return with his debtor, doubts began to grow in his mind. Was this really a risk worth taking? Had he allowed his personal feelings to get in the way of good business? If he had, that was something he had never done before.

Perhaps, initially, there was sense of relief when the men returned battered and bruised and without their quarry. But it was only initially, then the two men encountered the full force of their master's rage. How dare they let him get away and allow all the money he had spent ensnaring Barabbas to go to waste. They would be sorry.

But not as sorry as Zacchaeus was. He hated losing money almost as much as he hated Barabbas. Yet he had lost both. He felt physically sick contemplating that this opportunity to destroy the man had slipped through his fingers. He knew the reality was that he may never have another chance at revenging the wrongs done to him in his youth.

Zacchaeus spent the next two days confined to his sleeping quarters. It was only as he revisited in his mind all that had gone wrong for the umpteenth time that a new thought startled him and set his mind working in a new direction as he considered again the official from Jerusalem and who he represented and wondered why a man of such influence would be interested in a lowlife such as Barabbas.

PART TWO
GALILEE 30 AD

CHAPTER THIRTEEN

I KNEW SHE WAS A prostitute, but she was so beautiful. I was captivated the moment I set eyes on her, finding it amazing that a girl that good looking was on the game; normally the prostitutes in Galilee were anything but easy on the eyes. But Naomi was different.

'Right, it's time for me to go — unless you want to pay for anything extra.'

I groaned inside as I rolled over to find the space next to me still warm but already empty. I looked up bleary eyed able to see only the shapely outline of Naomi picking up her clothes from the floor as the morning sun shone in through the window. Quickly rubbing the sleep from my eyes, I sneaked a look in time to clearly see her body disappearing under the dress she was putting on.

'Well,' she asked, 'is there anything else I can do for you?'

There was plenty Naomi could do but I had run out of money. Somewhere in my brain I was still trying to figure out why I had used the last of my money so that one of the local prostitutes had somewhere warm and safe to sleep the night away. But, like any man, I knew exactly why — it was the best half shekel I had spent, and I did not want her to leave. It made no sense, but right at that moment, I longed to feel some form of affection.

'Can I see you again?'

I hoped my discomfort was not too obvious. It had been a long time since I had tried to chat up a woman rather than negotiate a price with her.

'Sure, you can, blue eyes, if you want to pay me something now we can make an arrangement for later on this evening.'

For the first time in my life, someone had referred to the colour of my eyes and made it sound like a compliment. It was all the encouragement I needed to voice my hopes.

'Oh, I wondered if I could see you as a friend . . .'

But even as I spoke the words I could hear how stupid they sounded. Naomi was a prostitute. Why on earth would she want to see one of her customers on a social level? I wanted to take my words and stuff them back down my throat. I could feel the embarrassment welling up as my face burned. At that moment all I wanted was for Naomi to get out of the house as quickly as possible and to never see her again. Instead, she sat on the bed next to me and stroked my face.

'That would be lovely, but if I see anyone as a friend I miss out on earning money and I can't afford to do that. It's sweet of you to ask, though.'

I hardly heard her words. The touch of her hand on my face was enough to stir up new passion within me as I desperately tried to remember if I had any more money in the room. But I knew it was in vain. I had given her all my money last night.

She sprang up from the bed just a little too hastily.

'But now I must be going. Perhaps I'll see you again tonight.'

And with that she was out of the door. I rolled over onto my back and cursed. I wondered how many of Naomi's other clients had made a similar suggestion to mine as I realised how well practiced her gentle refusal line was. I was an idiot. I cursed again, this time at my wastefulness at having paid her good money just to sleep in my bed for the night. I should at least have negotiated on the price. But then, when had negotiating ever been a strong point with me?

Once I, Izzy, Josh, and Dan had arrived in Galilee two years ago I had tried to negotiate a job working for the Romans collecting taxes. I had reasoned that tax collectors were never poor and that I could stand being a hated collaborator if my pockets were bulging with money. But

I had timed it wrong. I had arrived in the village of Capernaum still recovering from the attentions of Jericho Zac and his henchmen. I had looked like a gladiator who had lost every one of his combats. Looking back, I realised there was no way I would have been given a tax booth to run looking like that. Even now I was still trying to work out why I had not waited a few days for my injuries to heal up. In the end an old guy called Zebedee had given me some casual labour mending fishing nets. It was going to be only temporary, but here I was, two years on, still smelling of fish most days and still scratching around for every last coin.

I may have left my debts to Zac behind in Judah, but I had not left behind the debtor's life. It had taken me no time at all to start running up new debts in the north of the country. As I laid in bed, looking up at the cracked and flaking ceiling above me, I wondered if my life could ever change. I could barely remember the times of my childhood when money had been plentiful, and life had seemed so simple. Now every day was a struggle and a disappointment — just as Naomi had been.

I decided to get up. I stood on the floor and straightened my aching back and rotated my shoulders as I tried to get my body fully working. I was starting to feel old. Thirty-three was not ancient, but nobody had told my body that. It ached every time I bent over to mend the fishing nets or pull them in after a catch. As I looked for the clothes I had left scattered all over the floor last night, I decided today could be good day to take it easy and renew my strength. But then I rejected the idea almost as soon as I had thought it. No work today meant no money, and no money meant no Naomi tonight — and she was definitely worth getting back ache for.

'Hey, Barabbas, how are you doing?'

Izzy walked casually into the house. I was still naked, but Izzy was totally unfazed by the sight that greeted him as he walked in.

'Morning, Izzy. I'm all right.'

I smiled as I pulled on my clothing. When you share a small home with your brother and two cousins, modesty and privacy are out of reach. Looking back, it amused me to think how, when we were growing up, Izzy was so particular about not seeing me naked or being seen naked himself. The situation between us, though, had changed. Since our mother had run out on us, we'd grown closer than we'd ever been, although neither of us discussed where Mother might be.

'How was the party?' I asked once I was dressed.

'It wasn't a party. How many times have I got to explain to you? We were being taught.'

It was always the same, Izzy would deny that he and Dan and Josh were feasting with his new mates and claim instead that they were being instructed by Jesus in the ways of life and God. But everyone knew Jesus loved a good party ever since he provided gallons of wine for a friend's wedding reception when he first arrived in Capernaum. But I wasn't worried what Izzy and his cousins did when they spent their nights out with Jesus. I appreciated the opportunities it gave me to bring back the likes of Naomi to the house without having them shouting encouragement from their corner of the room.

'So, where are the other two?'

'I don't know. They didn't stay to listen. I thought they might have come back here. Must have gone off somewhere else instead, I guess.'

'No doubt they'll turn up eventually.' I looked around for my sandals. 'But I'm off to try and earn some money.'

'We'll just have to hope that you can still find some work then.'

I wondered what Izzy meant as I walked past him and out of the door. I soon realised as I first looked at the people around me and then at the sun in the sky. Judging by its position and the industry of the people, it must have been about midday. I should have noticed when the sun silhouetted Naomi's body as she got dressed this morning that it was later than I had thought. She had not left me at the crack of dawn and I had not gotten out of bed early enough to find any work that day. I stood motionless outside my home uncertain of what to do next.

'You didn't realise you'd left it too late to go job hunting, did you?'

'I'll have to try to find something,' I replied. 'We need the money and I can't borrow any more. We've got nothing saved and nothing to eat.'

'Why don't you come with me and spend some time with Jesus and the guys.'

I was shocked. Since we had travelled from Bethany, Izzy had never encouraged me to spend time with his group of friends. Even on the journey up to Galilee, Izzy had tried to stop me from getting to know the rest of the group. It had suited me at the time. I was struggling to keep up with the party because of my injuries, but my pride had stopped me from saying anything. Being left on my own meant I could concentrate on walking rather than having to make any sort of conversation with my fellow travellers. Once we arrived in Capernaum Izzy had kept with the group and I, along with Josh and Dan, had been left to sort myself out.

I had found the casual work with Zebedee and not worried too much about what Izzy got up to until Zebedee's two sons, James and John, had joined Jesus' group.

I could still remember the look of amazement on Zebedee's face, which quickly changed to fury, as his two sons got up and left their work on the fishing nets to go off with Jesus. It had left Zebedee in a real mess, but it had worked out well for me. I told the deserted father that Izzy had done something similar to our father. This had earned me extra work and a bumper wage that day with regular casual work ever since.

But not today. For all of my good standing with Zebedee, all the work would be done down on the shore of the Sea of Galilee by now and there would be nothing else happening until the boats put out this evening. I looked around. There was no one looking to hire workers now in the village and to wait around hopefully would be a waste of time. A neighbour who

I had occasionally gone drinking with walked past with his wife. I went to acknowledge him when the wife grabbed her husband's arm and determinedly walk by, ignoring me. She must have seen Naomi leaving the house and realised what she was. It would be a long time before the wife let her husband spend time with a man who brought prostitutes back to his house and slept with them all morning. She'd also be quick to tell the other women in the area about her immoral neighbour. I did not have any close friends and even the number of my acquaintances was reducing.

That made up my mind.

'Sure, why don't we go and see your Jesus. It'll beat hanging around the house all day and dying of boredom.'

'Great.'

Izzy could be a great actor, but it was his eyes that gave him away. He had obviously expected me to turn him down and while his mouth smiled at my acceptance, the panic at what he had let himself in for was clear to see in the widening of his eyes. I wondered what Izzy had to hide and my determination to find out gave me a new enthusiasm for going with him.

'So, where do we go?' I asked.

'I'm not sure, I was going to find out once I'd had something to eat.'

'That's great, I'll join you for your meal. But where were you going to get the food from?'

'I was going to buy some at the market . . .'

Before Izzy could say another word, I had him by the throat, pinned up against the wall of their house. I was overcome with fury.

'And where were you going to get the money from to buy the food with?' I spat in his face.

This time Izzy did not try to hide his panic. He scrambled and wriggled, trying to get free of my grip but it was no use, I had him and there was no escape.

'I've got a few coins on me,' he managed to gasp out as my grip pinched his airway.

'And where did those few coins come from? You don't do any work.'

I waited for his answer. It was only as I noticed Izzy's face was slowly turning blue and that his normally bright eyes were starting to dull that I released my grip, allowing him to breathe again. Izzy slumped back against the wall and took some deep breaths. I waited to see the colour come back to his face before I placed both my hands threateningly on Izzy's shoulders.

'Well, I'm waiting for an answer. Tell me where you got the money from or next time I won't let go of your throat as soon.'

Izzy looked at me, knowing he was beaten and that he would have to reveal his money source.

'I look after the money people give Jesus.'

'What do you mean, the money people give to Jesus?'

'As He goes round teaching, people give Him money. Not a lot, but some. I look after it. Sometimes I borrow some of it.'

Izzy looked thoroughly ashamed. Here he was admitting to a murderer and mugger that he was a petty thief and yet he felt ashamed of his crimes. I began to chuckle. Then I began to laugh. Izzy looked at me.

'What? You think it's funny that I steal money from someone who's a good man?'

'No, I think it's funny that you look after the money. How much is it? We could use it ourselves and no one would find out. Well, not for a while anyway. I think it's a great idea for me to come and see Jesus today. You could be sitting on a gold mine!'

'No, Barabbas, I'm going to pay back the money I've borrowed. I won't steal from Jesus. I won't take advantage of Him.'

Suddenly my hand was back around my brother's throat. But there was no fury in my actions this time, just cold calculated menace.

'Listen to me, you little runt. I've spent years of my life in squalor and poverty because of you and now you're going to make it up to me or I'm going to kill you. The choice is yours.'

The fight went from Izzy's face. As much as he was able to, he nodded his head in acceptance. As I released him I felt a pang of sorrow as I realised that the improved relationship we had enjoyed over the past couple of years had ended. There could be no going back now. Izzy was under my control and fearful for his life. We would never be friends again. For a moment I regretted this turn of events. But then my stomach growled, reminding me of my hunger and of the days of hunger and misery Izzy had been responsible for in the past. It was time for him to pay me back. And that payback started today.

'Right,' I said as I shoved Izzy away from the wall of the house and towards the village centre. 'Let's go find something you can buy me to eat and then let's go and find this Jesus of yours.'

Izzy did not say a thing. He hung his head and set off towards the market.

CHAPTER FOURTEEN

THERE WERE THOUSANDS OF THEM, literally thousands.

I stood in wide-eyed amazement as I saw the hordes of people who were flocking to see Jesus. When I was a young boy I went up from the farm with my family to Jerusalem for one of the main festivals. I've never been sure which festival it was, and I don't remember much of what we did; but I always remembered being astonished by the number of people who made the journey to the country's capital city. We had passed large groups of people on the roads into Jerusalem and the city itself had been packed with Jews observing, what was it, Passover, Pentecost? I'm really not sure.

But just outside the small village of Capernaum, miles away from the Holy Temple in the centre of Jerusalem, it seemed as if even more people had congregated to see Jesus. I knew that there would be many more people in Jerusalem in a few weeks for this year's Passover, but somehow the crowd here was more impressive. Perhaps it was the sense of expectation which everyone in the throng had as opposed to the resigned boredom which some in Jerusalem would have at attending yet another festival.

I knew why the people here had that sense of expectation. The people were drawn to Jesus because it was said he healed the sick. Izzy had mentioned about some blind people being made to see and other men he had told me of who were the friends of a cripple had lowered their friend on a mat through a roof and Jesus had healed him. I did not buy any of these stories. Over the years there had been no end of people who had made claims about being able to heal, but I knew all of them had been fakes. One of them had even 'healed' Josh of a lame foot. Josh had never been lame, but he had been broke and the denarii he had earned that day had bought the family a good meal — now *that* had been a miracle.

Jesus' reputation had yet to be tarnished and so the crowd was made up of blind people being led by seeing friends and cripples being carried by naïve but well-meaning family members. But there was something else that drew this huge crowd. It was obvious to anyone watching and could be heard on the lips of some of those in attendance. People were talking about Jesus being the Messiah — the longed-for new leader of the Jewish people who would free them from the Roman occupying forces and make the nation great.

Jesus was following a long line of would-be Messiahs, and he was certainly building up the largest following of any which I was aware of. It was a good job that we were miles away from Jerusalem because if the Romans based there, or the High Priest who ran the city, heard about Jesus and the size of the crowds he was pulling there would serious trouble.

But I knew Jesus was not the Messiah. Izzy had told me that Jesus had grown up in the northern town of Nazareth, whereas Jewish kings came from the southern end of the country. There was also a significant question mark over his parentage. His mother was unmarried when she became pregnant with him and it was said that the man she eventually married, Joseph, was not the baby's father. Illegitimate children were not found on the thrones of Israel. To the man's credit, Joseph brought up Jesus as if he were his own son and they worked together as builders in the construction of Sepphoris, a new city that had been built just a few miles from Nazareth.

As an illegitimate jobbing builder from the wrong part of the country, Jesus did not have the credentials to be the longed-for Messiah. But I realised how much the people wanted him, or someone, to be the Messiah and I knew they would conveniently overlook the shortcomings of Jesus' claims to be their king. Hence the crowds that were flocking to see him today. I stood, lost in awe at the impact Jesus was having on so many people, my brother included.

'See, Jesus is big news. People love Him, some of what He says is unbelievable . . . '

It amazed me how resilient Izzy was. It was only a little while ago that I had been throttling the life out of him and forcing him into swindling Jesus out of his funds. Our relationship had changed at that point and we both knew it. But now, here was Izzy chatting away to me as if everything was still the same. Perhaps that was the impact Jesus had on him. However, the rest of my brother's speech on the qualities of his new hero was lost on me as I spotted someone I knew in the crowd. I would have recognised that figure anywhere, particularly when I had enjoyed its finer points only the night before. Naomi looked even more attractive in the bright light of day than she did in candle light. Izzy noticed that I was not listening to him and followed the direction of my gaze.

'Oh, I see you've noticed Naomi, can't blame you for that.'

'You know her?'

'Yes, she hangs around a lot with us, I'm pleased to say.'

Not for the first time that day I could have throttled my brother. Was this the reason why Izzy had wanted to keep me away from Jesus and the others? Was he interested in Naomi as well? I decided at that moment that if I could not have Naomi then I would not let my brother have her. Did he know what she did at night? Or was Izzy another of her paying customers? Before I could take those thoughts any further, two other familiar faces appeared on the scene.

Josh and Dan sauntered across the landscape. As they ambled along I shook my head in resignation. They had to be two of the most dim-witted men in the midst of the crowd. Not for the first time, I found it hard to understand how they could drift through life without any purpose or any worries. But, then again, perhaps it was me who had got life wrong. They were always happy enough in their stupidity whereas I spent most of my life feeling miserable and hopeless. I called them over.

'Josh, Dan, come here I've got a job for you to do.'

The two looked worried.

'There are so many people here,' I continued, 'that some of them are not going to be as careful with their possessions as they could be. You are going to find those who are not looking after their purses and relieve them of their wealth.'

Before I could go any further, Izzy interrupted me. 'No, Barabbas, you can't do that, not here.'

Both of the cousins turned to look at Izzy, but I ignored his interjection and continued to address Josh and Dan.

'You know how to do this without getting caught. We will meet at our house this evening and share out the proceeds. Don't try to swindle me of anything because I will know if you try.'

'What are you and Izzy going to be doing then?'

I was unsure if Josh was trying to stand up to me or if this was a genuine question.

'Don't worry about me and Izzy. You and Dan do your bit and Izzy has his instructions. When we meet up this evening all of us will be bringing along cash to share out.'

Josh and Dan both looked satisfied with this answer. They knew it would not do them any favours to argue, and, in a strange way, I knew that they trusted me. Izzy, on the other hand, looked far from satisfied. He hung his head. But I knew him well enough to know that he would be at the house this evening with the money he had taken. I also knew that once my brother had drunk a few glasses of wine, paid for from the bounty, his guilt would disappear. But I had to make sure that the work was done first.

'Right, let's get to it! See you this evening.'

With that the other three left and merged into the crowd leaving me on my own considering my options for the afternoon. I had no intention of bringing in any money that day. The others would not like it, but none of them had the nerve to stand up to me. They would grumble as they handed over the money and probably curse me behind my back, but I could cope with that. I was going to enjoy my afternoon risk free. The question was, would it be in Naomi's company?

Most of the crowd had walked past me now, moving on to a green bank by the Sea of Galilee where Jesus was going to speak to them. If I was going to spend time with Naomi I would have to move quickly in order to catch her. I was just wondering if she was worth the trouble and beginning to decide that she was, when suddenly every plan I had for the rest of the day changed instantly.

My stomach turned and a flush of colour came to my face as I looked to see the last of the stragglers make their way towards Jesus. Standing there in the crowd, looking straight at me, was my mother.

CHAPTER FIFTEEN

I WAS FROZEN TO THE spot. The shock of seeing Mother again after two years stupefied me. There were so many questions to ask: where had she been? Why had she left? What had she been doing? But, as I stood there, the only question that screamed in my head was 'Can I run away and pretend that I'd not seen her?'

However, that option was soon robbed from me as the woman I'd not seen for months strode purposefully towards me with the glint of fury in her eyes.

'Fine son you are, running off and abandoning me like that.'

Despite my shock and the stinging reprimand, I had to smile. Mother had obviously not changed. At that precise moment I realised how much I had not missed her or her vicious tongue one bit. But rather than being angry myself I found the only emotion I felt was pity. It had to be hard living every day of your life with such constant bitterness. However, I still was not going to let her get away with her barbed accusations.

'As I remember it, Mother, it was you who ran out on me and Izzy after I was taken off to see Jericho Zac.'

'What? You stupid boy, I didn't run out on you, I was trying to help . . .'

' . . . by taking off?' The pity was quickly giving way to fury. But I was not going to allow her to rile me now as she had done so many times before. I had moved on. It may not have been to a particularly better place, but it was certainly better without her. I stopped myself from launching my own tirade at her and instead turned to walk away.

'I'm sorry Mother, but I don't have the time or the inclination for this, or for you.'

My mother reached out and grabbed my arm. It was all I could do not to swing around and knock her to the ground. But there were too many other people around. People who would not begin to understand what this woman had made me suffer through the years. They would just see a huge thug attacking a poor, old, defenceless woman. There would be only one of us who would gain the crowd's sympathy, and I knew she would milk it for all it was worth. Some of the people around us were already starting to take far too much notice of this family reunion for my liking already. As I fought the urge to push her away, I made myself stand still, and then turn back to the woman who had given birth to me. As I did so, a pain in my head started banging relentlessly. It must have been the stress.

'I'm sorry, Son, I shouldn't have called you stupid. Please forgive me.'

I was stunned; it was as if I had been transported to another world. I struggled to remember the last time I had heard such tenderness in my mother's voice. Then I remembered, it was as she said goodbye before Jericho Zac's thugs had dragged me off to Jericho. Perhaps she had left the house to try to help, but I found it hard to understand what she could have done that would have helped me, her or Izzy.

'So, if you were trying to help, what did you do. Where did you go?' I asked.

'It's complicated. I can't explain it here. There are too many people about. But I promise you, I was helping you.'

Incredibly, tears started to run down her old, wrinkled cheeks. I wanted to believe her, I really did, but I could not see how her running off and leaving the family would have been any help at all.

'But where did you go?'

'Barabbas, I can't tell you that now. Please, stop all these questions. It was a long time ago and it won't do you any good.'

She was lying. Instinctively I knew it. My mother had only ever looked after herself. I knew I meant nothing to her.

'You're a lying cow. You've never done anything to help me. Not ever. And certainly not when Jericho Zac had me naked and beaten in front of him. I was saved by some mystery man on a horse and if I ever find out who he was I'd kiss his backside. I wouldn't even waste my time to kick yours, though you deserve it!'

With that I strode off. I started heading in the opposite direction to the rest of the crowd, back towards home. People began to shout at me as I pushed my way past the last of the Jesus hoard. I didn't care if it was women, children, or cripples who got in my way; I was too blinded with fury to care who I was shoving. I thought I might have heard my mother calling after me, but it could have been just the noise of the melee. Even if I'd been certain, I would not have turned around or responded. She had walked out of my life, and I was not going to let her back in again.

It was amazing how quickly my day was turning sour. It had started so well, waking up within the company of a beautiful woman. But now it was difficult to see how it could get any worse — but it was just about to. As I rounded the corner of the lane my house was in, I saw two men, both bigger than me who didn't look as if they were there for a social visit. I had never seen them before, but I remembered too clearly other men like them. They were hired muscle.

There was only one reason why hired muscle ever came looking for me. I was behind with my debt repayments and these two were here to collect what was owed. After my night with Naomi, a day without any work, and with Izzy, Josh, and Dan yet to come back with their pickings, I was not yet in a position to be able to make any payments.

I wanted to try to get away without them seeing me. I was still a way off from the house, so I stood a chance of them not seeing me. But then they turned and looked in my direction. I could have tried to plead my way out of the situation, but the two men did not look as if they dealt much in polite conversation. Without waiting another moment, I turned and ran.

It took them only a few seconds to realise who I was and that I was not intending to make any sort of payment. They shouted as they chased after me. My brief sight of them led me to guess that they were anything up to ten years younger than me and I knew that they would eventually catch up. My only hope was that the headstart I had on them would be enough for me to reach the crowds which had come to see Jesus. Once I reached them, I hoped I would be able to lose myself in the masses.

It also surprised me how much extra energy sheer fear gives and how easy it was to ignore the banging in my head after my encounter with Mother. I sprinted towards the outskirts of the people. I wanted to look behind, to see if the two men were gaining, but I feared looking back would lose me vital seconds. I kept looking forward, but the crowd seemed to be constantly moving further away, although the rational side of my brain was telling me that the people were standing still and not moving at all.

At any moment I expected to feel a hand on my shoulder, pulling me back. In blind panic, I pushed my way headlong into the throng of people without breaking my stride. The same people I had pushed aside a few moments before as I made my way home were now being shoved out of the way as I went in the other direction. Suddenly my left foot hit something hard and sharp sticking out of the ground. Before I had the chance to realise it was a stone, I was stumbling forward and in just a couple of seconds that stumble turned into a fall. I landed flat on my face, exhausted and winded by the impact with the ground.

I shuddered as I waited for my pursuers to catch up and haul me away. Slowly I turned around and came face to face with two men bending over me. But they were not the two thugs from outside my house. Instead there was only concern as they offered their hands and pulled me gently back onto my feet.

Having looked around and realised that I had lost my pursuers in the crowd, I thanked the two men who had helped me and began to wander further into the crowd. Unfortunately, it was a hot afternoon and many people there stank, but I was more concerned about putting distance and people, lots of people, between me and the debt collectors. Just as I was congratulating myself on my escape two hands sprung out from the crowds and grabbed me.

'Barabbas!'

There had been many times in past when I had come close to killing Izzy and this was another time to add to the list. It took only a couple of seconds for me to recognise him and realise that there was no danger, but what was actually a fleeting moment had felt like a lifetime. My entire stomach had churned at the prospect of being captured. I was about to launch a volley of abuse at him, but Izzy did not give me the chance.

'Mother's here!'

'I know, I've already seen her. But I want nothing to do with her. She's abandoned us once and I'm not going to give her opportunity to do it again. You need to forget about her.'

'But this is our mother. The woman who gave birth to us. We can't just ignore her, we've a responsibility to look after her.'

Jewish society expected sons to look after their widowed mothers if they were too old to marry again. But I knew that what Izzy really meant was that I had a responsibility to look after her as Izzy had never taken a responsibility seriously in his life. I sighed.

Was this really my lot in life? To be lumbered with the responsibility for my mother, brother, and two idiot cousins? When I had first come to Capernaum without Mother and with Izzy so caught up with Jesus, I had enjoyed a degree of freedom I had never experienced before. But slowly that had been eaten away as my debts piled up and Izzy spent more time in the house. Now Mother had returned. I briefly remembered the time I had spent last night with Naomi and realised that would never happen again with my mother back. Life was so unfair.

The pounding in my head increased. Perhaps I would have been better off being caught by the two thugs.

I allowed myself to be guided through the crowds by Izzy, assuming I was being led to wherever my mother and cousins were. I wondered if my day, or even my life, could get any worse as Izzy directed me towards a small group of people slightly set away from the rest of the crowd. As I got nearer I could see Josh and Dan and Zebedee's two sons, James and John.

Suddenly another figure in the group came into view. Naomi was there. It crossed my mind that she might be a guest of Izzy but then decided it did not matter even if she was. Her company, even in a crowd, would make the whole experience a pleasure. Instinctively, I straightened my shoulders and walked purposefully towards the others who were all paying rapt attention to Mother.

'Anyway, I came back just two days later from Jerusalem and found my sons and my nephews had moved, leaving me abandoned and alone in the world.'

It was a lie. Since Mother had been sick she had never been anywhere near Jerusalem, or any other large town. Her sickness meant she was excluded from polite society and her poverty meant she had no place in it anyway. In fact, as I watched the scene of her animatedly telling a fictitious version of her abandonment I realised that it had been many years since she had been the centre of attention. The people around her were evidently unconcerned that her illness meant she was impure and appeared to be enjoying her tales.

'I didn't know what to do. Barabbas had left behind a mountain of debt and I had no idea where he was. But Lazarus and his sisters told me he had joined the others and gone off with Jesus. It's taken me this long to track them all down.'

James, John, and Naomi all looked at her sympathetically, but I knew full well that it would not have taken two years to find us. But then why let the truth get in the way of another good story? Mother was evidently warming to her theme and enjoying her role of story-teller. She had a sparkle in her eyes and she began gesticulating with her hands to add extra emphasis.

'I can't believe I've finally found them. It's been so long since we were last together. But I can remember that last time as if it were yesterday.'

'Yes, so can I. But then again it's not every day that you discover that you and your brother have different fathers.'

A silence suddenly descended and hung over the group like a swarm of gnats: totally unwanted but nobody knowing how best to dispel it. I could have kicked myself. I had wanted to bring Mother back down to size again. I resented the way she was painting me as the bad son and herself as the doting, respectable mother. But I had spoken out of anger and my tone of voice had betrayed that fact.

All of a sudden, Izzy turned around and walked quickly away from the group. Mother called after him pleading with him to come back, but her pleas fell on deaf ears as he determinedly walked away. I knew the shock that he would be feeling now as it would have been similar to mine, but at least I had been told in private and not, as with Izzy, in the company of a crowd of people, some of whom I barely knew.

Everyone else looked uncomfortable. Rather than bringing shame to Mother for her loose morals thirty-odd years ago, I had merely confirmed the bad son image she had painted. After all, good sons never brought shame to their mothers and their families.

Josh and Dan were looking at each other in disbelief as they tried to take in the news. Nobody, including Mother, seemed to know what to do next when the moment was broken by a total stranger who stood a few feet from us. He was too far away to have heard any of what had been said. The man's excited shout caught everyone's attention.

'There He is!'

En mass all the people around us turned to see Jesus. My group's discomfort disappeared completely as every member looked up to see the builder from Nazareth. Izzy even turned around and sprinted back to the group as Jesus looked straight over to us and nodded at me in recognition. I was surprised that one journey we had made together two years ago had stuck in the man's mind.

Then I realised my mistake. Jesus was acknowledging James and John, and even Izzy. I was surprised at how well in with Jesus Izzy was. I thought he had exaggerated their friendship, but obviously they were on good, friendly terms. My shock at this revelation was cut short as my mother moved and stood alongside me.

'Don't you ever shame me like that again,' she hissed in my ear while everyone else's focus was on Jesus. 'I think what I know about you would be far more interesting to other people than anything you could say about me.'

'Don't threaten me, woman,' I barked back, far louder than I meant to, but she had gotten under my skin again, just as she always had.

'Barabbas, what are you doing?' This time Izzy, despite the confusion he must have been feeling, had decided to speak up for his mother.

'Keep out of this,' I retorted. 'You have no idea what she's put me through.'

'I was there. Of course I do.'

'Not for the times when you went off with the family's money and ruined us.'

I was so blind with rage that I was ready to square up to Izzy, Mother, or anyone else who wanted to take me on. Nevertheless, I was still surprised when the man who had signalled Jesus' arrival shouted at me.

'Give it a rest. We're trying to listen here.'

I was aware that all the people around us were staring at the scene of domestic disharmony — even Jesus, who I had been vaguely aware of talking about sheep and money a moment ago, had stopped his teaching. I looked around. There were so many people that there was no obvious path to go down in order to walk away. So instead I cursed loudly, spat on the ground, and turned my back on my family which allowed Jesus to continue speaking.

'This is what God's like,' the travelling preacher continued. 'There was a man who had two sons and the younger one asked his father for his share of the inheritance. The father divided up his property and gave the younger boy his share. That younger son took the money and left the family home and wasted his money on wild and reckless living . . .'

I could not believe what was happening. Jesus was telling the people my life story. Over the time that Izzy had known Jesus he had obviously told him about what had happened when we were younger and now here was the would-be Messiah telling everyone else about it and saying that it was what God was like. Jesus may not be using any names, but it still enraged me to hear my story being told. And anyway, if that was what God was like, then I decided I would rather take my chances as a sinner.

There may have not been an obvious path for me to take from the scene, but I did not care. I was not going to hang around and hear some stranger tell people about things that had happened to my family. Disgusted with the situation, and with myself, I pushed my way past the on-looking crowd and made my way back home again.

CHAPTER SIXTEEN

I LOOKED AROUND AT THE place I called home and was reminded again that it was no more than a dingy hovel. There was one room in which I lived, cooked, kept the animals and sometimes slept if the upper room was already full. It smelt of the animals, but also of the four men who inhabited it. Neither aroma had much going for it, and, with the sun now setting, the house seemed unnaturally gloomy. None of which helped the growing sense of claustrophobia I could feel creeping up on me and taking control.

I knew that my surroundings were only a part of my problems, though. My mother's return had set things back to how they were before. I reflected that earlier on in the day I had asserted myself over Izzy and we both understood that I was the boss. However, with Mother around, and with Izzy discovering that we did not share the same father, I wondered how things would now progress.

The reappearance of Mother had opened up old emotional wounds within me and new ones in Izzy. There were days, sometimes weeks, when I would forget that I did not know whether or not the man who had brought me up was my biological father. Now, though, my head was swimming with all the old questions about who my father may have been and why my parents had never told me that rather important piece of information before. It would have explained so much about my childhood.

As I sat with my back against the wall facing the closed front door, I knew if I opened it the fresh air coming in would help to alleviate the stench of the house. But I didn't want anyone to know I was in. I wanted to be left alone, to brood, and to try and work through the thoughts that were plaguing me, but it was not working, all I had done was make my headache worse and allow self-pity to envelop me.

My life was a mess. It had always been a mess and would continue to be a mess for however long it lasted. Now, to add insult to injury, the local preacher man was using extracts from my life to teach about God — although I never felt that God had taken any interest in me throughout my time on earth. I was also convinced that Jesus' popularity would last only a few more months, perhaps only weeks. Would-be Messiahs had a very short timespan because, in the end, the crowds would grow bored as their latest hero failed to live up to expectations. I knew that once his time was up no-one would remember Jesus' stories, but I was still furious that Izzy had told him about our past.

My self-pity began to subside and was replaced with an ever-growing anger. Anger at Izzy, Mother, Jesus, and life in general. This was not what I had expected as a boy, but that was what came of being illegitimate.

I decided I needed to get up from the floor. I stood and stretched and wondered what to do next. I had no idea how long I had sat there but it had started to get chilly. I walked to the centre of the room in order to rekindle the last embers of the fire. There was no food simmering above it — that had run out the day before. I needed my brother and cousins to return so that they could divide the money they had stolen and then get some food.

As if my thoughts had somehow drawn them to the house, the front door opened and Izzy, Josh, Dan, and Mother entered.

'It stinks in here,' my mother complained.

'It's better in the upper room,' Izzy replied. 'You can sleep in there tonight.'

My heart sunk. My mother was moving back in. She may not have put it that way to the other three, but I knew once her feet were back under the table she would never leave. Another mouth to feed, but, far worse than that, a mouth that never shut up and only ever spoke to complain. I hoped that the other three had stolen enough money to buy enough food for the five of us.

'What did you lot get hold of then?' I asked.

Three guilty faces looked straight back. But I knew the guilt they felt was not because they had stolen but because they had not followed my instruction and had come home empty handed.

'Nothing?' I was incredulous. 'Were none of you even hungry?'

The three men looked down at their feet, studiously studying the floor rather than giving me any eye contact. They knew this was going to be bad.

'They didn't need to steal because Jesus fed us all.'

Mother looked defiantly at me.

'Jesus didn't feed me,' I replied trying my best to keep my voice steady, hoping it would not betray the loathing I felt at that moment for everyone else in the room.

'Well then, Son, you should have stayed.'

'So, Jesus fed every single one of the thousands of people who were there this afternoon?' The sarcasm dripped off my tongue.

'Yes, He did. Someone gave Him a bit of food and somehow, He made it feed every one of us. Shame you could never feed five of us, let alone five thousand.'

Mother's stance had not changed. She continued to stare at me as she stood in the middle of the room with the open door behind her. The last light of the evening was fading behind her and I couldn't help but think about Naomi's silhouette which I had so admired and lusted after this morning. The stark contrast between Naomi's figure and that of my mother only served to remind me of the way my day, which had started so well, had fallen into serious decline as the time had moved on.

'So, tonight it's only me who's going to go hungry then,' was the only response I could muster.

'Sorry, Barabbas, we got caught up in Jesus' teaching.'

If I had been in a better mood, less hungry, and had my day worked out better, I could almost have admired Josh for having the courage to apologise. But I was not in a better mood, I was starving, and my day had been a disaster.

'I don't care how sorry you are. And I'll tell you something else!' I realised I was shouting now. I was on the verge of losing all control, but I needed to keep control if I was to stand any hope of stopping Mother from taking back the authority I had gained over the family in the last two years. I took a deep breath and lowered my voice.

'I don't like Jesus telling everyone our life story. Izzy, you have got a big mouth which you need to learn to keep shut, especially considering what you found out about our family situation today.'

'He didn't know Jesus would use the story.'

It was my mother who spoke. I realised that she didn't want her past infidelities brought up again and spoke to stop the conversation going in a direction she was not comfortable with. As she did so, I could feel the status quo of my earlier life returning. Mother sticking up for the waste of space that was my younger brother.

'Anyway,' she continued, 'Jesus said that the way your father acted, accepting Izzy back into the home after all that had happened was just how God reacts when sinners go back to Him.'

'And I suppose God also treats us as harshly as I was treated?' I couldn't keep the scorn from my voice.

'Of course not,' Izzy replied very matter-of-factly. 'Jesus said no one can be as good as God, but people can sometimes show His character in the way they act. I guess that's what our father did.'

'But he wasn't my father,' I was trembling with rage. 'If that man acted like God, does that mean God spends his time sleeping around like a whore-monger?'

The slap caught me off guard but the resulting sting on my face was somehow familiar. It also caused me to calm down from the hysteria that was beginning to take control. I looked at Mother wanting so much for her to drop dead on the spot. But the selfish old bag just stood there and continued to breathe.

'So, did I feature in Jesus' story at all?'

'Oh, yes,' said Izzy enthusiastically. He obviously hoped knowing the story also featured me would somehow defuse the current domestic situation. 'He said you wouldn't come to the party our parents held. Which, of course you didn't.'

'But He never said my husband died that same night when you were so angry.'

If there was the hint of accusation in Mother's words neither my brother or cousins appeared to pick up on it. I looked into my mother's eyes and realised that she knew I had killed her husband, who may, or may not, have been my father.

As I considered what to say or do next, I saw some movement in the doorway behind the others. As I looked over I saw the two thugs I had escaped from that afternoon. I cursed my luck and I cursed myself. I had become so wrapped up in my own misery that I had forgotten all about my pursuers. Having lost me in the crowd, it was only common sense that they would return to the house once the crowds watching Jesus had dispersed. And here they were now.

Their combined frames blocked the doorway and if I moved towards the window they would easily get there first. There was no escape. But I didn't care. The fight had left me. Today had taught me that I had no control over what happened to me and that, if God was real, he obviously delighted in kicking a person when they were down. Right now, I felt as if I had spent my entire life down and normally out.

My mother's reactions were obviously slowing with age. It took her a few moments to notice that everyone else in the room was staring behind her at the door. She turned around and started at the sight of the two men behind her, but she soon recovered herself.

'And what do you two want?' she asked without any concern that either of them could have broken every bone in her body with one arm tied behind his back.

'We want Barabbas,' one of the men replied. 'Jairus wants to ask him about some money which is still owed.'

My mother turned to look at me.

'You don't change much, do you?' she said.

As I went off with the hired muscle I could not help but think that if Izzy, Josh, and Dan had actually stolen some money rather than meeting her, I might have had some money to pay back.

But I stayed tight lipped. What would be the point of saying anything?

CHAPTER SEVENTEEN

'WHO'S HE? WHAT'S HE DOING here?'

Jairus was a very different kettle of fish to Jericho Zac. There was the physical difference. Jairus would have towered over the tax collector. He stood as tall as me but was much slimmer in build. Then there was the matter of his priorities. The only thing that mattered to Zac was money. He had no family that anyone knew of, whereas Jairus had a wife and young daughter. However, despite his family, Jairus' first focus was on religion.

He was the leader of the local synagogue and his high reputation in the area reflected his position. Money came some way down the pecking order for him. Which was a relief as the one thing Jairus and Jericho Zac did have in common was that I owed them both money and was behind in my repayments.

However, Jairus' off-hand reaction caught me completely unawares. It evidently surprised the two hired muscle men who had been sent out to bring me to him.

'This is the debtor who owes you money, sir. You asked us to bring him in.'

'Did I? Did I?'

It was obvious to everyone in the room that Jairus was utterly distracted and I guessed it was not because the synagogue floors needed cleaning. In fact, looking at the pristine condition of the town elder's home, the synagogue was probably always as spick and span as the large room we were in. It was immaculately clean and every piece of furniture was in its place. This one room alone was the size of my entire house. The distance between the two of us in terms of wealth was huge even though the distance between our actually properties was no more than a few miles.

As I was wondering what was going to happen next a stunningly handsome woman entered the room. I watched her walk towards Jairus, her skin glowing in the lamp light which lit up the room. The subtle lighting only added to her attractiveness. But it was more than just her looks, her body language oozed confidence; this was the mistress of the house. Before she reached her husband, he held out his arm to her imploring her to come to him.

'Is there any change?' he asked. 'Is she any better?'

Jairus' wife said nothing but the sadness with which she hung her head gave all the answer that was needed. Jairus dropped his outstretched arm before she had the chance to reach it and so she stopped still and did not enter any further into the room. Night time has a quietness all of its own, and a silence hung heavily in room before the master of the house spoke.

'My daughter, my poor daughter.'

The anguish poured from Jairus. One of the men who had brought me in coughed in order to get his attention and to remind him, no doubt, of the presence of an outsider in their midst. Jairus looked around distractedly. As I looked at him, a glimmer of hope began to rise up within me. I could see in the other man's eye that the fight had gone from him and that an outstanding debt paled into insignificance compared to whatever problem he had with his daughter.

'I'm sorry,' said the synagogue leader as he tried to turn his mind to the people in the room with him. 'What did you say this man is here for? I really can't remember asking you to get him. My mind's been on my poor Deborah. She's become sicker and sicker as the day's gone on . . .'

Jairus' voice trailed off as his thoughts returned to his sick daughter.

'He owes you money, sir.'

'Well, I can't deal with that now. Let him stay here until the morning and I'll see to him then.'

'When we tried to find him earlier, sir, he ran. He may do the same again tonight.'

'Then stand guard outside the door and make sure he doesn't.'

The tension and strain of having a sick daughter were clearly taking their toll on Jairus as his concerns as a father far outweighed any debt that might be owed him. My hopes continued to rise that things may go well with this creditor.

Briefly my mind flew back to my last encounter with Jericho Zac and the way that had played out far better than I could ever have dreamed with my saviour on a horse. It had been years since I had last given that man a thought, but he had returned to my mind on the same day as my mother had returned and I had been dragged away again because of my debts. I was not expecting a mysterious man on a horse to come riding to my rescue this time. However, I reckoned that, if I was clever, I might be able to save myself this time. A plan began to form in my mind, but as I was grabbed by the two men I realised I would have to act quickly and take a wild chance.

'I think I can help you with your daughter,' I said as I was being frog-marched out of the room.

'What? Don't take him yet.'

This man was desperate to see his daughter well and he was even willing to listen to a debtor.

'Well?' Jairus continued once his hired men had stopped our progress towards the door. 'How can you help my Deborah?'

'I know a man called Jesus who heals people who are sick. I can take you to him. He'll listen to me if I ask him to help you.'

It wasn't completely true, but in the situation I was in I was willing to take that risk.

'Could you?'

With those two words and the renewed look of hope in Jairus' eyes I had a new best friend in the synagogue leader.

'Jesus is in the area at the moment. He was teaching down by the Sea of Galilee earlier today. I could take you to him tomorrow.'

'And what would you want in exchange?'

I was caught off guard by the soft voice of Jairus' wife. I turned to look at her. Even as the lamp light glowed on her skin, I could see an iron-like hardness behind her eyes and in that moment realised that she had already given up hope on her daughter ever recovering from whatever ailment she had. She was not convinced by the thread of hope being offered.

'I suppose,' she continued, 'that you'll want your debt cancelled.'

'And it will be if Deborah is healed.'

The look his wife shot Jairus showed who had the real power in this relationship. I suspected that the position Jairus held in the town and probably a fair proportion of his wealth came from being married to a hard-hearted woman who knew how important business success and status were. She was clearly displeased with the rash promise of a debt being cancelled but she was not going to allow her husband to know that. Instead she smiled at Jairus and walked towards him.

'Of course, you'd be right to do that,' she said as she linked her arm through his. 'But what will you do if this man is wasting your time and his friend can't help Deborah to get well?'

'But I've heard about this Jesus and I've heard that he has healed people.'

'Of course, you have my darling. But this man may be lying. He may not know Jesus at all. You would have to sell him into slavery to settle the debt if he was lying, wouldn't you?'

'I would, I'm not stupid you know.'

Jairus abruptly pulled his arm away from his wife. She hung her head and walked away from him, suitably chastised. I was surprised at the way she had over-stepped the mark in her wifely role. Perhaps she was not as clever as she first appeared. But then I saw the smirk on her face as she walked away from Jairus and realised how clever she had been. A small reprimand now was worth having the assurance that I would be suitably punished for wasting their time and giving her husband what she thought was false hope.

As I looked at her our eyes met and hers clearly displayed the disdain with which she held me. Her husband was oblivious to it all.

'We'll go and see Jesus tomorrow,' he said. 'This man can stay here and take us to him in the morning.'

I was grabbed and taken towards the door by the two men who had brought me to the house. As it creaked open I heard again the soft voice of Jairus' wife.

'And don't forget my husband told you to guard the door.'

There was to be no escape for me that evening and my future freedom hung by a thread. I just had to hope that the thread was strong enough to pull me out of the mess I was in.

CHAPTER EIGHTEEN

IT WAS MY MOTHER'S RETURN rather than my debts that had kept me awake that night. Her return had opened up the old wound of not knowing who my father was and added to that was guilt about the way I had allowed Izzy to discover that we were only half-brothers. I had no idea as to why I felt guilty about that. Izzy had never been a good brother to me and there was no reason why he should be protected from the truth. But I could not shake the guilt.

As I had laid awake, trying desperately to sleep, other memories from the past began to plague my mind. I hadn't given Reuben a thought for many years, but now his memory haunted me as I remembered how he had swindled me and stopped me atoning for my family losing the farm. It struck me that since my escape from Jericho Zac's clutches I had given up on any plans to regain the old farm. I did not even know if it was still there or what had happened to its ownership.

As I struggled with all these questions and emotions I saw the light of dawn coming through underneath the door and with it came another emotion. One that I had not felt for years. It was hope.

I realised that so much of what had kept me awake were things I had already escaped from before. It had been a long time since I had last considered my paternity, my mother, and the problems I had left behind in Bethany and Jericho, and I was confident I would be able to escape from them again.

I had no idea whether Jesus was able to heal Jairus' daughter but I really did not care. Truth be told, I doubted if Jesus could help. However, I was certain that the synagogue leader did not have the guts to actually sell me into slavery despite the promptings of his wife.

Would it really be fair, I could argue to Jairus, to punish me when I had only been trying to help? And I would only have to argue that if I hadn't already escaped. So many people were attracted to Jesus that it would be easy to get separated from my creditor and his henchmen in that crowd. Once I'd gotten away I would move on again to a new area as I had done with Zac. And just as moving on that time had separated me from Mother, so this time would have the same result. In fact, on this occasion I would move on without Izzy and the cousins as well. I didn't think it likely that someone like Jairus would pursue my family for the debt, and even if he did, I had had enough of always worrying about them. They would have to sort themselves out.

With this plan in mind and certain that the day would be the start of a whole new chapter for me, I had finally gone to sleep, but it wasn't long before one of Jairus' servants brought me some breakfast. It was only dried bread and some wine, but it must have been the first time I had ever been brought breakfast in bed. I decided it was an omen that this was going to be a good day.

I looked outside and saw that the early-morning sun had been replaced by grey clouds which threatened to bring rain. I hoped any bad weather would not stop the crowds gathering to see Jesus as I would need them to help my escape.

But my concerns about the size of the crowds evaporated as the two thugs who had brought me to Jairus entered the room. The smile that had been on my face was lost completely as I saw that they had brought a pair of shackles with them.

'I said to the boss,' one of the men said, 'we wouldn't want to lose you in the crowd like we did yesterday.'

The sneer on his face left me in no doubt that they had second guessed my plan. Even though their boss was so desperate about his daughter that he had not thought of it, his two muscle men obviously had.

They shackled me to the biggest of the two goons as we walked down with Jairus and some of his other servants towards the crowds who were gathering by the water's edge waiting for Jesus. To add insult to injury the threatened rain materialised and soaked me to the skin. The certainty I had felt over my future when I first woke up had been washed away in the deluge.

Despite the weather, the crowds were as large as the previous day, perhaps even bigger. Now the throng that I had hoped would be my salvation were presenting me with the problem of how I was going to get anywhere near to Jesus. We had been walking around for hours trying to find the miracle man and work out how to get to speak to him. With each change of direction, each dead end, and each minute that passed, a growing sense of dread built within me. Today was not going to go the way I had planned.

'So, how do we get to see Jesus? You did say you knew him.'

Jairus' words, spoken with such hope and anticipation, only served to deepen my dread and lack of hope. My intention had been to slip away early so that my lack of familiarity with Jesus would not become evident. I desperately tried to think of what to do, of how to buy myself some more time.

'I can't work out where he is yet,' I replied. 'But I'll keep looking.'

'Mind that you do. Deborah's in a desperate state.'

That was true. If his daughter's sickness had left Jairus distracted the previous evening, this morning it had left him distraught. Her condition, which had come upon her suddenly, had deteriorated significantly over night and, by the whispered conversations between the servants, it was only a matter of time before Deborah died. If I was still a captive when that happened having failed to take Jairus and his party to Jesus, I shuddered to think what the outcome would be for me. Perhaps it would have been better to have perished at the hands of Jericho Zac, unless another secret saviour on a horse was going to come galloping to my rescue. Somehow, though, I thought that an unlikely scenario.

The guy I was shackled to suddenly gave me a mighty thwack to my midriff. Having been joined to me all morning, he probably realised that I had no more of an easy route to Jesus than anyone else in the crowd. With my wet clothes clinging to me I was already feeling uncomfortable, but my current predicament was providing a new level of discomfort. I desperately needed something to go my way, but for that I needed my own miracle.

Then my miracle appeared. I saw one of my boss' sons just a few yards away. I needed to get his attention quickly or the opportunity would be lost. In a moment of blind panic, I could not remember which of the sons it was. The man was already walking on ahead when I suddenly remembered.

'John!' I called out after him. 'John, son of Zebedee!'

For a moment, the noise of the crowd seemed to have stopped John from hearing, but to my relief the man turned around. However, there was no look of recognition on John's face, not even a hint that he knew who I was.

'I'm Barabbas. I work for your father.'

John looked at me and then at the shackles I had on. It would have been bad enough if they were just attached to my feet alone, but to be chained to another man gave me the look of a desperate criminal. In truth that was an accurate description, but it was not the impression I wanted to give John. It was clearly, though, the impression he got.

'Look, if you've done something wrong there's nothing I can do about it. I can't get involved. If you work for my father you'll know I don't spend much time with him and the boats anymore, I spend most of my time with Jesus now.'

I was aware that Jairus was listening to John and the look on the synagogue leader's face told me that he was beginning to doubt my closeness to Jesus and his people. John started to turn to walk away. I could see the opportunity slipping through my fingers. I had to do something, anything to save my skin.

'No, you misunderstand me. I'm Izzy's brother.'

'Of course, you are,' John turned and looked squarely at me, recognition dawning on his face. 'Now I remember you. You were the one who had a row with your mother yesterday. You threw a tantrum and went stalking off. It was really quite funny.'

The smirk that had started to spread across John's face turned into a belly laugh. He was only a young man, possibly not yet twenty, but my row with Mother yesterday had obviously amused him and he was arrogant enough to show that fact. I desperately wanted to punch the lad and put the smile on the other side of his face. That was the trouble with kids who had rich fathers; they always had a tendency to be arrogant and consider themselves more important than anyone else. I would have taken great delight in cutting the young whipper-snapper down to size but that would not have helped my current situation. So instead I just stood there and bit my tongue so hard it hurt.

'So, does Izzy know about your current difficulties?' John asked when he realised no one else was going to join in with his merriment.

'I don't know. Maybe.'

'I still don't know what I can do for you, though.'

'I don't want you to help me.' I tried to level my tone so as not to sound petulant. 'There's a good man here called Jairus and he needs to see Jesus.'

'What? The synagogue leader?'

Of course, John would know Jairus. A synagogue leader and a local businessman such as John's father would move in the same circles.

'Yes, it's me, John. I need Jesus' help. Deborah is very sick, at death's door. I need her to be healed. Can Jesus do it?'

The look of desperation on Jairus' face was evident for everyone to see. A flicker of shock briefly crossed John's face. Normally a man in Jairus' position would look refined and distinguished without a hair out of place. After a sleepless night and a soaking in the recent down-pour, Jairus looked almost as unkempt and dishevelled as me. His current appearance and the emotional agony which he was so obviously going through was enough to convince John that he had to act.

'I can get you to Him,' he said. 'But we're going to have to be quick because I think He's got plans to move on soon.'

'The quicker the better,' replied Jairus, his voice taking on a new sharpness. 'We've wasted enough time with this fool leading us round in circles.'

And so, the party set off. John and Jairus led the way followed by the household servants who had come with them. I brought up the rear with my two guards. I was wet and tired, and the ordeal of trying to find Jesus had left me physically drained. I struggled to keep up with the others; the shackles were rubbing my ankles forming painful blisters. But, despite this, a small modicum of hope returned. We were now going to find Jesus. Even if the preacher failed to heal Deborah, I had at least tried to help which may yet stand me in good stead.

I tripped and stumbled, almost pulling my shackled companion over on top of me. Instead he reached out and pulled me back to my feet, wrenching my shoulder in the process. I gave out a loud yell of pain, and yet no one in the party took the slightest bit of notice. I cursed and carried on walking, only to find that the rest of the group had already come to an abrupt stop. There, just a few feet in front of us, Jesus was speaking to the crowd.

'Barabbas, what are you doing here?'

Of course, Izzy would be right by Jesus listening to his every word. Somehow, he had managed to miss the rain and stood looking his normal smug self, making me look even more like a drowned rat. Worse still, standing next to Izzy was Naomi. She was as captivating as ever. She looked over but barely appeared to recognise me. I must have looked even worse than I imagined. At some point my luck must be due to change, but it was clearly not going to be now.

Before I could reply to Izzy's question, John moved forward with Jairus at his side.

'This man's daughter is desperately sick. He wants Jesus to heal her.'

'Well, we can't interrupt Him,' Izzy answered. 'He's teaching at the moment, but we can speak to Him once He's finished.'

'Who is this man?' Jairus was in no mood to wait.

'This is Barabbas' brother, Izzy,' John explained. 'And he's right. I know we need to get Jesus to Deborah as quickly as we can, but Jesus will want to finish His teaching first.'

Jairus looked less than impressed at having to wait. His whole party knew any delay could be fatal. In normal circumstances I would have been concerned about the wait, but my attention had been taken by Jesus who was teaching the crowd by telling a story.

' . . . after the man who had been attacked by the robbers had been left by the priest and the Levite, a Samaritan came by. He went to the man and tended to his wounds. Then he put him on his donkey and took him to an inn where he paid for the man to have a room.

'The Samaritan paid for more treatment and paid the inn keeper for two more days' stay for the victim saying that if the bill came to anymore he would pay it on his return.'

I wanted to yell out — to stop Jesus telling this new story from my own life. I swung around and grabbed Izzy, sending a wave of agony up to the shoulder the guard had wrenched a few moments earlier. The pain did not help my mood.

'What have you been doing? Is there any event in my life you've not told Jesus about?'

Izzy looked shocked and bewildered at my reactions.

'He's not mentioned you were part of the thieves and He's not even said it's a true story,' he said as he pulled himself free. 'I've heard Him tell this one before actually. He's trying to make people see that even people like the Samaritans can be our neighbour and that we have to look out for people whoever they may be.'

'I don't care what he's trying to get the people to see,' I hissed back, my face contorted with frustrated rage. 'I don't want him talking about things that have happened to me. You should learn to keep your mouth shut. Nobody needs to know about my past.'

Before Izzy had the opportunity to reply a new buzz came over the crowd. Jesus had finished his story and John and Jairus had told him about Deborah. Jesus had clearly agreed to go to the synagogue leader's house and the crowd were moving on with him. I was pulled away from my brother as my guard moved off with the rest of Jairus' party. Izzy followed, too, but at a safe distance from me. He was clearly keen to avoid having to answer any more of my questions.

I began to wonder how many of Jesus' stories featured me and decided that if this mess with Jairus was ever resolved, I would spend more time listening to the builder-turned preacher from Nazareth.

It was a fair distance from the shore of the Sea of Galilee where Jesus had been teaching to Jairus' house but we were covering it quickly as Jairus set a fast pace back to his home. The pain from my blisters was getting worse and I was struggling to keep up as the party pushed our way through the accompanying crowd of people. I was relieved when I saw Jesus stop walking. It was obviously an unexpected stop because Jairus continued on a few more steps before turning and realising that Jesus was no longer at his side.

'What is it?' he asked. 'Why have you stopped? We need to get back. She's so sick.'

'Somebody touched me.'

I could not understand what Jesus was doing. Why had he stopped just because someone had touched him? Of course someone had, probably dozens of people would have pressed or pushed against him in the crowd which was with us. Jesus' close followers plainly felt the same.

'With this number of people around you that's not surprising, teacher.' John did his best not to make Jesus look stupid.

'Now, can we move on?' Jairus was beginning to panic.

'No,' said Jesus. 'Someone touched me because they wanted to be healed. I felt the power come out of me. Who was it? We won't move on until I know who it was.'

There was an uneasy restlessness within the crowd. Jesus had contradicted someone of the standing of Jairus. That did not happen every day, particularly when his desperation was obvious to everyone there. The crowd wanted to know what would happen next. Would Jairus force Jesus to move on or would whoever had touched him own up?

'We're wasting precious time.' Jairus was close to tears as he tried to fathom how to deal with Jesus who clearly did not operate to the same rules as everyone else.

'I just need to know who touched me,' replied Jesus calmly.

'It was me.'

I would have known that voice anywhere. Unlike the rest of the crowd who turned towards the direction the words had come from, I did not have to look to see that it was my mother who was walking forward towards Jesus and Jairus.

'I'm sorry,' she continued. 'I have been ill for so many years and I thought if I could only just touch Your cloak, Jesus, that I would be healed.'

'Who are you?' Jairus snapped at her. 'Who is this woman?'

'This is my mother,' Izzy spoke up. 'It's true, she has been ill for many years, all my family's money has been spent on paying for doctors who have done no good at all.'

'Your faith in me has healed you,' Jesus said, looking straight at her with a kinder look than she had ever received from me.

'Never mind her.' Jairus had started to physically pull Jesus along, determined to get him to his daughter as quickly as he could. 'It's this way to my house.'

As he was pulled along Jesus smiled at my mother and she responded with a smile that lit up her whole face.

'Thank you,' she mouthed.

I wondered how long the smile would last once she got home and realised that she had not been healed and that nothing had changed.

As it turned out, the party's restarted journey ended abruptly. A man coming from the opposite direction to the rest of the crowd pushed his way through the oncoming melee. He was shouting out calling for Jairus. When the synagogue leader saw him the flush of colour which had been on his face from the brisk walk drained quickly away as his servant fell prostrate on the floor before him and said the words the whole party were expecting.

'Your daughter is dead.'

CHAPTER NINETEEN

'I BLAME YOU ENTIRELY FOR this. You and your family.'

I could easily have predicted Jairus' response to the news of his daughter's death. It was not a fair response or even particularly accurate, but when a parent loses a child it is only natural for them to look for someone to blame. Naturally enough, that person was me.

I wanted to protest my innocence. Surely it was the fault of the illness she had developed, and, in my opinion, it would have been extremely unlikely that Jesus could have healed Deborah anyway. But I knew that any defence I could muster would not be listened to and would probably make my situation worse — if that were possible.

I stood silently, head bowed, and allowed Jairus to vent his fury. I wondered, somewhat fearfully, what the final outcome would be.

'You told me you could take me to Jesus,' Jairus raged, his eyes bulging and every vein on his neck visible. 'But you took hours just to find one of his followers. Then your brother stops us from speaking to Him and your mother — your mother — delays our trip back so that she can get healed herself. All of this and my daughter dies. Do you have any idea how that feels?'

As I stood there I noticed that some of the shoots coming up from the ground were beginning to flower. Spring was on its way, but I feared I would not live long enough to see the summer. Then I realised that Jairus had stopped speaking. I looked up to see the synagogue leader obviously expecting a response from me. In truth, I had stopped listening long before he ceased to speak, and I wondered what I was expected to say. I tried to think of something which should be relatively safe.

'Sorry.'

It proved not to be as safe as I had hoped. Jairus strode forward and pushed me to the ground which resulted in my shackled companion crashing to the dirty road as well.

'Sorry?' Jairus was clearly losing any fraction of self-control he had previously been clinging to. 'Sorry? I'm going to make you sorrier than you have ever been in your entire life. You are going to suffer in ways you could not even begin to imagine . . .'

The words of the town elder trailed off as Jesus gently helped me and my guard to our feet. I was stunned. It was the last thing I had expected. I went to say something, but Jesus spoke before I had the chance.

'Jairus, don't worry. Your daughter will be all right.'

'All right? Haven't you heard? She's dead — and it's your fault as well.'

Jesus looked at the finger pointing straight at him and then looked up at Jairus' face which was twisted in a mixture of rage and grief.

'I heard what they said just as you did. But now, Jairus, hear what I'm saying. Deborah will be all right. Let's go to your house. Don't lose your faith.'

I struggled to understand what Jesus was doing. He knew the servants would only come and tell their master his daughter was dead if they were certain that she was. I was astounded that Jesus was giving this man false hope. But Jairus was accepting it. Confusion passed through his eyes before paternal desperation gave rise to the hope that his daughter was still alive.

'Really? Are you sure? Come on, come on, let's get back.'

A murmur from the crowd began to grow into an excited din. No one knew what was going to happen next. The daughter was dead, the servant had been sure of it, but now Jesus was saying she was going to be all right. That made no sense at all and the mass of people following on to Jairus' home knew it.

Something spectacular was going to happen. Either Jesus was going to do the impossible and bring Deborah back to life, or he was going to land himself in a huge amount of trouble with a powerful man. Nobody wanted to miss the outcome, it would be talked about endlessly in the months to come.

Meanwhile, my blisters were still sore, and I was being dragged along at a rate far quicker than I would have liked. But slowly I began to find my own new ray of hope. There was no way Jesus could bring Jairus' daughter back to life, but, by giving the synagogue leader new hope, Jesus would take the renewed and intensified fury of the grieving father, and that might just allow me the opportunity to come out of this situation alive. I would undoubtedly still be in trouble, but it would be Jesus sharing that yoke with me.

It took me by surprise when we came to an abrupt halt. I looked around and realised we were outside Jairus' house. Since we had left that morning a crowd of people had gathered outside and many of them were weeping and wailing in grief. For most of them the grief was not real but some of them would receive payment from the household for their show of sorrow. Later that 'sorrow' would quickly turn into a drunken delight when they bought ale with the money they would earn now.

'Why have you brought the teacher back with you. Didn't you get my message?'

Jairus' wife now cut a sorry picture of misery. But even with the red rings around her eyes and glistening tears on her flushed cheeks, there was still the beauty I had recognised in the previous day's candlelight.

'He said that Deborah would be all right if He came back with us.'

One day when I had been mending the fishing nets, a vicious storm had blown up on the Sea of Galilee. One of the boats that had been out on the water had been wrecked by the wind and waves and sunk. I'd been called upon to rescue the only survivor of the sinking boat. The man had clung onto a piece of drift wood and had allowed the currents to buffet him towards the shore. I had never forgotten the look of desperation on the man's face as he firmly held the wood hoping that somehow everything would turn out all right. I saw the same look on Jairus' face as he spoke to his wife. He was desperately hoping against hope that his daughter would survive.

Judging by the look on his wife's face, she did not share his hope. Her look was one of contempt that her husband was not man enough to accept that their only daughter was dead.

'There's nothing he can do,' she announced coldly. 'Deborah is dead. I've seen her myself.'

Jairus did not reply. Instead he sunk to his knees and wailed so pitifully it sounded as if his heart might rip open at any moment. By this time the crowd gathered around the synagogue leader's house had become silent as they watched the unfolding picture of grief and misery in front of them. All eyes were on Jairus until someone close by moved a step forward. It was Jesus.

'Get up. Don't worry. Deborah's not dead. She's just asleep,' he said as he gently pulled Jairus to his feet.

Nobody in the crowd said a word; we were all totally absorbed by the scene playing out in front of us. I tried to fathom what Jesus was playing at. His actions and words made no sense at all. Suddenly there was laughter, a woman's laugh. I looked away from Jesus to see Deborah's mother laughing. There was no mirth, though, only mockery and scorn. Soon others around her were also laughing and ridiculing Jesus. But he took no notice of them and instead guided Jairus into the house followed by Zebedee's two sons, John and James and another of his followers who I thought was called Peter.

Others from the crowd were about to follow them in when John turned around and shut the door behind them. Jairus' wife soon stopped laughing when she realised she had been shut out of her own home, but her good breeding meant that she did not open the door and follow the men inside.

As everyone waited to see what was going to happen next the rain started to fall again. I sighed at the thought of another soaking and looked around to see if Izzy and Mother had found anywhere to shelter. That was when I discovered that my family were nowhere to be seen. After the stinging rebuke they had received from Jairus they had evidently thought they would be better off keeping out of the way, leaving me to face my problems alone.

As I bent forward to move the shackle around my ankle, trying to gain some relief for my blisters, my mind went back to the time I had been imprisoned by Jericho Zac. On that occasion my family had failed to be any help as well, and I had been forced to rely on the actions of a mysterious stranger on a horse to save me. 'A friend in high places' Zac had called him. Even two years further on I still had no idea who that 'friend' had been, but I decided that if I ever got out of this present predicament it would be my mysterious rescuer I would go looking for rather than my family.

Those thoughts were interrupted by the sound of the front door to the house opening. It creaked on its hinges but the sound of the complaining, rusty mechanism was drowned out by the collective gasp from the crowd as a young girl, probably around twelve years of age, stepped out into the rain shower and hugged her mother.

'Mummy, I'm feeling so much better now,' her young voice rang out clearly. 'I had a good sleep and now I'm hungry.'

Deborah's mother instinctively flung her arms around her daughter and then proceeded to sob uncontrollably. All good breeding, all composure was gone at the sheer relief and joy of having her daughter back. As I looked on at the scene of maternal love I tried to recall my mother acting similarly. My memory failed me on the matter.

As the other onlookers tried to make sense of what their eyes were telling them, Jairus appeared at the door with Jesus. Both of them had beaming smiles on their faces.

'He was right. He was right.'

Jairus was beside himself with joy.

'Jesus told her to get up and she did. It's a miracle . . . '

Without any apparent warning the smile vanished from the synagogue leader's face as he saw his daughter and wife embraced just in front of him.

'Deborah!' he almost screamed her name. 'Get in. It's raining. You'll catch your death of cold.'

With that Jairus took hold of his daughter and bundled her and her mother into the house. Once he had seen them safely back inside Jairus turned around to face the crowd again, the smile returning to his face.

'Friends, I can't begin to tell you how grateful I am to Jesus. I really thought I had lost my precious, precious Deborah — but, as you can see, I haven't! Listen to this man,' he continued, pointing at Jesus, 'He is surely a man of God.'

As he was speaking Jairus looked around the assembled crowd and his gaze fell on me.

'And you, my good friend,' he said as he walked towards me, clasping an outstretched hand on my shoulder, 'are no longer in my debt. Whatever it is you owe me, forget it. As I promised you last night, my daughter is well, so your debts are forgiven.'

He turned to the hired man who had been shackled to me since breakfast.

'Release this man and let him go.'

With that Jairus withdrew his arm and turned to find Jesus.

'Now come and have some food with me,' he said to his new best friend as Jairus took his turn to guide Jesus into the house.

My shackled partner looked less than impressed at having to release his prisoner without first giving me a good kicking. But Jairus had spoken in full sight of the assembled masses and so there could be no doubt that I was a free man and not to be harmed. So, he did what he had to do. He released me from my chains and grunted. I decided to take the grunt as the acknowledgement of my freedom and turned and walked away.

Earlier I had intended to leave the area alone without returning to my family. But as the rain got steadily harder and I became wetter, I told myself that it made sense for me to return to home in order to get dry before starting my journey. That is what I told myself, but deep down I also knew there was another reason for wanting to go home. After what I had witnessed with Deborah I was beginning to wonder how Mother was.

CHAPTER TWENTY

THE RAIN WAS PELTING DOWN as I approached home. The dirt track that led to the part of Capernaum I lived in had become so saturated that it was beginning to resemble a small stream rather than a road. I cursed loudly as I skidded for the umpteenth time. Soaked to the skin, the rough material of my clothes felt even more uncomfortable when wet, and the rain itself was falling so hard that it stung my eyes. Although when I rounded the corner to reach my house I suddenly became aware of a benefit of the deluge as my stinging eyes saw Naomi standing by the front door.

The rain had soaked through her clothes as well, but the material she wore meant that her dress clung tightly to her body. The thin fabric had become almost translucent as it absorbed the rain. I desperately tried to compose myself before speaking.

'Hi.'

I was disappointed when Naomi did not reply immediately, neither did she smile. She looked uncomfortable. As I approached she raised her right hand and scratched at her left ear. Her arm covered her chest. Even as she stopped scratching her ear, her arm remained awkwardly in front of her. I was taken aback with her newfound modesty.

'Oh, hello, Barabbas,' she said as her face turned crimson. 'I've just been with your mother. Izzy and your cousins left her in the crowd and she couldn't remember her way home. I brought her back.'

'I'm glad you could remember the way. Perhaps you can find your way back here tonight – I'll make it worth your while.'

'No, I'm . . . I'm sorry but I can't. I've decided to change . . . to find another way of making a living . . . I'm sorry.'

As the words stumbled from her, Naomi turned to leave. Before she took more than a couple of paces, and before I realised what I was doing, I grabbed her arm and turned her towards me.

'Then be my girlfriend . . . my partner . . . my wife, whatever you want.'

I pleaded with Naomi, hardly realising what I was saying but then I saw tears welling in her eyes. At that moment she did not need to say anything for me to realise that I did not feature in her ideas for the future, but she spoke anyway.

'No, Barabbas. How could we have any sort of relationship? I don't know you. You were just another customer, a nice customer, but that was all. I need to find new people to be with. People who didn't know me as a prostitute. That's why I'm joining Jesus' group. He's shown me there's a different way I can live.'

She shook herself free of my hold and walked determinedly away. I felt sick with disappointment, and, in a surge of fury, decided that I would have her anyway. Who was she, a cheap prostitute, to walk away and deny me any satisfaction? I lunged at her, twisting her around as we fell onto the sodden earth so that my weight was pinning her to the ground as we landed on it. We were in the open, lying on the street, but I was too crazy to care. Fury and lust drove me on.

I looked at her face. Tears mingled with the falling rain. She knew what was going to happen.

As I struggled with Naomi, her eyes widened with surprise. Before I had the chance to wonder why, a crashing blow swept across the back of my head leaving me stunned. When a second blow hit I fell onto my face with only enough consciousness to sense that Naomi was pushing me away before standing up and running off to safety. A hand grasped a clump of my hair, pulling me to my feet. Then came a familiar voice.

'You disgusting wretch!' my mother hollered. 'I can't believe what you were going to do to that poor girl. Get inside now.'

I was so stunned and had such a large amount of hair being almost ripped from my scalp that I allowed Mother to man-handle me into the house. I saw the plank of wood she had hit me with being picked up by a neighbour who had evidently witnessed the whole scene. I was humiliated but I also felt a rising surge of shame from within. I thought I had loved Naomi, but I was no more than an animal, a brute. As Mother shut the door and let go of my hair I instinctively went over to the furthest corner of the room and curled up in a ball. Mother was ranting, calling me all manner of things, but I didn't hear a word. I was lost in my own world of self-hatred and loathing. I thought I had hit rock bottom before, but now I knew that this was really it. I'm not sure if it was a result of the blows to my head or a natural defence mechanism against the situation I was in but slowly, and without any attempt to fight it, I began to lose consciousness and escape my mother's verbal onslaught.

* * * * * *

I came to and tried to assess how long I had been unconscious. Not long, I guessed, as there was still only me and Mother in the house. She was cooking. I could not determine exactly what was in the pot, but the smell coming from it was making me feel sick and I retched.

'If you're going to be sick get outside.'

I gingerly got to my feet and headed towards the front door. The movement was enough to bring up the contents of my stomach. I managed to get outside the front door before I threw up a puddle of sick. I stood with streaming eyes and a stinging nose, bent over and made sure there was nothing left to come up. I was vaguely aware that the light had taken on the gloom of evening and realised that I must have been unconscious for much longer than I had originally thought.

I straightened up and became aware of a young girl, no more than eight or nine, staring at me before she giggled, evidently embarrassed, and ran off. At that point I noticed for the first time that I was standing in the street completely naked.

'Where are my clothes?' I demanded of my mother as I hurriedly made my way into the house.

'They were wet through,' she replied. 'You would have caught your death of cold if you'd stayed lying in them, so I undressed you.'

I was embarrassed. It must have been thirty years since Mother had last taken my clothes off me. But my embarrassment grew as I remembered what had led me to be out cold and needing Mother's help in the first place. I was surprised to find self-loathing soaring up again. I could not think of anything to say. Instead I looked around for some dry clothes to put on.

'I've spoken to Naomi,' Mother spoke coldly, in a matter of fact way that I found harder to handle than when she raged at me. 'She's said she'll not bring a complaint against you as long as she never sees you again. You are a very lucky man. I told her I thought pigs like you should be castrated.'

I still did not reply. I wanted to escape from the situation and could not look my mother in the eye. I had intended to leave her and the family behind and move to somewhere new. I wished now I had followed that original plan. It would have avoided this mess. Finding some clothes, I quickly put them on and contemplated walking out of the door and not looking or coming back. But before I had the opportunity to do so the door opened and in walked an excited Izzy.

'Mother, is it true? Are you better?'

There had not been many times in my life when I had felt any gratitude towards my brother, but this was certainly one of them. Izzy had always lived a self-absorbed life and so was totally oblivious to the atmosphere he had walked in on. My gratitude to him increased when, for the first time that evening, Mother smiled.

'Yes, it's true. The bleeding has stopped. Jesus healed me.'

The world stopped at that moment. Everything else that had happened that day became unimportant. Had I heard her right? After all these years of illness was my mother finally well?

'Really?'

'I'm not going to lie about something like this, am I?' she scowled as she turned towards me. But then it was gone, and the broad smile returned.

'Well, Jesus is working overtime for this family today,' Izzy said enthusiastically continuing the conversation. 'After all, Barabbas, He got your debts with Jairus cleared as well.'

'Just don't mess it up like you did last time with Jericho Zac.'

Mother's comment took me aback.

'What do you know about what happened then? You'd already run out on us.'

'Izzy told me about it after I heard Jesus' story.'

'What story?'

I was aware that there was a growing level of anger rising in my voice. Surely Jesus could not be telling another story that related to me? How much of my life story had Izzy told this wandering preacher from Nazareth? I looked straight at him, demanding to know more.

'Well, I told Jesus about what happened to you when Jericho Zac took you away,' Izzy mumbled, clearly uncomfortable about confessing; but one glance at me told him he would have to continue with the whole story.

'I told Him how Jericho Zac had cleared your debts but that you had demanded repayment from some other guy which made Zac furious and demand his money back from you again. Jesus never mentioned your name when He told the story, He was just showing how if God forgives us, we should forgive other people.'

It seemed incredible that the lie the father had told his son when I was stealing from him had now become the basis for a moralistic story. If I had been able to control my anger at my brother for blabbing family business to a stranger like Jesus, I might even have seen the funny side of it all. But Izzy had said too much, and I was not going to stand for it anymore.

'You total waste of space . . . '

Before I could launch into a stinging verbal volley of abuse Mother cut me off.

'Barabbas, enough!' She hit the side of the cooking pot with her spoon. The noise seemed to startle her and so she laid it down gently on the side of the pot. As she continued to speak I noticed a softer tone in her voice and a softer look about her face. The healing, or whatever had happened that day with Jesus, had evidently changed her.

'Haven't we all had enough of this constant anger between us?' she said. 'Why do we always have to be shouting and raging at each other? Wouldn't life be better if we just got along?'

I was about to redirect my fury from Izzy to her but she seemed to know what I was about to say.

'I know, I know,' she continued. 'I've been as much a cause of the shouting and cursing in this family as anyone else. But I want it to change. I want us to change. I'm well now and I want to enjoy my new life.'

'I would like to have enjoyed the last thirty-three years of my life,' I snarled back. 'But you did nothing to make that happen. Not you nor my father, no, not my father, your husband. Your affair must have really helped make his life happy.'

'I was raped.'

It was as if Mother had landed another physical blow on me. I reeled backwards from the words, reaching out to the walls to steady myself. I was my father's son: the illegitimate child of a rape victim, now the would-be rapist himself. The son of a monster growing into an even greater one. I sat on the floor and covered my face with my hands.

'Look, what's all this about?' Izzy looked more confused than ever. 'You said something about this before, but I thought it was all just heat-of-the-moment stuff. Don't we have the same father? Who raped you Mother?'

'I'm sorry,' Mother said, 'but it's true. You boys don't have the same father. I became pregnant with Barabbas after I was raped just before I married Simon and every time I have ever looked at Barabbas since, and the blue eyes he has, I've seen my rapist's face. I have relived every terrible moment of that attack. I never even thought about what effect it would have on you and by the time I realised the impact, it was too late.'

'What happened to him?'

There was no reply.

'What happened to him?' I looked at my mother insisting on an answer.

'He got away with it. I didn't know who he was.' The reply came in a whisper.

'Where did it happen?'

'Jerusalem.'

'Then I'm going to Jerusalem and I'm going to find him and kill him.'

The colour drained from Mother's face.

'No, Barabbas, don't do that,' she pleaded. Then a look of hope sprang across her face. 'Anyway, what hope have you got of finding him after all these years?'

'I don't know, but I've got to try.'

Despite my confident reply, inwardly I was trying to work out why I had to try. I realised it was because of all the bad things I had done in the past and failed to atone for. Killing my father, losing the farm, bankrupting the family. All the attacks, robberies, and crimes that I had committed. Somehow, I felt that if I could track down Mother's rapist and make some retribution, that it would cleanse me from the guilt I felt about the past.

But I struggled to see how I could possibly find the man. My only hope would be that the man's blue eyes would make him easier to find. But with thousands of people in Jerusalem at any one time, it would be like looking for a needle in a haystack. Hope and despair were whirling around inside me. Then the conflicting thoughts and emotions were interrupted by Izzy.

'Then it looks like we're all on a trip south.'

I had forgotten my brother was in the room. I looked across at him.

'But what about you?' I asked him. 'What about the fact that we don't have the same father?'

Izzy seemed to be contemplating his response. Part of me, the part I was growing to despise, but couldn't bring under control, wanted him to be devastated by this change in circumstances.

'Barabbas, we have never been close,' he said, 'and my father is still the person I always thought him to be. I don't have any changes in my circumstances.'

Without being able to help myself, I started to laugh. I had spent the past two years carrying the secret of us being half-brothers, not wanting to risk upsetting Izzy with the news. Yet my brother's total self-absorption meant he could shake off the news as lightly as if he had been told that supper would be late that evening.

However, my laughter was not shared by the other two in the room and particularly not Mother. She still looked anxious and I think she may have thought that my laughter signalled the end of my sanity.

'Stop your inane laughing,' she ordered. 'There is nothing to laugh about. You are to forget what I have told you and we will build ourselves new, better lives here.'

'Oh no, Mother,' Izzy responded. 'Like I said, I'm heading south. I came here to tell you that I'm off tomorrow with Jesus and the others to go to Jerusalem in time to celebrate the Passover. And you two can come with us.'

I looked at Mother, and she slowly shook her head, pleading with me not to go. I stopped laughing and looked away. I turned towards Izzy.

'I'll get packed this evening,' I said trying to work out why Mother was so afraid of me going to Jerusalem. If she did not know who my father was then why was she so afraid of me finding him?

The only answer I had to that question was that my mother was lying.

PART THREE
JUDEA 30 AD

CHAPTER TWENTY-ONE

THE TWO YEARS HAD BEEN more strenuous and frustrating than Zacchaeus had anticipated but he had eventually made some progress.

He had resolved to discover why a man of influence in Jerusalem would have been in any way interested in a scumbag such as Barabbas. It defied belief and two years ago Zacchaeus had begun his quest to try to discover why.

He had gone to Jerusalem. That had been a risky thing to do, forcing him to leave his business issues to his hired underlings who he was not sure were up to the job. There had been many sleepless nights before his curiosity eventually won and he made the journey to the capital city. It was there that his eyes were opened as to how little influence a provincial tax collector and money lender had outside of his designated region.

Zacchaeus was used to people stopping whatever they were doing to attend to him when he entered a room. In Jerusalem they barely even acknowledged his presence. In the big city, bereft of power, influence, and standing, Zacchaeus' notoriously short temper was tested to its limit as he found himself having to remain patient with men who, if they were in Jericho, would have been shivering wrecks if he had so much as looked at them.

What was also obvious was that he stood no chance of getting anywhere close to the man who had saved Barabbas. He discovered that he was not going to be granted an audience, but he guessed that even if he had, there would be no way he would be allowed to ask any personal questions.

However, Zacchaeus still had one hope. After Barabbas had escaped from Jericho, he had sent his men to Barabbas' home town of Bethany. They had come back with the news that he and his family had disappeared from the village. The obvious conclusion was that Barabbas' powerful friends in Jerusalem had set him up with a home and income in the city. Reassured that a man the size of Barabbas who had blue eyes would stand out, Zacchaeus didn't think it would take him long to find him even in the capital. But after searching high and low it was obvious that Barabbas had disappeared. After several frustrating weeks, he returned to Jericho unhappy, irritable, and ready to kill someone as soon as he looked at them.

His mood was not helped when he realised that not only had his time away been in vain, but his fears about the competence of his staff had been well placed. He had lost at least a fifth of his wealth through their sheer incompetence. As far as Zacchaeus was concerned, that could all be chalked up with what Barabbas already owed him.

Having wasted time in Jerusalem, his attention for the next few months was focused squarely on first restoring his fortunes to the level they had been at before his time away. Then he took them to even greater levels. As he worked he discovered that his trip to the city had not been entirely in vain. While there he had come across some new ideas on how to raise revenue. The extra bonus for him was that, should anyone in Jericho question what he was doing, he was able to inform them that the schemes were identical to those being practised in the Holy Temple which seemed to quell any objections. His vast fortune grew at a quicker rate than he had enjoyed for many years.

The months went by and, as Zacchaeus' businesses prospered, Barabbas slipped from his mind. Until the time came for the Feast of Tabernacles and he became aware that some of his neighbours were preparing to journey to Jerusalem to share the festival with family. Zacchaeus' mind again turned to the Temple and then, instinctively to Barabbas and his links, whatever they may be, to the authorities in the city.

Zacchaeus had built his adult life on destroying Barabbas and he had failed to achieve his goal. He looked around him and took in the splendour and grandeur of his palatial home; he vowed that he would be willing to lose it all if he could only destroy the man who had dominated so much of his life. It was irrational; he wondered if he might have been going just a little bit mad, but he knew he could never rest, content with his life, until he had brought Barabbas to his knees.

But in order to do that, Zacchaeus needed to know where the man was, and he did not have a clue. He started in the last place he knew Barabbas had been, Bethany. He realised he had to take a different approach to the heavy-handed thugs he had sent to the village the last time, but he wasn't sure how else to go about it.

He made the journey to what he considered to be the pig-sty of a village. He was gratified as he arrived to see that his reputation had gone before him and that people appeared to know who he was. It was probably his height, or lack of it, that first made people suspect his identity and, initially, that irritated him. Then he decided that he cared very little about why people knew him, he was just satisfied to see the fear in their faces as the truth dawned on them. However, that fear was making him as useless in gaining information as his hired muscle had been. People dispersed as soon as they saw him coming, just as quickly as if he had been nine feet tall and solid muscle.

There was somebody who, while not delighted to see him, could not afford to insult him by failing to offer some hospitality while in the village. Zacchaeus was not sure where Benjamin lived but he reckoned that in a small place such as Bethany it would not take him long to find him. He headed towards the part of the village where the houses were less shabby than the others, although there was not a lot of difference between the abodes of the villagers.

As he tried to work out how he was going to identify Benjamin's place, Zacchaeus heard his name being called. He turned and caught sight of Benjamin hurrying towards him. Obviously, the man had heard the gossip that he was in the vicinity and decided it would be advisable to come looking for him.

Zacchaeus raised his hand in acknowledgment while his attention was drawn to a younger man who was accompanying Benjamin. He noticed the man's good looks and slim build. He lowered his hand as a smile spread across his face and it was not at the prospect of meeting Benjamin.

'Zacchaeus, I had no idea you were coming to our village,' Benjamin said between pants as he tried to regain his breath. 'But you are most welcome, most welcome.'

Zacchaeus gave him the briefest of acknowledgments before turning back to look at Benjamin's companion.

'Come, you must come back to my home and eat,' the small-time money lender continued. 'It's just this way.'

Before he knew what was happening, Zacchaeus found himself being man-handled by Benjamin and being virtually dragged towards the man's home. He would have protested at the treatment, but as the other man was turning to walk with them he decided not to resist. It was only a few moments before Benjamin was opening the door to his home and the three men all made their way inside.

'What do you think you're doing?' Benjamin snapped at the third man. 'We'll resolve our business later.'

To his dismay, Zacchaeus realised the younger man was about to leave. He wanted to find a way to prevent that from happening. Without thinking, he said the first thing that came into his head.

'No, no Benjamin. Allow the gentleman to stay. I only have some brief business I need to address with you. Then you'll be free to attend to his needs. Perhaps I may also be permitted to do so.'

Zacchaeus silently cursed himself. He could get away with such comments in the cosmopolitan world of Jericho but not in a small backwards village such as Bethany. He saw the man shift uncomfortably at the innuendo, clearly not sure how to react short of screaming in fright and running out of the house. Benjamin also started at the words. Clearly his tastes were very different to

Zacchaeus' and he clearly did not know how to respond without the risk of upsetting his influential guest.

'Let me quickly get down to business,' Zacchaeus said, trying to regain some authority and control over the room. 'I need to find Barabbas Is—'

Before he could get the oaf's full name out Benjamin's companion gasped and then tried to regain some degree of control. It was clear he knew who Zacchaeus was talking about.

'What?' Zacchaeus demanded of him. 'What do you know of Barabbas?'

Before the man could reply Benjamin cut in.

'Lazarus knows nothing. He is nothing but a simple villager. However, I am sure that I can assist you with your enquiries.'

From the look on Lazarus' face, Zacchaeus was certain he knew plenty that would help him in his search for Barabbas and that Benjamin's intervention was only a ploy to ingratiate himself with his guest. The man from Jericho was going to have none of it.

'Lazarus is it?' he asked of the young man whose face contorted into a mask of horror as he tried to work out if he should help. 'I don't believe Benjamin is right when he says you know nothing. I believe you know a great deal and so I demand that you tell me.'

Lazarus hesitated for a moment. Zacchaeus thought he detected a slight indication from Benjamin giving him permission to speak.

'I knew Barabbas when he lived in the village, but he left Bethany about two years ago.'

Zacchaeus did not know what he had expected Lazarus' voice to sound like, but he hadn't expected the coarse whisper in which his words tumbled nervously out of his mouth. However, he decided he had no time to waste in sympathy and pressed on with his questioning.

'And do you know where he went?'

'I'm not sure exactly where he's settled. But he went up north with Jesus of Nazareth.'

'And I'm supposed to know who this Jesus fellow is?' Zacchaeus' attraction to the man was rapidly diminishing.

Lazarus looked uncertain how to respond. After a few tense silent moments, Benjamin rejoined the conversation.

'He's a preacher, the latest fad. They're saying he's the Messiah, or at least they were. I don't know if he's still trying to make a name for himself.'

'Oh, yes,' Lazarus suddenly found his voice again. 'He's still teaching up in Galilee.'

Zacchaeus was astounded. 'What? Barabbas has gone religious? I don't believe it!'

'From what I heard,' Benjamin replied, 'he needed to get out of town quick and Jesus and his people gave him the cover he needed to escape.'

Zacchaeus could not believe it. How on earth could a man claiming to be from God help a debtor and criminal escape from justice? He found it impossible to understand what made these peasant idiots tick. How could they not realise that money was the only god that could do anybody any good? His blood pressure rose and his could feel his face colouring with rage.

'I know this man owes you money, Zacchaeus. Allow me to send my men up to Galilee to look for him.'

'There's no need for that.' Lazarus stopped abruptly as Zacchaeus turned his attention to him.

'Why not?' he demanded. 'What do you know?'

Lazarus stood in front of Zacchaeus, defying him with his silence. His temper burst forth. He flew at the younger guy, easily knocking him to the floor and winding him in the process.

'Answer me!' he shrieked as he stood over the crumpled body on the floor. 'What do you know? Why don't we need to send anyone to Galilee?'

The fight, and the defiance disappeared from Lazarus' face.

'Because if he's still with Jesus he's on his way back. I've heard they're coming back to Jerusalem for the Passover.'

Before another word was said, Zacchaeus was out of the door and heading back to Jericho. He thought he had seen enough of Jerusalem, but, as he began his journey home, he was already considering what he would need to prepare for another trip to the capital city.

CHAPTER TWENTY-TWO

'I DON'T BELIEVE IT. HE'S just called Jericho Zac over to him.'

I sprang around to see where Josh was looking and saw a commotion by the side of the road. Three thuggish looking men appeared to be taking part in a dance routine around the trunk of one of the trees that lined the road. But I could not see the diminutive tax collector anywhere. Then I realised that what had looked like a dance was actually the three men reaching up into the tree and helping Jericho Zac to clamber down from its branches.

As the people gathered around realised that someone of the tax collector's importance had climbed a tree like a street urchin in order to see Jesus, they couldn't contain their laughter. Jericho Zac did his best to retain his dignity as he descended to the road. However, I failed to see anything funny in the situation. I groaned inwardly as I discovered that my old fear of Jericho Zac still had the ability to turn my bowels to water.

I hadn't wanted to come through the city in the first place. I'd joined with Jesus and his followers to journey from Capernaum in Galilee through to Jerusalem in the southern area of Judah simply for convenience and safety. It was always better to travel with a group, even when the group contained my pain in the backside family and a woman I had attempted to rape. Naomi had kept a considerable distance the entire trip and I could not blame her. At first, I was pleased, as it saved any awkward conversations. But as the group had journeyed on I had wanted to speak to her again and, staggeringly, to apologise for my actions although I could not understand why.

I never apologised, except occasionally to my mother. To be honest, I was struggling to come to terms with the new emotions I was feeling. I also noticed changes in my family. Now that she was well, Mother was a different woman. Despite her reaction to my attack on Naomi and the trip to the capital, she had been far more caring. Even Izzy and my two cousins seemed different and certainly less annoying. I wondered whether life could be better for all of us and if spending time with Jesus was actually doing us good.

But all these positive thoughts had come to an abrupt end the previous day. Word got around that Jesus wanted to make his way to Jerusalem via Jericho. There was no need to take in the smaller city on the way to Jerusalem but that was the route Jesus had settled on.

I still owed Jericho Zac money and there was also the small matter of the tax collector's hired man. But there was nothing I could do. I had reflected that it was probably safer to keep with the group, keep my head down, and hope I did not encounter him. That was certainly a better plan than for me to travel on to Jerusalem by myself. After all, I knew better than anyone how dangerous the roads into the capital city were.

Now, though, disaster had struck, and it was all Jesus' fault. A huge crowd of people had come out to meet the preacher and healer, and I had worried that Zac might have been amongst them. Just to be safe, I had stayed in the middle of the group which had come with Jesus. I was head and shoulders taller than any of them, but I hoped that, even a big man like me, could be lost in the melee that always seemed to follow Jesus. But now Jesus himself had called Zac over to him, within a few yards of where I was standing. This had the potential to go very wrong for me.

The short tax collector looked a mess with sycamore leaves caught in his hair. I was sure I saw some cuts and bruises on his face. Jericho Zac normally paid close attention to his appearance and the look on his face told everyone that he was not happy at the attention. I found it hard to imagine that anyone would have allowed the diminutive man an easy trip to the front of the crowd. Looking at him now, the red marks on his face and arms bore witness that some of the people had taken the opportunity a large crowd gave to punch and hit him without giving away their identity. This was humiliation on a large scale for a man used to instilling fear in others.

'Did you have something to say to me?' The tax man's surly tone was enough of a warning to the crowd that the laughter began to dissipate. No one wanted to risk their laughing being remembered by a man who delighted in revenge.

'Yes, Zacchaeus, I'd like to go to your home. I'm hungry and could do with a good meal.'

Jesus' response drew an audible gasp from the crowd. Jericho Zac was not known for his hospitality and no one with any self-respect would fraternise socially with a tax collecting collaborator of the occupying Roman forces. But here was Jesus doing exactly that. There was an immediate change in the people. A few seconds earlier they had been delighted to see Jesus and had enjoyed what they had taken to be his humiliation of a hated tax man. Now their hero was inviting himself to be the man's guest and to eat his food. I was shocked at how quickly Jesus had turned what was a good situation for him into a complete disaster.

'You want to come to my house for a meal?' Zac was evidently finding it as hard to take in the circumstances as the rest of the crowd. 'Well, of course,' he said as he started to regain some of his usual self-confidence, 'I'd be delighted.'

He began to walk just in front of Jesus, down the road towards his home, obviously expecting his self-invited guest to follow, which he did. The rest of the crowd also followed with the original murmur of surprised shock at Jesus' actions turning into a louder, more audible cry of anger. I desperately wanted to go in the other direction, but the sheer volume of people following, wanting to see what was going to happen next, made any change of direction impossible.

'What are you doing?' my mother asked. Panic was written across her face. She was only too aware of the danger I was in.

'I can't fight the crowd, I'm just being pushed along.' I could hear the panic rising in my own voice as I struggled helplessly against the tide of humanity which was sweeping me along in its current.

'God help you if Jericho Zac sees you,' was the last thing I heard my mother say as we were separated by the throng. I watched as she disappeared from sight.

As I turned to look in the direction the crowd was going I found myself looking Zac directly in the face. He had stopped by the front door to his palace-like abode. I knew by his double take that he recognised me. I wanted to turn and run but the mass of people all around made that a hopeless wish. Instead I found myself being propelled closer and closer to the little man who never took his eyes off me. His smile broadened.

He gave instructions to the three hired men who had helped him down from the tree and the three of them moved en mass towards me. The sight of the three thugs making their way purposefully into the crowd was enough to convince those in front of me to move. It was only a few moments before the men had grabbed me and against my will were dragging me towards their boss.

'Well, if it isn't my blue-eyed friend.'

As his confidence had returned so had his camp manner and I cursed my luck again at being born with such a distinctive eye colour for a man with my olive skin.

'I never forget a face, big boy,' he went on. 'Certainly not when its owner owes me a huge packet like you do. Take him inside, I'll deal with him later.'

As I was dragged past, the tax collector put a hand out on my chest to stop our progress.

'And this time there will be no let off for you. I think your high placed friends will be far too busy to worry about you. I'm going to make you pay for every penny you owe me.'

Jericho Zac indicated for me to be taken on into the house. As I was taken in I passed Jesus, the man responsible for my capture, and I wanted to kill him. Jesus looked directly at me without a scrap of emotion evident on his face.

* * * * * *

I was back in the same pitch-black cell I had occupied two years earlier. I realised last time I had been in so much pain and confusion that it had numbed my sense of fear. Pain free, I was now terrified as I sat in the darkness. But at that moment my fear was mixed with anger towards Jesus who had evidently handed me over to Jericho Zac expecting a generous reward.

That was the only explanation I could come up with during the hours I spent alone in the lightless room. There had been no need for Jesus to direct his group through Jericho in order to reach Jerusalem. There had been even less need for him to have made contact with the tax collector. And the only reason I could see for inviting himself to the collaborator's home was to negotiate the reward money he would claim for handing me over.

It was all Izzy's fault. If only he had kept his mouth shut about the whole incident with Jericho Zac. It had infuriated me that Jesus had used my brother's tendency to blab family business in order for the preacher to use it to make a moral point. But when I thought about how Jesus was now using it to line his own pockets, my blood boiled.

But I was also worried about what would happen next. Once my price had been agreed, Jericho Zac would waste no time in getting value for money and I was sure he would find value in my suffering. I shuddered involuntarily. Death would be better, but I knew that easy option would not be given. If Zac was having to pay for me he would want a good return on that money and so I would be sold into slavery, and face abuse and violation on a daily basis, particularly if a Roman or Greek bought me.

Just at that moment the door opened, and I saw the familiar silhouette of Jericho Zac before he entered the room.

He turned to the servants with him. 'Get him out of this house.'

With that the little man turned and walked out of the room.

I was stunned and wondered if I had heard correctly. I must have misunderstood what he had said, that I was going to be forgiven my debt a second time. Without any warning an avalanche of pain exploded in my gut. I doubled over and realised I had not been paying attention to the two men in the room. One had just thrown a heavy punch to my stomach knocking the wind out of me.

'You disgusting pig,' the man yelled. 'Get out.'

Bewildered as I was, I needed only one invitation to leave the home of Jericho Zac. Despite the pain in my stomach I scuttled past the two men and out into the area I remembered from my previous time in the house. I was surprised at how well I recalled the route to the kitchen and from there out into the open air and freedom. As I looked around I saw a mass of people standing outside the house. They were cheering and, in amongst them, I could make out the form of Jesus who was receiving the plaudits from everyone else.

I tried to make sense of what was happening and attempted to breathe deeply and recover from the earlier punch. At the same time, I tried to recover my senses. I wondered if my saviour on a horse had ridden by again and saved me, although I thought that unlikely. Last time Zac had been furious about having to cancel the debt. This time the debt appeared not to bother him. I could also not understand why the people were again treating Jesus as a hero. Just a few hours earlier they had regarded him as the scum of the earth as he invited himself to such a hated man's home for a meal.

None of this made any sense. I looked around, trying to decide what to do next. Then I caught sight of Naomi on the edge of the crowd that surrounded Jesus. Without thinking of what might happen, I made my way straight over to her. She was smiling and cheering with the rest of them.

'Naomi.'

She turned and immediately her face turned to one of bitterness and anger.

'I told your mother that you were to keep away from me.'

At last, I thought, someone is behaving in a way that made sense. But could I persuade her to explain to me the rest of the madness that surrounded us? I needed to know if all that was going on was real or some elaborate hoax; because if it was, I knew that my life could be in danger.

CHAPTER TWENTY-THREE

I KNEW I HAD TO act fast or else Naomi would turn tail and run away. I spread my hands out to try to indicate that I didn't mean her any harm.

'I know I'm meant to stay away, but I haven't got a clue what's going on here and you're the only one I know to ask.'

Her face softened, not by much, but just a little. She looked around her. I guessed that she was weighing up the risks. She was surrounded by a crowd of people, many of them who probably knew her. As I had just come out of a dark room and still recovering from the hired muscle's thump, I probably looked less threatening than I had for some time. She sighed, pushed back a few stray strands of hair that had fallen onto her forehead and took two paces towards me. Initially my heart soared that she was coming closer, then I realised it was so that she would not need to shout above the noise of the crowd.

'It's Jesus,' she said. 'He went in and spoke to Jericho Zac. No one knows what He said but a little while ago Zac came out, cancelled all debts to him, and said that he would pay back anyone he'd cheated out of money and give them compensation as well.'

I was amazed that anyone could change Jericho Zac so completely and so quickly. The man was a money grabbing, selfish, self-centred egotist. Men like that did not forgive debts and did not repay people. It all made no sense, and I had the impression that, unlike last time, Zac had decided to cancel my debt voluntarily.

'Looks like he's let you off as well.'

Naomi's words brought me back from my thoughts.

'Yes . . . he has,' I stuttered out a reply. There was so much I needed to speak about to Naomi. I knew she had no wish to speak to me, so I had to make the most of the opportunity currently available.

'Look Naomi, I'm sorry I attacked . . . it was wrong . . . I shouldn't have done it. I want us to be friends . . . '

I was falling over my words. Ideally, I would have wanted the time to plan what to say as nothing was coming out as I wanted it to. Nor was any of this what Naomi wanted to hear.

'Friends? Us?' She began to laugh, but there was no mirth in it. 'With our history friends is the very last thing we could ever be. I don't wish you harm, Barabbas, but I don't want anything to do with you either. I told you before, I want a new start with people who don't know what I was.'

'But it doesn't matter to me what you were before,' I was pleading pitifully, but I did not care.

'You can never forget it, though. How long will it be before you decide you want another taste of what I've already given you? And how many times will you let me say no before you decide to try and take it for yourself again, like you did before?'

Naomi turned away.

I was sure she was crying but I could see only the back of her head as she ran off into the crowd. I wanted to call after her, but she would have ignored me, and I didn't want to draw attention to myself. I looked around for somewhere to go to get away from the cheering crowd whose euphoria I did not share. Of all the people who were celebrating Jericho Zac's actions I had most reason to be elated.

Just a few minutes ago I had been readying myself for physical abuse, slavery, and who knew what else. Now I was free from those fears. No one else in this crowd had experienced the same narrow escape. Yet I was unable to be half as pleased as they all were. Confusion reigned in my mind: surely the improvement in my financial situation was the most important thing.

What did it matter if some woman had spurned my advances? She was not the first and, I reflected, she was unlikely to be the last. But it did matter, and it mattered to me more than anything. I found myself wondering if I was actually in love, but I had nothing to compare it to.

Lost in my own thoughts, I was growing less and less aware of what was going on around me. Then I caught sight of my mother, brother, and cousins and a more familiar emotion of anger returned as the world around came crashing back into focus.

The four of them stood around Jesus laughing and joining in with the others who were obviously congratulating the man from Nazareth on his work on Jericho Zac. I forgot all about the pain in my stomach as my blood boiled. I was furious that those people who were meant to be closest to me were sucking up to the man who had caused me to be taken prisoner and potentially put me in a position where my life had been in danger. I may have been released, but at that moment my family were more interested in Jesus than they were in their own flesh and blood.

I stormed towards them and as I got closer I heard Izzy questioning Jesus.

'But why bother with someone like Jericho Zac? He was just a no good low life.'

'No,' Jesus corrected him, 'he is a Son of Abraham, a Jew like you and me. I've come to save the people who have lost their way – and there weren't many in Jericho who had lost their way more than Zacchaeus.'

'And by changing him You've rescued a lot of other people from the nightmare Jericho Zac was responsible for.'

Izzy played the part of sycophant well. As I approached them I was beside myself with fury. I could not believe that my family were more interested in singing Jesus' praise than they were in my welfare.

'Oh, very cosy,' I snarled as I reached them. 'Glad to see you having a good time together rather than worrying about how I was getting on at the hands of Jericho Zac.'

'But Zac said that he'd forgiven all his debtors, so you were going to be all right.' Mother seemed genuinely surprised at my anger.

'You knew that for sure, did you?' I snapped back at her. 'You specifically checked that I was going to be released.'

'No, she didn't. I did.'

I was shocked by Jesus' words. It had never crossed my mind that the man who had landed me into the trouble in the first place would take any action to help get me out of it.

'What? You asked Jericho Zac if he was going to release me as part of your conversation with him?'

'When he told me he was going to forgive his debtors I asked him about you and he told me he would release you.'

'Well, if it weren't for you insisting on seeing him in the first place I wouldn't have been his prisoner.'

The words sounded childish and petulant even as I spoke them, but I was still struggling to take on board everything that had happened in the past few hours.

'I knew that if I went to see him that your debts would be cleared. I'm sorry for the unpleasantness you had to experience this afternoon, but I think in the long term it's worked out well for you, hasn't it?'

Before I had the chance to respond Izzy was adding his own contribution to the discussion.

'Yes, Barabbas, do you realise how much you've benefited from Jesus? Jairus let you off the money you owed him because Jesus healed his daughter and now He's convinced Jericho Zac to cancel what you owe him. I don't know why you think you've got any right to be angry. A few weeks ago you owed a fortune to two very powerful men. Because of Jesus, all your debts have cleared. You should be here thanking this man, not shouting the odds at Him.'

As he finished speaking I realised that I was impersonating a fish washed up on the sea shore. My mouth was opening and closing at a rapid rate as my mind tried to catch up and decide what words should be coming out. I knew that Izzy was right and that my freedom from debt was down to Jesus, but I was also angry after spending several hours in a pitch-dark room imagining my life coming to a very unpleasant end. It had been a huge gamble by Jesus and it had been at my expense.

'But if you had failed,' I was looking directly into the preacher's eyes, 'you would have been responsible for my death. I don't like having my life put on the line like that.'

To my amazement Jesus chuckled, reached out his right hand and squeezed my shoulder.

'You've been putting your own life on the line for as long as you can remember,' he told me. 'And, besides, I don't ever fail.'

With that Jesus turned away from the family group and was immediately faced with another group of grateful and excited people. They knew it was their turn for a few minutes with the great man and they were determined to make the most of it. As Jesus became absorbed by this latest group my family all turned to face me.

'He certainly told you, Barabbas.'

'Yeah, you're such a loser.'

Dan and Josh had enjoyed watching every moment of my encounter with Jesus. I knew that, as far as they were concerned, I had lost it hands down. Normally fear would have stopped them from saying anything like that to me, but even these two idiots could see that today was a day when the normal order of things was different. The two of them laughed as they made their way out of the crowd, leaving me fuming at my inability to get back at them either verbally or physically.

'I'd better go with them. Make sure they don't get into any trouble.'

Now that Jesus had gone Izzy was also keen to also put some distance between us. He had spent too many years of his life having to cope with my temper and if he could find a way of escaping from it he would. Before either his mother or brother had a chance to say anything, Izzy had gone off after Josh and Dan. Knowing they would all be drunk by sunset did nothing to help my mood.

'Take no notice of any of them.'

I knew Mother was trying to calm me down. I turned to face her but could not find any words to say.

'It's been an unbelievable day,' she continued. 'Let's find something to eat. Then we'll make our way back to Bethany. With your problems with Jericho Zac fixed there's no reason why we can't settle down there again and start a new life.'

'Oh no, Mother,' I contradicted her, 'I'm not settling anywhere yet. I'm on a trip to Jerusalem and nothing's going to stop me.'

The relaxed look on Mother's face was lost in an instant.

'Barabbas, leave it. There's no need for you to go to Jerusalem. The other three are going there with Jesus to celebrate the Passover. I'll need you to stay with me.'

'Not a chance. I started this journey to go to Jerusalem and that's where I'm going.'

'Then I'm going to have to come with you. I can't risk you doing anything stupid.'

As my mother spoke, I discovered a new determination within me to go to the capital and to find my father. The worry on her face and her fears that I might do something stupid told me only one thing – Mother knew exactly who my father was and where to find him.

I had failed to atone for killing the man who raised me as I had failed to regain the farm. But this gave me the opportunity to bring about some sort of justice for Mother. She may have been unkind, uncaring, and a nightmare to live with, but she was still my mother. I was determined to bring her some sort of restitution for what had happened to her in the past – whether she liked it or not, and whatever way I could.

CHAPTER TWENTY-FOUR

IT HAD BEEN YEARS SINCE I had last been in Jerusalem for Passover. All good Jews tried to ensure they celebrated it in the country's capital city. But I was not a good Jew and it must have been fifteen years since I had last been to celebrate the festival in the city with the rest of the family. That had been before Izzy had ruined the family and Mother had become ill. Any trips to Jerusalem had been curtailed from then on.

I had only a hazy memory of my last proper Passover. I could remember the noise and the people and the excitement of the time. In those days it had been an excitement I had shared in. On the whole, life had been good and it felt as if we were blessed by the God we were worshipping. However, since Izzy's actions and my response to his homecoming it was clear that God had forgotten about all of us. Even as I walked towards the city, struggling to keep up with the rest of the crowds, I wondered why I had decided to come.

But the answer to that was all around me. The people, the excitement, the feeling of being at one with my culture again. Then there were also the potential opportunities occasions like this gave. Pockets and purses were there to be picked. In a city as crowded as Jerusalem would be over the next few days I knew I could get away with it. My debts were cleared, but I would still need money for food and accommodation. Anyone visiting Jerusalem at Passover would expect to be relieved of some of their money – it was an accepted hazard of the festival.

There was something else that kept me with the crowds, though. Today, four full days before the Passover proper, there was a tangible feeling of celebration and optimism. I looked around and found it hard to take it all in.

There were hundreds, perhaps thousands, of people packing the road. The people were shouting and cheering, waving arms, hands, and palm leaves. Some had taken off their cloaks and laid them down on the road in front of the travelling party I was with. There was plenty of pushing and shoving as well. I had seen Naomi pushed over earlier. My instinct had been to run over and help her back to her feet, but to my intense irritation Izzy had been close enough to give her his helping hand first. In fact, I'd come to realised that Izzy always seemed to be remarkably close to Naomi and I was sure that it could not be put down to coincidence.

To make me feel better, I went over to the man responsible for knocking Naomi over and laid him out cold with a solid right hook. I was not sure I had actually identified the correct man, but it had made me feel better and it had certainly reduced the amount of jostling I received as others in the crowd decided that keeping their distance was a good idea.

The jostling had increased, though, the nearer we got to Jerusalem. It seemed as if half the city had come out onto the road and I knew why. They had come to see Jesus. I laughed to myself at the mob mentality that had caught up so many people into this Jesus craze. News of his teaching and the healing had performed had swept through Jerusalem and now everyone wanted to see him. Although I was still baffled by Mother's claims to have been healed – with an illness such as she had, no self-respecting son was going to ask for proof – it seemed everyone had been taken in.

I could see how charismatic Jesus was, but he came from the wrong town, the wrong class, and even the wrong profession to be what the people were now proclaiming him to be – their king. It worried me. I followed because of the safe passage it gave me and the petty pilfering opportunities that came with that. But the rest of my family appeared to be as convinced as the rest of the crowds on the road that the man currently riding a donkey into the city was the real thing.

I knew enough Jewish traditions to know what Jesus was demonstrating by riding that donkey. The teachings of Jewish scriptures said that the new Jewish king who would free the people from oppression would come into the city riding one. Jesus was telling the crowds that what they thought about him was right, that he was their new king. That was rubbish.

As I continued walking in the crowds, I knew that Pilate, the Roman ruler of Jerusalem, would not hesitate to kill Jesus if he thought his claim to be king was supported by a growing number of people. Pilate had not reached the heights of Roman power without being completely ruthless. I wondered why Jesus would make such a scene entering Pilate's territory; the only conclusion I could draw was that Jesus was either completely mad or just insane enough to think that his supporters were right, and he was going to end up ruling over Israel. As far as I was concerned, there was as much chance of that as me ruling over it.

Despite their delusion, I still found the crowd's enthusiasm intoxicating. It had been many years since I had felt part of anything. My years toiling at the family farm, the resulting years of trying and failing to keep the family solvent and life as a hopeless debtor had been a very lonely time. What I was experiencing now was something unfamiliar. With the notable and understandable exception of Naomi, I had been accepted into the group of men and women who had followed Jesus for the last three years and, nonsense though it was, the excitement was now tangible. I looked around me and my head spun at the sights and sounds. Despite the ridiculousness of it all, I found that, for the first time, a glimmer of hope had entered my soul. Perhaps I really had stumbled onto something good and something that was going to change things.

That glimmer of hope quickly left me when my left foot skidded through a pile of dung deposited by the donkey carrying Jesus. It was still warm as it spilled over the soles of my sandals and squelched between my toes. A couple of people nearby began to laugh. Without thinking about what I was doing, I kicked my foot forward in such a way as to flick off some of the dung.

'Hey!'

Josh turned around obviously not pleased to find animal faeces sprayed up the back of his legs. His shout caught other people's attention, including my mother.

'What's going on?' she demanded.

I realised that she had journeyed all the way to Jerusalem with the rest of the party keeping pace with all of us. This was something new. She had spent the last twelve years struggling for any sort of physical endurance. She should have stopped days ago and rested but she seemed to be as fit and able as all of us. She spoke without any trace of breathlessness.

'Oh, Barabbas, can't you look where you're going even at your age? We'll stop off just outside the city gates and get your foot cleaned up.'

I felt like a child again. Mother was humiliating me in front of anyone who could hear. Fortunately, the level of noise meant that the number of people able to hear her amounted to the two of us and Josh and Dan. To make sure no one else heard the conversation, I quickly agreed to her suggestion and decided to bear the discomfort and embarrassment of having walked too directly behind Jesus' donkey.

As the city gate loomed into view, so the excitement of the crowd grew with every approaching step. The cheers and songs steadily built up in volume and speed as the crowd clamoured to get nearer and nearer to Jesus. My size helped me to cope with the volume of people. But now, as the crowd funnelled down to get through the gate I found myself having to help Mother keep her footing in the crush.

'Get me away from all these people.'

I would have to have been deaf to have missed the growing panic in my mother's voice, but I was being pushed forward by the weight of the crowd all around. I looked around, trying to see a way out from the crowd. Just as I was starting to lose any hope, I noticed a few other people were obviously feeling the effects of the mass of people and there was a funnel of folk breaking away to the left of the crowd.

Without saying a word of warning to her, I scooped Mother up under one arm and pushed my way to the left. As I cut across the crowd someone fell in front of my path, but I didn't have time to adjust my pace and I stepped forward placing the whole of my weight on the person's rib cage. I had to get my mother through the melee and to the safety of the edge of the crowd.

'That was frightening.' The fear in Mother's face reflected the reality of her words. She sat down with the others who had moved away from the crowd, clearly relieved to be away from the uproar.

'It's okay, Mother, we're safely out of it now.'

'Give me a moment to catch my breath and I'll sort out your foot. Take your sandal off while I sit here for a moment.'

I was reluctant to remove my footwear and even less willing to give Mother my foot to wash. The dirty, unmade roads of Palestine always resulted in filthy feet for anyone who walked any distance on them. Dirt and dung were everyday travelling hazards and, as far as me and my ilk were concerned, something for the traveller to sort out for themselves. Even the rich and powerful would only allow the lowest of their slaves to wash their feet for them.

A few months ago, the thought of my mother degrading herself to wash my feet would have made me chuckle with spite. But now, for some unknown reason, things felt different and I could not allow her to shame herself in such a way. Instead I moved a few steps away.

'Don't worry about my foot. I've walked through worse over the years. You rest yourself here and I'll go into the city and see where the others have got to.'

'No, Barabbas, don't go. I'm begging you to stay out of Jerusalem. No good will come of you going there.'

I was certain I had misread the situation and had been tricked by my mother. She had no intention of helping me with my dirty foot. I was an idiot to ever think that she had. This was a diversion, a tactic to delay or possibly prevent me entirely from entering the capital. I was not pleased with the deception.

'You're not stopping me. I'm going in there to find my father and when I do I'm going to make him pay for what he did.'

'Oh, Barabbas, what makes you think you'll ever find him?'

'Your determination not to give me the chance. The only reason you don't want me to go looking is because you're terrified that I will find him. I think you know exactly who he is and where he is and when I find him I'm going to be asking him why you're so keen to protect him.'

'It's not him I'm trying to protect. It's you.'

It had never occurred to me that my mother may have been working for my own good. But who could I need protecting from? It made no sense at all and as that realisation dawned on me so did the certainty that this was just another of her manipulative lies.

'I'm sorry, Mother, I don't believe you. I'm going to find that scum and I'm going to make him sorrier than he has ever been in his life. Now, you clearly know more than you're letting on so, tell me, who is he and where can I find him?'

She sat on the grass mound and defiantly shook her head. I took that as my cue to leave. I turned and walked again towards the city. The crowds were still attempting to make their way in after Jesus and so I changed direction and began to walk towards another gate which was further around the city wall. It would mean it would take me some time to find Izzy and my cousins but I would find them and then I would find the man who was my father.

I thought I heard Mother call out after me but it could have been other people shouting in the crowd, so I ignored it and kept my face set towards Jerusalem and what I was sure was my destiny. Had I known at that moment all that would happen over the next few days I would have taken my mother's advice and returned to Galilee to mend Zebedee's fishing nets.

But I did not know, and so I entered the city.

CHAPTER TWENTY-FIVE

AS THE CAPITAL OF THE country, Jerusalem represented the centre of all Israel and at its centre stood the temple. For the religious fanatics it marked the centre of the entire world but, even with my limited education, I knew that was positioned many miles away in a city called Rome. However, I gasped as I encountered the holy building for the first time. I had heard that King Herod had rebuilt it and spent a fortune on it, but nothing had prepared me for the sight that greeted me on my return to Jerusalem.

I craned my neck back as I tried to take in the many stories in front of me. The building exuded money, power and the hub of human life. People came and went, passing on the steps leading up to the temple's magnificent front doors. Although it had been reopened for more than a decade, there was still construction work going on. The outer courts were being built by labourers who, by their features and skin colours, had evidently been drafted in from across the Roman empire. I noticed that women were entering and concluded that some of the essential courts, such as those for women and non-Jews, must have been completed. I was surprised at my eagerness to enter the building and by how much I wanted to see what it looked like inside – or at least as much of the inside as a ceremonially unclean person like me could see. But it would take time to get in. This was Passover season and even if the temple was not the centre of the world it felt as if the whole world was visiting it.

As we stood there waiting to enter, from within the building we could hear the panicked sounds of animals going through their death throws as they were sacrificed. The noise was unsettling the animals the people around me had brought with them to sacrifice. As I mounted the steps the stench of blood and dung assaulted my nostrils – the place looked impressive, but it stank.

'I've got a shekel, so I'll pay for both of us.'

'Thanks, I'll pay you back with a couple of drinks this evening.'

I had been so awe-struck at my first visit to the rebuilt temple that I had not taken any interest in the people around me, but this brief exchange between the two men in front brought me back down to earth. I had forgotten about the temple tax I would have to pay to enter the place. I did have the required half shekel to pay the tax, but I was reluctant to part with it. I wondered if I could slip in and avoid paying, but everyone knew that was impossible.

The temple officials responsible for collecting the money never missed anyone. If you entered the temple, you paid the tax. I considered turning around and finding an inn, somewhere to spend the money on some drink, but Izzy had told me that Jesus had intended to come straight to the temple on entering Jerusalem. I was still to formulate a plan to start looking for my absent father so, at this point, I just intended to stay with my brother and cousins and they were bound to stay with Jesus. Although I knew it would do me no good, it also helped that they would be staying near to Naomi, too.

I continued my slow progress into the magnificent building. I would have cursed the pitfalls of following a religious fanatic such as Jesus, but I looked around at the crowds of people also at the temple and decided that, if I set the family to work, there was far more than half a shekel to be procured through pinching some purses.

I began to rummage around in my purse hoping I would have a half shekel of good enough quality to pay the temple officials. If the coin was chipped or not of the right make, I knew they would refuse to accept it and make me exchange my old coin for a more acceptable one. Unfortunately, the exchange was not free. The money changers, as they were known, demanded a surcharge for swapping coins. Everyone knew it was a scam designed to line the pockets of the officials and I wondered why they were allowed to get away with it. Perhaps it was because they did it in the name of God and no one wanted to risk upsetting Him, although I wondered if I would chance it as I surveyed the battered old coins I had on me at that moment, but I wasn't sure.

A loud crash from within the building brought everyone walking with me to a sudden stand still. There was an instant silence – even the animals appeared to be struck dumb as the crash was followed by the sound of metal, a lot of metal, hitting the temple's stone floor. I was about to push my way forward to see what was going on when there was another crash with a voice shouting. I strained to hear what was being said but the mood of the whole crowd had changed in just a few seconds. Something was kicking off inside the temple and everyone wanted to see what it was. There was no need for me to push my way forward. I was carried into the building by the tide of people who bypassed the temple's tax collectors and surged into the money changers court.

I had always considered myself a man of the world and reckoned I had seen most things in life, but the scene that confronted me as I entered the court was astounding. Following his flamboyant entry into the city, Jesus had certainly let the world know he had arrived in the temple. He stood, isolated in the centre of the money changers' tables, incandescent. He single-handedly threw over the tables, scattering the money all over the floor. The acoustics of the high ceilings amplified all the sounds in the place and each table turned sounded like a clap of thunder directly overhead.

'You're a bunch of thieves!' Jesus shouted with every vein on his neck bulging beneath his puce face. 'This should be a place of prayer not corruption,' he added as he sent another table tumbling to the floor.

I could not believe my eyes. No one liked to be ripped off or to pay the temple tax that was demanded, but Jesus' reaction was wild in the extreme. Not for the first time I questioned the man's sanity as I looked around the room to try to spot Izzy and my cousins. I saw them no more than a few yards away although that distance was increasing as they were edging further and further into a corner obviously hoping not to be identified with Jesus' insane actions.

I could see a look of incredulity written all over Izzy's face. It was matched on the faces of virtually every other individual in the temple. Although it had been refurbished only in the last ten years or so, a temple had stood on this site for the best part of a thousand years and it had never hosted a scene such as this. Even the money changers themselves, whose wealth was being scattered, failed to respond to Jesus' actions. It was like watching a man rage against life-like statues as everyone stood awestruck by the scene.

That quickly changed, though, when Jesus produced a whip and started directing it at the temple officials. Pandemonium broke out in the crowd. I could almost read the minds of the massed ranks of people: if Jesus was physically attacking the money changers, how much longer would they be safe? I, however, remained rooted to the spot, I wanted to see what would happen next. I didn't know from where Jesus had got the whip, but I guessed that he had brought it with him. In that case, I realised, this had been planned by Jesus and there was a purpose behind it.

'Come on, Barabbas, this is our chance.'

I was so absorbed by Jesus that it shocked me when Dan shouted in my ear above the din of the rumpus which surrounded us both. I looked around to see my cousin had scooped up an armful of coins from the floor and was carrying them in the fold of his cloak. I was startled when I realised that my normally dim-witted relative had seized an opportunity quicker than me. As I looked around I saw other men taking advantage of the uproar by helping themselves to the money which covered most of the floor and which had been abandoned by the officials as Jesus chased them out of the temple. Immediately my brain switched into gear. There had to be bigger opportunities available than some small loose change to grab.

Then I saw it. On the far wall there were a collection of jars sat on a ledge. When I first saw them, I thought they had been made of ordinary clay, but as I looked again I saw they were made of the more expensive alabaster. They were pricey pots and I reckoned that whatever was in them would be valuable.

'Drop those coins and come with me,' I barked at my cousin.

Dan looked perplexed. He had no wish to abandon his newly found bounty. He stood defiantly not wanting to give it up.

'Come on!'

Out of the corner of my eye I had caught sight of temple guards rushing into the court we were standing in. The opportunity Jesus' actions had brought was already slipping away. I reached out and pulled Dan's arm and yanked him across towards the jars. The money he had been holding fell again onto the floor and Dan shouted vainly in protest. But I was bigger and stronger than him. He put up little resistance once the money was gone and the two of us were soon over by the jars.

The chaos which had surrounded us was slowly being replaced by order. As I looked around to ensure I was unobserved I noticed that there was no longer any sign of Jesus. He had obviously left the temple and moved on somewhere else. It was not important what fate had been dished out to him, I wanted to make sure I took full advantage of the opportunity provided. Satisfied that no one was taking any notice, I looked at the jars on the ledge. One by one I tipped them forwards and saw that each contained an oil I did not recognise. I swore under my breath – I had hoped they would contain something expensive such myrrh or frankincense, but I didn't want Dan to sense my disappointment. It was typical of my luck; the chances were that the money Dan had previously collected would have been worth more. In sheer desperation I picked up the largest jar I could.

'We'll take this,' I told Dan as I turned towards the door to leave.

Order had been restored to the temple almost as quickly as it had been lost. The temple guards were pushing the people out of the court so that the tables could be righted, and the scattered money sorted out – I could see that was going to take quite some time. At the door other guards were searching people as they left to ensure that the temple treasury was not deprived of any of its income. I was impressed at how efficiently the guards had done their job restoring some semblance of order and beads of sweat began to break out on my brow as I approached the exit.

The man in front of us began to fidget as he approached the guards. I guessed he was carrying some money that did not belong to him and the guards also spotted his agitated behaviour. Ignoring his protests, they pulled him to one side and began a full and thorough body search. It took only a few moments for them to discover his cash of coins. I fleetingly wondered how the man had managed to hide so much money, but I knew I needed to concentrate on getting out of the temple with the jar. I hoped that accosting the man in front would divert the guards' attention and with a nod of my head I directed Dan to change his position in the queue so that he obscured the view most of the guards had of both me and the jar. The now steady trickles of sweat that were running down my face were a giveaway to my own agitation, but fortunately the guards all looked to be preoccupied with the thief they had caught in front of me.

'Excuse me, I think I'll take that jar off you before you leave.'

I felt my heart sink into my boots. I was only one step away from leaving the temple and getting away with the theft when a young, eager, and obviously officious guard stepped forward from the other side of the doorway intent on blocking our path. For a split moment I thought about trying to run. I was bigger than the guard, but probably more than ten years older. Would my additional physical strength be enough to out run the younger man? The thoughts whirled through my mind, I shifted my foot as I decided to give it a go when Dan reached out and grabbed my arm, preventing me from making my escape.

'No, you won't. We paid for this fair and square,' he said as he took the jar from me.

'A couple of peasants like you? I don't think so.'

The guard's words sounded certain enough, but I could see a look of doubt flicker across his eyes as they darted between me and my cousin. I had to admire Dan. I had always thought of him as being the dimmest of the whole family, but he had out thought me twice now and if we both bluffed well I gambled that we might just get away with it.

'Peasants?' I tried to sound as incredulous as I could. 'So, because we have travelled a great distance and come straight to the temple to do our religious duty, you accuse us of being peasants? Who is your superior?'

The panic on his face told me that we had convinced the young guard he had made a dreadful mistake. Looking at him more closely I guessed he was even younger than I had first thought, and, in the heat of the moment, he had probably overstepped his authority. Now he was calculating how much trouble he was going to be in and the answer he was coming up with was a lot. I seized on this new opportunity.

'Actually, I can see you're young and I'm willing to accept that you've made an honest mistake with the best of intentions. Therefore, my cousin and I will leave without saying any more about it.'

I was sure I heard Dan begin to snigger even as the guard began to stutter out an apology. It was clear that Dan's spell of genius was coming to an end and he was now reverting to stupid again. His laughter was certain to give away our pretence. Before that could happen, though another voice cried out in a thick Eastern accent.

'Stop those thieves! That's my alabaster jar!'

An elderly man was making his way from the ledge the jar had come from and was pointing an accusing finger at me and Dan. His interruption took the attention of the now thoroughly confused guard. Without hesitation I elbowed him in the neck. The guard's eyes bulged in surprise at the attack before he crumpled to the ground without making a sound.

At that moment Dan and I started to sprint out of the temple's door, alerting the other guards to the incident who darted to the doorway. But when they saw that it was only the theft of some foreigner's jar they decided not pursue us. The treasury's money was far more important.

CHAPTER TWENTY-SIX

'WILL YOU GET OUT OF here you, pesky cat!'

I couldn't help but chuckle as Lazarus threw a stone at the feline which had intruded into his home. It dawned on me that I had found myself laughing a number of times since my family and I had intruded into Lazarus and his sisters' home. The cat, though, obviously decided there was no joy to be found in the house and disappeared back through the window and into the evening air.

It was the third evening we had spent in the house since returning from Jerusalem two days ago. On escaping from the temple, Dan and I had encountered Josh and he told us Jesus and the rest of the group were leaving the city and going to Bethany. I hadn't reckoned on a return to the village I had called home for a few unhappy years. I was not keen to follow especially as the hovel we had once lived in was occupied by a new tenant. However, my cousins were insistent, and as I had nowhere else to go, we all returned.

It turned out to be a great decision. As we entered Bethany we had passed Lazarus' house and I remembered the youngest sister, Mary, who had tended to my wounds after my first encounter with Jericho Zac. I remembered that they had originally been friends of Jesus and so we chanced our luck and knocked on the front door to ask for somewhere to stay for the Passover. The door had been opened by the older sister, Martha, who grudgingly said that, if her brother was agreeable we could stay for the festival. Lazarus, no doubt remembering my reputation as a thug, obviously felt he was in no position to refuse us. But he was not as keen to provide hospitality to a set of wild cats who were currently plaguing his home.

'I don't know why they keep coming in,' he complained. 'But I wish they'd find somewhere else to go.'

He picked up the stone he had thrown in the now departed cat's direction and put it back on a pile he had in the house for the purpose of keeping the cats at bay. There was a way he bustled about the house and got so annoyed with the cats that I found amusing and I could not wipe the smile off my face. It was easy to be happy when I was in a good house with every home comfort. In the room I was in, there were six seats. When we had lived in Bethany our one-room house contained just one stool.

'Perhaps it's your sister's cooking.' Mother's suggestion brought me back to the conversation in the room.

'Martha has fed us wonderfully since we've been here.'

Here was another change I was having to adjust to. Since she had claimed that Jesus had healed her, Mother had mellowed into a far happier woman. The bitterness that had been eating way inside her had gone, even her features seemed somehow softer and the viciousness of her tongue had dissipated. When I had met up with her again outside the wall around Jerusalem she had, at first, been alarmed to hear that I had gone to the temple, but as I recounted what had happened her concern was replaced by an unnatural keenness to return to Bethany.

I had always been convinced that she had wanted to keep me away from the city but based on her reaction to me going to the temple, I now had an inkling of an idea that if I were to return to the temple I may stand more chance of finding my father. Not that I could work out why – surely no one connected to such a holy place could be violent enough to rape a woman. But then I thought about the men who were involved with the killing of the animals and decided that, perhaps, it wasn't quite as inconceivable as I had initially thought.

But over the last two days even my enthusiasm to search for the man responsible had lessened. It was in part due to the comparative luxury I was now enjoying and partly due to the company. Mary had blossomed over the past two years into a real beauty. I was far too old for her and my reputation in the village meant she was very quiet when around me. But spending time with such a beauty, who was currently sitting directly opposite me and looking as stunning as ever, was a great bonus. It even helped to take my mind off Naomi.

Naomi herself had disappeared from sight, along with Izzy and those who were closest to Jesus. The preacher from Nazareth was indeed using Bethany as his base but had gone into Jerusalem for the past two days to teach in the temple. It astounded me that he had been allowed back after the fiasco of his visit at the start of the week. As I had not seen Jesus, Izzy, or anyone else who had returned to the temple with them, though, I had not been able to ask how they had managed it. In fact, I didn't even know where they were staying once they returned to Bethany. That was surprising in a village of Bethany's size. I was certain people would be talking about me and my family staying at Lazarus' but as far as I was concerned they could talk as much as they wanted to.

My tranquil moment was brought abruptly to an end as the door flew open and Josh and Dan crashed into the room.

'What's for dinner tonight, Martha?'

The fact that my cousins were enjoying her cooking did not seem to please Martha. Having four unexpected guests thrust into her home had clearly upset her sensibilities. She was a good housekeeper and well organised, but she had not planned for this intrusion and she was not accepting it in good grace.

'There won't be anything to eat if you two louts keep hanging around here to get under my feet,' she snapped, but Josh and Dan seemed oblivious to her foul mood.

'All right,' said Josh, 'we'll go out for a while and let you get on. You coming with us, Lazarus?'

My cousins and Lazarus were probably around the same age, but I could see a depth and a maturity in our host that were clearly missing in both Josh and Dan. Lazarus was not the type to go charging around like a mad man in the way my cousins were. However, Lazarus lost the opportunity to turn the invitation down when Martha, who clearly felt she was the head of the house, spoke for him.

'No, he isn't,' she said. 'Have you forgotten what he went through just a few days ago? The last thing he needs now is to go charging round with a couple of idiots like you two.'

Lazarus had been ill up until a few days ago – then he had died only for Jesus to bring him back to life. Well, that was the story I and just about everyone else had been told. However, I knew that corpses did not come back from the dead. Lazarus had just been mistaken for dead and it had taken Jesus to come along, as he had done with Jairus' daughter, and point out the mistake.

Unfortunately for Lazarus, though, the mistake made over his mortality had resulted in him spending a few days in a tomb which, understandably, had left him and his sisters very sensitive to the whole episode. However, it had added to the weight of people's claim that Jesus was a miracle worker sent from God and probably the Messiah King as well. It took more than a couple of misdiagnosis of death to convince me, although I could understand why some people, my own family included, had been taken in.

Lazarus himself had said very little about the whole episode just as he was saying very little at that precise moment. A woman should never speak for a man and Martha had crossed that line. However, Lazarus loved his sisters and would not have wanted to embarrass either of them in front of comparative strangers. It was a disposition I had marvelled as I would not let anyone answer for me.

Josh and Dan looked at Lazarus to see if he would defy his sister. When it was obvious to them that he was going to remain silent and inside the house they turned and walked out of the door looking suitably dejected. A couple of moments later there was a knock on the door and I thought they had returned.

'Come in,' sighed Martha, once again superseding her position when her brother was in the room. Her tone made it clear, however, that she thought similarly to me and was expecting to see the two men return to the room. Her surprise was obvious when Jesus walked into the house.

'Oh, my Lord, do come and sit down, let me get You a drink. Lazarus, get some water to wash His feet.'

I noted the way Jesus appeared to overlook Martha's insensitivity to the normal customs as he settled himself on the last remaining couch in the room. I also noticed that Mary immediately got up from where she was sitting and sat at Jesus' feet. I was surprised by the pang of jealousy I felt.

'Martha, please don't fuss,' Jesus said. 'I've told you before not to worry so much about everything.'

Although the words were said gently Martha looked suitably downcast by the reproach. She sat down and said nothing.

'What brings You here?' Lazarus asked.

'I wanted to see how you are. I've been so busy going back and forth to Jerusalem.'

'So, what have you been doing in Jerusalem?' I surprised myself as I joined in the conversation.

'People are so mixed up about God and religion. I want to show them the real way to know God and to worship Him.'

I was about to ask what made Jesus think he knew better than the priests and the rabbis who had been teaching the people for years when Lazarus spoke first.

'That can't make You very popular with the religious leaders at the temple. You need to be careful or they'll come after You and they won't stop until they've shut You up for good. I've already heard rumours they're plotting against You.'

Lazarus' words sounded melodramatic, but I knew that there had been others who had upset the High Priest in Jerusalem and ended up dead. If what I had been told in the past was right, it was around the time of my last visit to the temple. The High Priest, Annas, had executed religious rebels. He had lost his job for that, but his punishment had still left those who had upset him dead. Jesus, confident as ever, seemed unperturbed by Lazarus' warning.

'You worry too much, my friend, I know exactly what I am doing. But I didn't come here to talk about me. I wanted to see how you all are.'

'Isn't that lovely?'

I looked across at Mother, surprised that, as a woman, she had joined in the conversation. Her face was glowing with pleasure at this meeting with Jesus. I wondered if she realised that Jesus had come to see the family whose house this was rather than any guests they may be hosting. But then Jesus turned directly to face her.

'And I've told Izzy he should come over and see you,' he said.

I thought my mother would burst with joy. Not only was Jesus talking to her, but he had told her son that he should visit her. If it was up to her, Jesus would not only be the new king he could take over as God Almighty as well.

There was another knock at the door and Izzy walked into the room. I knew for Mother this would count as another miracle. Jesus spoke the words prophesying his return and immediately Izzy walked into the room. She leapt to her feet and embraced her youngest son. I wanted to get out – the scene of domestic bliss liberally seasoned with messianic adulation sickened me. The happiness I had been feeling was rapidly evaporating.

Before I had the chance to move, the harmonious picture was broken by another wild cat appearing at the window. Lazarus leapt to his feet and grabbed another stone.

'Get lost!' he yelled as he threw the stone, striking his target on the side of its head. It was enough to convince the feline to leave the scene at a rapid rate of knots.

'That was some throw, Lazarus,' Izzy sounded suitably impressed.

'I've had enough practise. We've been plagued by cats for the last couple of day. I just can't work out why.'

'The last couple of days, you say.' There was more than a hint of mischief in my brother's voice. 'You mean ever since you took in my family. Have they smelt that bad?'

I rolled my eyes while Lazarus looked uncertain of how to reply. Mother laughed a little too enthusiastically, demonstrating her own unease with Izzy's joke.

Jesus got up and made towards the door.

'Well, I'm glad you're all well but it's getting crowded in here, so I'll leave you to it,' he said as he opened the door.

Martha started to bustle around again.

'Oh no, we're fine here. There's plenty of room. Don't go yet,' she pleaded.

'I'll come back and see you again when we've all got a bit more time.'

As he spoke Jesus walked out of the door and shut it firmly behind him. Martha turned around and glared at us obviously feeling that if it had not been for the self-imposed guests the latest local celebrity would have stayed in her home far longer. She said nothing but instead left the room muttering something about the evening meal. Her sister, who had only just made herself comfortable on the floor where Jesus had been sitting was equally put out by his early departure and promptly followed her sister into another part of the house. Lazarus looked uncomfortable and I found myself disappointed that I no longer had Mary to admire.

'But seriously, I wonder why you keep getting these cats coming in.'

I could not decide whether my brother really was totally oblivious to the atmosphere in the room or if this was a genuine attempt to cover up the situation. With Izzy it was so hard to tell, but whatever his reasoning, he obviously wanted to get to the bottom of Lazarus' cat problem.

'Apart from my family being here has anything changed recently or are they trying to get into any other room in the house,' he enquired.

'No, just here and, without wanting to sound rude, nothing's changed except your family staying here. But it can't be them because the cats aren't trying to get into their bedrooms.'

'Is this really necessary, Izzy?' I was already starting to find my brother intensively irritating.

Izzy totally ignored me and instead made his way over to the alabaster jar I had stolen from the temple. I had put it on a shelf just along from the window. I hoped I could leave it behind once we went back to Galilee. There was no point in carrying the extra weight when it was not particularly valuable.

'What's this then, Lazarus?'

'I don't know. Your brother brought it with him.'

'Did he now? I won't ask you how you got it Barabbas, but you can tell me what's in it.'

'I don't know.' For a reason I could not identify I was finding my brother's interest in the jar annoying. It was obvious it had nothing to do with the cats and I was about to tell him to shut up when Izzy swore loud and long.

'Watch your language, my boy,' Mother cut in. 'We're in good company here.'

'But you don't understand, Mother,' Izzy explained. 'This jar contains pure nard.'

'Pure what?' I asked jumping up from my seat and joining Izzy at the shelf.

'Pure nard. It's an oil from the East. I came across it when . . . when I was away from the family.'

I was surprised at the discomfort Izzy showed in talking about the time he had gone off with a third of the family's fortune. In any other circumstances I would have jumped at the chance to have added to his awkwardness, but I was intrigued by what Izzy knew about nard.

'So, does that mean it's worth something then?'

'Worth something? It's worth a fortune! The amount of nard you've got in here has got to be worth more than a year's salary.'

I held my breath waiting for him to say something more. I thought he was going to explain why, in this particular instant, this jar was the exception and was worthless. But Izzy remained silent. I examined his face and could see a real sense of excitement in his eyes. As far as Izzy was concerned this was the real deal. I looked around at Mother. She was also silent, waiting to see how this was going to develop. The question etched on her wrinkled face was clear for all to see: had the family's luck changed at last? I allowed myself to wonder if, finally, I was again a man of money. But I had raised my hopes in the past only for them to be dashed. Experience had taught me to be cautious. After all, I only had my brother's opinion about what was in the jar, I needed more.

'So, just by looking at it,' I quizzed Izzy, 'you can tell that this is nard?'

'Sort of,' he replied. 'But it's mainly the cats.'

'The cats?'

'Yes. For some reason, cats are attracted to nard. There's something about it they like.'

'And we've certainly had plenty of cats pestering us since it's been in the house.'

This time it was Lazarus' turn to join in the conversation. I had forgotten he was in the room. 'If this was a valuable jar of nard, it would need to be kept away from outsiders,' Lazarus concluded.

I had found it easy enough to steal two days ago; now I was adamant no one would get the option to do the same to me. This jar could be the end of all my problems and the beginning of a brand-new start. One year's salary could change everything.

Suddenly I found myself thinking again about our family farm. Since I had lost my money to Reuben I had given up any thought of ever getting it back, but that thought, and the dormant hope of atoning for killing the man whose raised me, resurfaced. But all this was only possible if I could keep the jar and decide for myself how the money it would bring in would be spent.

First, I had to get the jar away from Lazarus without causing him offence and my family members without raising any suspicions. I knew all of whom would have their own ideas about how the money could be spent.

'I'm not willing,' I told those assembled in the room, 'to just accept that this is nard just because of a load of cats.' I picked up the jar. 'I'm going to find someone who can confirm that it is what Izzy says it is.'

'What, at this time in the evening?'

I had to steel myself not to react to my mother's question. She may have developed a more pleasant nature, but she still had her wits about her. I knew that she would think that I was planning to run off with the jar and the money and leave them in the lurch. It was so annoying, but I could not allow my emotions to show.

'Of course, Mother, you're right. There'll be no one around to examine it now. We'll wait until the morning.'

I intended to be long gone by the morning. A midnight flit would see me and the jar in Jerusalem before the crowds gathered. There I would sell the oil and then look to reclaim the farm before my family could decide how they thought the money should be spent. I would find it hard to wait, but that was my only hope. Suddenly the dream of buying back the farm was within touching distance again. I just had to show a few more hours of self-control.

Then Izzy killed those dreams in an instant.

CHAPTER TWENTY-SEVEN

EVERY PROBLEM I HAD EVER had in my life originated with my brother. If he hadn't gone off prematurely with his share of the family's money, then we would never have run into financial problems. If he hadn't returned and convinced the rest of the family to take him back, I would not have killed the man who raised us. If he had pulled his weight after that happened, we might have kept the farm running as a going concern and I would not have had to run up such bad debts.

And now, his intervention was going to ruin my plans to get the farm back and all because he could never keep his big mouth shut.

'I reckon Matthew could tell us if I'm right. He'll still be with Jesus now.'

I don't know what stopped me from screaming a string of obscenities at Izzy at that moment. I did not want any more people knowing about the potential wealth which had fallen into my hands and certainly not a toe-rag tax collector who had taken to following Jesus. The more people who knew, the harder it would be to keep the wealth secret which would mean having to pay a higher price for the farm. Although I did have to accept that as someone responsible for taxing anything and everything of worth, Matthew would be the person to back up Izzy's claim that the jar contained nard.

'What a good idea. Why don't you take it to Matthew now, Izzy?'

Mother smiled sweetly as she spoke, but I knew she thought I was planning to run off with the jar and keep the money all for myself. She was simply scheming to stop me from doing that.

'Can I remind you that this jar belongs to me and if anyone is going to show it to Matthew it will be me?'

I picked up the jar again and stood as tall and solid as I could. No one in the room came close to me in stature and I hoped that reminding them of the fact would ensure that no one argued. It worked; no one did argue, but Mother still had not given up.

'Of course, it's yours, Barabbas. But why don't you take Izzy with you? He knows that lot better than you do and he'll get you to Matthew quicker than you would alone. Once you've spoken to him, you and Izzy can bring the jar back here.'

Her emphasis on her last few words made it clear to me that I guessed correctly about the assumptions she had jumped to. Fortunately, Izzy was too mesmerised by the new-found wealth in my hands to notice. I just hoped that Lazarus was preoccupied enough not to notice either.

'What are you waiting for, Barabbas, let's get this over to Matthew.'

'Where is he?' I asked.

'He'll be over with Jesus at Simon the Leper's house.'

Despite the firm grasp I had on the jar, I almost dropped it on the spot.

'Simon the Leper? What is Jesus doing there? Don't tell me he's got leprosy.'

Simon had been a relatively wealthy and influential man in the village of Bethany until he contracted the dreaded skin disease about three years ago. Most villagers would have been physically sent out of the area but Simon, with his large house on the outskirts of the community, was allowed to stay as long as he remained in his property at all times. I was surprised to hear he was still alive. If I had given him any thought at all it would have been to assume that he was dead.

Simon had done well to last this long, but the only people who would go and visit him would be other leprosy sufferers. If Jesus did have the disease, what on earth had he been doing entering Lazarus' home just a few moments ago? More worryingly, though, as a result of that visit, was I now at risk of contracting the disease just as I thought my life was getting on track with the money I would earn from the nard?

'Of course not. You saw Him when He was here. He's fine.'

'So, what's he doing with the leper?'

'Jesus healed Simon and made him well when he was here a couple of years ago. And, before you start looking like that, Barabbas, a priest confirmed Simon as being healed and he's had no problems since.'

'Healed or not,' I retorted, 'I still wouldn't want to spend any time in even a former leper's home.'

'Then you stay here and let Izzy take the jar over without you.'

My mother's words were like a slap in the face. She knew there was no way I would let the jar be taken away from me. But I really did not want to go to Simon's house. Beads of sweat pricked my forehead as I tried to resolve my inner conflict between the need for money and my fear of contracting leprosy. I decided I needed to buy some time.

'I'll go with him over to the house,' I said. 'We'll see what happens when we get there.'

I did not wait for Mother's reply. Before I had a chance to change my mind, I strode towards the door with the jar leaving the others in my wake as I left the room and the house. Marching purposefully away, I tried to remember the way to the part of Bethany where Simon lived. I slowed as I remembered that Lazarus' house was also on the outskirts of the village – the bigger houses always were – but was it the same end of the village as Simon's?

I was racking my brains trying to remember when Izzy caught up with me.

'What's the matter . . . forgotten the way?'

I wished I had my hands free so that I could knock the living daylights out of him. However, I knew that no matter how good that would make me feel for a few moments, it would not help. I needed my irritating little brother to get me to the leper's house and so I bit my lip, took a deep breath and tried to sound calm as I replied.

'I'm not sure I ever knew it. Does he live this side of Bethany?'

'Yes, he does.' Izzy seemed ready to respond to my self-control, and the mocking tone had been removed from his voice. 'It's only a few moments in this direction.'

Nothing more was said between us as we walked carefully in the half light of dusk, over the unmade road which led out of the village. We both wanted to avoid falling in any pot holes, particularly myself as I was worried that if I did I would drop the nard and the future it promised. I was still trying to decide what to do about entering the house of a former leper when Izzy took hold of my arm and pointed towards a large house just to the left of us.

'That's Simon's house.'

I wondered why he was whispering, but somehow, in the circumstances, it seemed right and so I whispered back.

'He certainly had some money then.'

The house was undoubtedly the largest house I had ever seen in Bethany.

'He still is rich,' Izzy whispered back. 'Since he was healed he's gone back to making a fortune again.'

'What does he do?'

'Something in the cloth trade. I'm not sure what, but it's enough for him to be able to put Jesus and rest of us up for the entire week.'

I cursed under my breath. That would mean there would be at least two dozen people staying in the house. I really did not want that many people to be aware of the nard. But my options were limited. As we had walked to Simon's house I realised that I needed a second opinion on the oil. If Izzy was wrong, and he could hardly be considered as reliable, my hopes for the farm would be gone and, more immediately, I would look a complete fool at the market tomorrow. I needed Matthew to confirm the nard. But as we stood there I realised again that I did not want to enter the house of someone who was or had been a leper. Izzy sensed my reluctance.

'Look, Barabbas, Jesus healed Simon. He's a healthy man now.'

I was struck by my brother's complete faith in Jesus. It was almost enough for me, but not quite. I did not share his faith in a man who was no more than a jobbing builder from the north of the country. I dithered over what to do.

'Give me the jar. I'll take it in.'

Izzy stretched out his hands.

'Trust me, Barabbas, I'll keep it safe. I'll show it to Matthew and then I'll bring it back and tell you what he said.'

Reluctantly I found myself handing over the precious jar without saying a word. Izzy took it and I watched him walk the few yards towards Simon's front door which he opened with his spare hand. As it opened the evening was flooded with light from the house and I heard the sounds of an evening meal being enjoyed by a large group of people. As the door closed I thought I heard Jesus' voice teaching and saying something about the Kingdom of God. I was not impressed. The sounds coming from the house made it clear there were more there than I had thought. More people knowing about the nard put it more at risk, I was not happy.

Nor was I happy when Izzy failed to return quickly. I began pacing up and down outside wondering what was taking him so long. Suddenly from the house there was a crash and the sound of people gasping in shock. My stomach somersaulted. I heard raised voices. Without thinking I dashed to the front door and was about to burst through it when it was opened by a harassed-looking Izzy.

In his hands was nothing more than thin air.

CHAPTER TWENTY-EIGHT

I KNEW IMMEDIATELY SOMETHING WAS wrong when I saw his face. My instincts had been proved right when Izzy's expression had turned to panic on seeing me. He had pushed past, running off down the street. I had turned and pursued him, but my brother was younger than me and not carrying as much weight. He took a good lead which had enraged me all the more. That was when I discovered that an angry runner can always outrun a scared one. The distance between us reduced until I had caught Izzy outside a smaller house in the centre of Bethany. I grabbed him by the throat and pinned him against a wall.

'It's not my fault!'

He could hardly speak. I realised I was throttling the life out of my brother. At that moment it felt good, but I knew that a dead Izzy was not going to be able to tell me what had happened, and so I lessened my grip on his throat. Izzy began gulping in great amounts of air as the blueness faded from his face. However, I was not worried about his welfare. My blood was boiling, I wanted to know what had happened to my nard.

'What's not your fault?' I spat at him.

'That the nard's gone.'

Any air that Izzy had succeed in taking in was smartly knocked out of him as my fist connected with his stomach. He doubled over.

'Where's my nard?'

A swift right hook to his face resulted in Izzy collapsing to the floor. Now that I had started to unleash my fury I could not bring it under control. My foot smacked against my brother's back as he lay on the floor. I was about to unleash another kick when a woman's voice cut through the night.

'I don't know what you're fighting about but go and do it outside your own home.'

I looked up and saw the front door of the house we were at had been opened by a middle-aged woman. She had probably been sent by her husband who thought she was less likely to get hit. For a fleeting moment I considered proving the husband wrong, but then I realised that involving other people would escalate the problem. That was something I could do without. I reached down and grabbed hold of the back of Izzy's clothing before dragging him away from the housewife.

It was dark, and I was uncertain where we were going. I wanted somewhere quiet. We came to a rickety lean-to which was probably used during the day as someone's workshop. But at night it was empty and isolated and suited my purpose ideally. I dragged my whimpering brother into a corner and sat him on the floor against the wall. It was time, I decided, to assert my authority over my younger sibling. Izzy knew it and I could smell his fear.

'Tell me exactly what happened.'

Izzy whimpered unintelligibly in the corner. I swung out my boot.

'Tell me!'

'It wasn't my fault.'

The kick had brought a mumbled retort from Izzy, but it was a line I had heard before – too many times. I wanted more information so that I could make my own judgement about whose fault it was.

'So, you've said.' I was trying to bring my temper back under control. A fury-fuelled beating of my brother would certainly have brought some satisfaction, but I knew I had to keep my temper in check and my head clear. If the nard had been lost I would need cool, calculated thinking to work out how to get it back. I remained silent, knowing that, eventually, Izzy would tell me what had happened.

With me standing over him, Izzy shuffled on the floor clearly trying to make himself more comfortable. Behind that movement I knew my brother was also assessing the situation to see if there was any means of escape. His sigh of resignation told me that he realised there was no hope of escape. All that was left was for him to tell me exactly what happened and hope for mercy. It was going to be a vain hope.

'I went into the house. There were so many people there. I had to pay my respects to Simon as the host. I didn't want to take the jar with me as Simon might have thought it was a gift for him. So, I gave it to Naomi and told her I'd take it back once I'd spoken to Simon.'

My stomach lurched at Naomi's name.

'Why did you give it to her?'

'We've become . . . friends. Or, at least, I thought we had.'

The rage was stirring through my veins again.

'Friends? She's nothing more than some cheap prostitute!'

I was surprised at the kaleidoscope of emotions that were whirling around inside. It was certain that 'friends' meant Naomi and Izzy were far more than just that. Jealousy engulfed me. The tart had deliberately started sleeping with my brother just to get at me. And Izzy had been stupid enough to think that she had been interested in him. Now she had taken my jar of nard. I was going to make her give it back and then I was going to make her pay.

'I'm sorry.' Izzy was obviously sensing my growing wrath.

'Yes, you will be. But first tell me what that woman did with my nard. I'll make sure I'll get it back.'

Izzy hesitated before speaking again. As his breathing became more rapid I realised there was worse news to come. There was a sick feeling in my stomach and it got worse as Izzy continued his account of the evening.

'As I had finished speaking to Simon I heard something smash. I looked around and I saw that Naomi had smashed the jar and poured the oil over Jesus. It was like some sort of anointing.'

It was unbelievable. Just a few short weeks ago, I had enjoyed the sensation of feeling that long, rich hair being draped over my own body. I hated Naomi almost as much for taking that pleasure from me as I did for the loss of the nard. Almost – but not quite.

I had thought my life had taken a lucky turn. I had stolen a fortune from the temple. Enough to actually dream of getting the farm back. For a few brief hours the future had looked good. But now I was back to where I had always been: at the bottom of the pile in life. Even the cheap prostitute who had spurned me had risen above me in the pecking order. As my realisation of all that had happened that evening grew, so did my fury and desire for revenge.

It was the sound of Izzy getting back to his feet that brought my mind back into the ramshackle building we currently occupied. It was ugly and looked big enough at a glance from the outside. But a closer inspection showed it had no foundations and it was in danger of falling to pieces, just like me.

I decided, if I was going to fall, I was going to take others with me. I had had enough of being the dirt on everyone else's shoe.

It had been a while since either Izzy or I had said anything. He evidently took that as a sign that he might get away with his involvement in the evening's fiasco and, encouraged by the thought, he started to speak again once he was fully back on his feet.

'I wasn't the only one outraged by her behaviour,' he continued in his tale. 'Some of the religious people there thought it was disgusting. And I pointed out how much the nard was worth, and people said it could have been sold and the money given to the poor.'

'We were going to do that!' I silenced him. 'We are poor, and we were going to get the money if you hadn't given the oil to Naomi.'

I took some deep breaths, trying to keep my temper in check.

'Anyway, what did your precious Jesus have to say about the whole thing?'

Izzy looked away. At first, I wondered why but then I realised he wanted to avoid answering the question. I stretched out my hand and grabbed his jaw.

I jerked his head around so that he was facing me. I hoped the look in my eyes told Izzy that I was not going to accept silence for an answer.

'He said she had done a beautiful thing that would be remembered for years,' he said, pulling his face free.

I was as surprised as the guttural roar which came from me which clearly terrified Izzy. He cowered, holding his hands up to his face to defend himself from the physical onslaught he was evidently expecting. I, though, turned away and began pacing around in circles not knowing how to contain the wrath which was consuming every portion of my body. How dare Jesus say something such as that. It had not been Naomi's nard to anoint him with. It was not for a loose woman like Naomi – who had rejected me – to drape her hair on someone like Jesus. It was not for that jumped-up arrogant peasant to say that it was a beautiful thing.

I had been irate with people before, my family in particular. But this was fury at a whole new level. There was obviously something going on between Jesus and Naomi. That was the only sane explanation. She was probably sleeping around with the whole party.

I had had a belly full of Jesus. The way he told people how to live their lives, claiming to be some sort of new king. I had also had enough of Jesus interfering with my family. I knew Jesus would be long gone once Mother stopped deluding herself and realised she was just as ill as she had ever been. It would be me who would have to support Izzy, Josh, and Dan when the wheels fell off the bandwagon and they went back to their normal lives again. Jesus would not be around for that. And the life which the whole family would have would still be one of poverty because Jesus' little woman had stolen the oil which was going to make us rich and set us up for the future.

As I paced around the confines of the small lean-to I swore that Jesus was going to pay for all that he had done. I was going to make him suffer big time. I just had to work out how.

'Barabbas, what are you going to do?'

There was concern etched on my brother's face. He was worried that I was going to take out my fury on him. I knew Izzy deserved to be punished for giving away the nard, but that would have to wait until I had sorted out the other two.

'I'm going to make Naomi pay for what she's done and then I'm going to make Jesus suffer.'

'Jesus? It wasn't Him who wasted the oil.'

'No, but it was his woman.'

'What? Jesus and Naomi? No, you can't be right about that. He doesn't treat the girls like that.'

'Oh, come on, wake up. Why else would she do what she did? I told you she's a prostitute. You won't be the only one sleeping with her.'

'I'm not . . . '

I laughed even as Izzy failed to finish his sentence.

'You're not sleeping with her? Oh brother, you're losing your touch. Even I've had her.'

The smack in the face took me totally by surprise. I could not remember a time when Izzy had ever initiated a fight between us. On any other day it would have been his death warrant. But not today. There were too many other issues to be resolved. Instead I took a step back and raised my hands, palms outwards, in a gesture of defence.

'Okay, okay, whatever. We can argue about Naomi later. But surely even you can see that what she did tonight proves there's something going on between her and Jesus?'

Izzy bowed his head in defeat. Somewhere in the deepest recesses of his brain he had already realised about the two of them and my words had only confirmed his suspicions. I saw a way to exploit the situation.

'Look, we've both been taken for mugs by Naomi. Who knows how long this thing between her and Jesus has been going on, but during all of it she's been leading me and you on.'

I was surprised to find that my initial rage had subsided. Now I felt no more than a steely determination to destroy Jesus and, with him, Naomi as well. Nobody made me look like a fool and got away with it. Naomi had made me feel a fool and Jesus had used my life story as a manual on bad living. It was time to start settling some scores. As Izzy raised his head to look at me I saw that same determination in his eyes. Nobody took on the Iscariot brothers and came out on top.

'So, what are we going to do about it?'

I smiled. Izzy was mine and would do whatever I told him to. The trouble was, I had no idea how to get back at Jesus and how to make him pay. He was so popular with the crowds that I could not see a way to get to him even for a preliminary beating. As my mind raced Izzy pushed for an answer.

'How are we going to make her pay?'

Then I realised I had misread my brother. His determination was to hit back at Naomi but as far as I was concerned she was small fry in comparison to the larger target. Then I remembered how sometimes you have to use a sprat to catch a mackerel.

'We make her pay by destroying her boyfriend.'

'What? Jesus? No, I'm not sure about that . . . '

Before Izzy could say anymore I had him by the throat again and this time the blocking of his wind pipe was not unintended.

'You had better be sure,' I hissed, 'otherwise I might concentrate on the fact that it was you who gave away the jar in the first place.'

I released my grip just enough to allow my younger brother to speak.

'All right, we destroy him,' he croaked before I totally released my grip. 'But how?' he asked as he rubbed his neck in obvious pain. 'Since his outburst in the temple the authorities have been out to get him but he's never alone. When he's at the temple there are always hundreds of people around him. Even tonight there was a big crowd at Simon's house.'

'There must be times when he's not in a crowd.'

'Yes, when he's arranged times to spend with those of us who are closest to him. But there's at least a dozen of us so you'd need a small army even then.'

At that point a plan formed in my mind.

'A small army, or a band of guards?'

It was a rhetorical question, but Izzy failed to grasp that fact.

'What do you mean?'

'Who else did you say wanted to destroy Jesus?'

'The temple authorities, the high priest, and that lot.'

'Yes, and they have a band of temple guards who would be able to overpower the small group of Jesus' friends at those quiet times. All they would need to know is when and where they were.'

'But only a handful of us know that. Otherwise the crowds would follow him.'

'Exactly, a few of us know. You could tell them – for a price.'

'You mean betray Jesus?'

'Well hasn't he betrayed you with Naomi?'

Izzy looked unsure. I reapplied my grip to my brother's throat.

'Or should I just blame you for losing me a fortune?'

Izzy shook his head and I moved my hand away.

'So, go to the High Priest tomorrow and sell them Jesus. Not only do we destroy him, but we also get our money back on the nard.'

'How much will we ask for?'

'Well, Judas,' I said, deciding that on such a momentous occasion it was better to use my brother's actual name rather than his nickname, 'I should think sixty silver coins should do it.'

CHAPTER TWENTY-NINE

THE TEMPLE LOOKED JUST AS impressive in the half light of evening as it had in the middle of the day. However, I was in no mood to stand back and admire the architecture of the Jews' most holy building. It had been almost twenty-four hours since I had hatched the plan to betray Jesus and each of those hours had dragged so much that it felt as if time had stood still.

Once Izzy and I had left the lean-to the previous evening I told him to go back to Simon the Leper's house and to stay there until I called for him. Izzy was not keen, and I was concerned that spending time in Jesus' company would encourage him to change his mind. But it was a risk I was willing to take in order to keep him away from our mother. If she got the slightest hint of my plans she would do everything possible to stop them.

I went straight back to Lazarus' house where I shouted and raged about the waste of the nard in front of the whole household. In truth, it was a rage I no longer felt now that I had formulated the plan to walk away with sixty silver coins – the equivalent value of the lost nard oil. I hoped, though, that my acting skills would be believable and, judging by the worried looks on the faces of Mother, Lazarus, and his sisters, they were. They had been visibly relieved to see me end my performance by striding out of the door and slamming it shut.

No one had bothered to come and look for me that night; they probably thought I was drowning my sorrows before passing out in a doorway somewhere. When I failed to turn up in the morning, I imagined they thought I was sleeping off both my hangover and my rage.

In reality, I spent the night back in the lean-to. Before the sun was completely up I left my hideaway and walked to Jerusalem in time for the opening of the city gates. Just as I had done three days before, I went directly to the temple because I wanted to discover the best time to approach the high priest with the offer to sell out Jesus. As I wandered around the building speaking to officials and asking their advice, it dawned on me that for the past few hours my dream of buying back the farm had taken my attention from my original intentions of discovering my biological father. I decided that if I could return my family to their old home my need to avenge my Mother's rape would be removed – but somehow, I knew that my curiosity would one day bring me back to Jerusalem to find him. Although I planned that to be as a man of wealth and property.

However, being in the temple was a worrying time. With my physique and blue eyes, I was not someone easily forgotten, and I was concerned that the guard who had caught me stealing the nard would be on duty and recognise me. It would have been so typical of my luck to get arrested when I was so close to realising my dream. Fortunately, the young guard was nowhere to be seen and I safely gathered the information I required. Perhaps this was to be the day my luck finally changed.

The advice had been to come in the evening. First thing in the morning was actually the best time to gain an audience with Caiaphas the High Priest and I had worried I would have to wait until the next day. But then an older official who had worked at the temple for more than forty years had explained that, if it was an important matter, the priest could be seen in the evening. I never said what I wanted to see the High Priest about, but I was confident it would be viewed as important by everyone concerned.

However, as I walked through the temple entrance leaving the setting sun behind me, I could feel the butterflies in my stomach as I anticipated a life changing few hours.

'So, why do I have to go on my own to see Caiaphas?'

Izzy sounded terrified. I guessed it was something more than mere butterflies that he was feeling at that precise moment.

'I've already told you.' I was doing his best not to let my irritation show. 'The High Priest won't see groups of people in case they're a threat to his safety. Only one of us can go to him and as it's you who'll be able to tell him when he can get his hands on Jesus it makes sense for it to be you.'

'Yes, and we'll be right here waiting for you.'

I was less than impressed at having Dan and Josh as company in the temple. I had been furious when I collected Izzy from Simon's house to find that he had told our cousins our plans. My brother's stupidity never failed to astound me. Dan and Josh were two unreliable fools and Izzy had told them that he intended to betray Jesus. In the short term the problem could be solved by bringing them along to the temple. That would stop them blabbing to anyone back in Bethany. The bigger problem would be keeping them out of the way until Izzy had his chance to hand Jesus over. It rankled with me to think that the first thing I might have to spend my silver on would be accommodation for my cousins. But that was the only way I could think of to keep them away from Jesus' supporters and telling them what had been done.

As we walked towards the priest's chambers my head began to ache. The throbbing grew worse as I worried if Izzy could really be relied on to speak to Caiaphas.

We came to the entrance of the High Priest's court. I swallowed hard, feeling the nausea seeping up from my stomach, but I knew I had to ignore it and look confident. If Izzy had any idea of the worries I had he would back out of the whole enterprise. I looked Izzy in the eye and tried to appear confident and unworried.

'You're on your own from here,' I said. 'Just remember what we practised this afternoon, say exactly what I've told you to say and take the money up front.'

It startled me to see tears in my brother's eyes. 'I can't do this.'

'You can, and you will you snivelling git. Now get in there.'

I pushed him through the doorway and into the priest's chambers. It was the finest part of the temple on public display. There were gold and silver carvings attached to the marble, but I had only the briefest of glances before I retreated back to stand with my cousins.

'I don't think he should have gone in, Barabbas. I don't think he's up to it.'

'Shut up, Josh,' I snapped back. 'Of course, he is.'

I wished I felt as confident as I sounded as I sat on a wooden seat a few yards across from the doorway and waited for Izzy to reappear.

* * * * * *

The waiting in itself was bad enough. What made it worse was having Josh and Dan for company. I wondered if one day they would eventually grow up. They behaved as if the whole enterprise was a game for the first few minutes but then boredom set in and they complained endlessly about how long Izzy was taking.

I could not make up my mind if the long wait was good news or not. It could be that there were a lot of people to see Caiaphas. On the other hand, it may be that the meeting was going on because the High Priest was so eager to discuss the proposal Izzy had brought to him. I found myself swinging from despair to hope and back again. My whole future was in my brother's hands. Izzy had been responsible for destroying my life, now I hoped that he would restore some of what he had robbed me of.

I was just about to tell Dan to shut up when the door opposite our seats creaked as it opened. Izzy walked through, and I felt the nausea rise up in my throat again. Izzy looked as if he had the weight of the world on his shoulders. His head was bowed, and his face bore a look of abject misery. He had failed, I knew it in an instant.

'What went wrong?'

Izzy looked up and walked away from the door and towards me.

'Nothing. We're all set to go. They'll have Jesus by the end of the week.'

Dan and Josh cheered as they jumped to their feet in excitement. Their euphoria was abruptly halted by one look from me.

'So, what went wrong?' I asked again, concerned that Izzy's countenance did not reflect the success of his mission.

'What went wrong?' My brother looked squarely at me with real hatred in his eyes, taking me by surprise.

'I'll tell you what went wrong,' he continued. 'I've just betrayed one of the best men I have ever met.'

'Is that all?' I found that I was laughing. Izzy suddenly developing a conscience was the least of his worries. 'Once we've set ourselves up with the money we're getting from this you'll soon forget him. Anyway, what's the worse they can do to him? Give him a flogging? Banish him from the temple? He'll be back in Galilee in a few weeks and all of this will have been forgotten.'

'You just don't understand.'

'I understand all right. I understand that we've just earned ourselves sixty silver coins.'

'Thirty.'

'What?' My good humour disappeared as quickly and suddenly as it had started.

'When I said we wanted the money up front they said they would only give thirty coins – but I have them here.'

Izzy held up a cloth purse which jangled with the money inside it but I was not impressed.

'Thirty? You accepted half the amount?' I knew I was shouting and drawing attention to us, but I did not care. 'You stupid . . . '

Before I could tell Izzy exactly what I thought of him I noticed more movement from the door opposite. I stifled my outburst as a small man dressed in ornate robes walked into the outer temple court. He looked as old as God and his poise indicated that he considered himself just as important.

As far as I was aware, nobody from my family had ever seen the High Priest before but this had to be him: the confidence with which he carried himself, the arrogance that seemed to pour from every inch of him. He reminded me of Jericho Zac but with far more class and power.

'Is that him?' I asked Izzy. I wondered if I spoke to the priest now if I could renegotiate the price. Although as more people followed him through the door I knew that would be difficult if not impossible.

'No, that is Annas, his father-in-law. He was High Priest himself years ago.'

'So, which one's Caiaphas?'

'That tall guy just walking in now.'

I looked to where Izzy was pointing. A man about our mother's age was walking through the doorway. In his youth he had clearly been a giant of a man. His stature, height, and skin colouring were similar to mine. Then my world came to crashing halt when I saw the man's face.

He had the same piercing blue eyes as me.

CHAPTER THIRTY

TO SAY THAT THINGS HAD not worked out the way Zacchaeus had expected either in the short or long term would have been an understatement. In the long term he had expected to continue to make huge amounts of money for the next few years before entering into a retirement that would have seen him enjoy the many fruits of his labour. He had been on course to fulfil that plan until he had encountered Jesus and his long-term plans were now very different.

In the short term, Zacchaeus' plans for Barabbas had changed. He was amazed that, once again the man who had loomed large in his life had escaped his clutches, just when Zacchaeus thought revenge had been handed to him on a plate. But now he had a new short-term plan as far as Barabbas was concerned.

He was still amazed at the way a chance meeting with Jesus has so altered his life. He had hurried back to Jericho from Bethany after Lazarus had told him that Jesus and his group – which, he hoped, included Barabbas – were heading to Jerusalem for the Passover. He was heading in the wrong direction for the capital city, but he wanted to get home and prepare for the trip. Passover was still more than a week away and he knew he would have had the time to make all the arrangements and still be at the temple in time for the festival.

However, all his plans changed as he got to the outskirts of his home city. Jericho was far bigger and more cosmopolitan than the little village of Bethany, but in terms of cities it was a small and uneventful place to live. So, when Zacchaeus encountered large groups of people on its outskirts, he knew that something significant was afoot, but he had no idea what.

He accosted a couple of young women who were excitedly giggling, looking out at the road that led north, and asked them what was happening. Their reply astounded him.

'They're saying that Jesus of Nazareth guy is making his way here,' they said, wide-eyed and excited.

Their excitement, though, could not match that of Zacchaeus. He had never considered himself a lucky man – hardworking and scheming, yes, but not lucky – but his luck had taken a real turn for the good with this news. If Jesus was coming to Jericho, then his group of followers would be with him as well. He would know by the end of the day whether Barabbas was with them which would save him the trip to Jerusalem which he was pleased about given how much business he had lost in his last visit to the city. Having Barabbas on his own turf also meant that Zacchaeus' thugs were on hand to take him prisoner was well.

All he needed to do was make sure that Barabbas was with the group that he could already see nearing the city. Outside the city would be too soon to encounter them. He needed them deeper into the city boundaries, closer to his home to make sure that Barabbas did not see him while the oaf still had the chance to change his mind and leave the area. Zacchaeus made his way towards the city centre, hardly able to contain his excitement. However, his mood quickly changed as he found himself engulfed by the crowds that had also come to see Jesus.

Zacchaeus was alone, none of his hired muscle were at hand and there were people in the crowds who took full advantage of the situation. Sly digs and the odd kick became a full-on assault as the people around him realised that Zacchaeus was alone and unable to identify his attackers in the melee of people around him. His excitement gave way to sheer fear as he realised he had no hope of reaching his home and the safety it provided him. But he needed to get to some form of safety or he was in danger of not surviving his current circumstances.

His salvation came in the form of a sycamore tree. Its low thick branches risked obscuring people's view of Jesus and so it stood isolated by the edge of the road. Zacchaeus was small and nimble enough to make lunge for those branches and use them to make his way to the top of the tree and away from his anonymous attackers who could not risk identifying themselves by individually making their way up the tree after him.

From his advantage point, Zacchaeus was able to see the crowd below and his attention was immediately drawn to three of his men who stood just yards away from him. They were obviously also waiting to see Jesus and totally unaware of their master's presence in the vicinity. Even though it hurt his bruised ribs, he yelled as loudly as he could to alert them of his precarious situation. It took them a few moments to realise that his voice was coming from the top of a tree, but when they did they immediately made their way over to him and gathered at the bottom of the trunk trying to work out how to help Zacchaeus get down.

It was at that point that Jesus and his party turned up. The good news for Zacchaeus was that it distracted a lot of the attention away from his predicament as he tried to work out how to get down from the branches. However, his relief at no longer being the centre of everyone's attention was short lived as Jesus made his way directly over to him, called him down from the tree, and told Zacchaeus that he expected him to provide some hospitality! In the normal course of events Zacchaeus would have enjoyed having the latest sensation single him out and would have taken great delight in telling him to get lost and to refuse to accommodate him, thus establishing his own place in the hierarchy of life.

However, having scrambled down from the tree flustered and embarrassed, he felt he had no option but to agree to allow Jesus to his home. He was seething with resentment and anger until he noticed that within Jesus' entourage was Barabbas. Suddenly the embarrassment and humiliation were worthwhile. That fool Jesus had brought his enemy straight to him. If the price of getting his hands on Barabbas was to provide a meal for some two-bit preacher from somewhere in the back of beyond it was a price worth paying.

The occasion had started off well enough. Barabbas had been thrown into the depths of Zacchaeus' home to await his fate while his captor had spent a pleasant couple of hours dining in the company of Jesus who proved to be a great guest. Zacchaeus looked at him and tried to assess the man so many people were drawn to. He could see why they would want to spend time with him: he was more muscular than the average fella, he looked like he might be a builder by trade, but he was not particularly good looking. However, there was a depth to the man's eyes that Zacchaeus would not have been able to explain if his life had depended on it. His voice had a tone which gave it real authority and the things he spoke about were interesting with witty observations and clever phrases.

Just as Zacchaeus thought that this was definitely going to be one of his better days, everything changed, and his life was never going to be the same again. Jesus asked if there was somewhere private where he and Zacchaeus could speak, and Zacchaeus surprised himself as to how eager he was to find out what Jesus had to say him. He took Jesus out from the group and into a small anteroom where he and his guest sat down.

In the space of just a few moments Zacchaeus' life changed completely. He listened open-mouthed as Jesus told him his life story. For the first time in his life Zacchaeus was being told the truth about his background, his upbringing, and the life he had created for himself. He had no idea how Jesus knew what he did, but he knew that this preacher man was telling him the truth because so much of his life made sense for the very first time as he heard what Jesus had to say.

Suddenly Zacchaeus realised that things were meant to change. Jesus made him see that although he had built up a huge fortune and a luxurious lifestyle, it had not brought him the happiness and fulfilment he had expected to come with it. In a blink of an eye Zacchaeus decided he didn't want this life anymore and told everyone that he was going to be giving away the money that ultimately had failed him.

In the days that followed there were times when Zacchaeus regretted his action. Adjusting to such a dramatic change in his circumstances was tough. But even the regret was tinged with the excitement of what life could offer him now. The start of a new adventure. He had no idea where it was going to take him, and he felt real freedom in the fact that he could no longer control what was going to happen next after he had told the authorities that he was no longer going to be collecting taxes. He had expected a bit of bother from his bosses, but they knew it would be easy enough to find someone willing to take over the role – and Zacchaeus felt sorry for whomever it was.

But work aside, he still had unfinished business with Barabbas. Almost as soon as he gave the order for Barabbas to be released, he regretted it. The history the two of them shared went back an entire lifetime, even if Zacchaeus was the only one of the two of them who realised it. He needed to get hold of the other man – as far as he was concerned there was still a payment that had to be made. He knew, though, that Barabbas would not willingly cross his path again and he did not blame him for that.

Zacchaeus would have to track him down and the way to do that, he reasoned, was for him to stick with Jesus and his group. So, Zacchaeus had travelled with the rest of them to Jerusalem and then back to Bethany even though it was a village that repulsed him. He had even taken his life in his hands and gone with Jesus to the house of Simon the Leper, but he had not seen Barabbas anywhere. Then the brother, Izzy, had come to the house. Zacchaeus had noticed him give a pot to some woman who had then broken it and anointed Jesus with whatever oil was inside. Zacchaeus had initially been disgusted with the waste, but then thought about the way others would look at his actions when he had encountered Jesus and realised that they would have been perhaps even more amazed by his behaviour. Jesus seemed to bring out the crazy in people, although, to Zacchaeus at least, it wasn't clear why that was.

What was clear was that Barabbas' brother had not intended the woman to break the pot. He looked horrified and left the house almost straight away looking harassed to the point of tears. When he returned later that evening it was clear that he had been on the receiving end of some rough treatment and Zacchaeus instinctively knew it was at the hands of Barabbas. He saw Izzy talking to Barabbas' cousins. Deciding that this might be his chance to discover the whereabouts of the man, Zacchaeus subtly made his way towards the three men hoping not to draw attention to himself.

As he approached he heard them talking in whispers but made out the words 'Barabbas,' 'Jerusalem,' 'temple' and 'tomorrow.'

That made up Zacchaeus' mind. He would be going to the city the next day with the intention of meeting with Barabbas. He did not care what anyone might say about how crazy his intentions were. He would meet with Barabbas, there were debts that had to be paid – one way or another.

CHAPTER THIRTY-ONE

'IT IS YOU – YOU'RE not getting away this time!'

Suddenly I was hauled back into the world around me as two pairs of hands grabbed me. For a few fleeting moments my world had stopped after I had seen High Priest Caiaphas for the first time. Could it possibly be that the most important Jew in Jerusalem was my father? He was the first person I had seen in my entire life who shared both my eye and skin colouring. But Caiaphas was a Holy man, the man who met God every year when he entered the temple's Holy of Holies. How could someone such as that be capable of rape as Mother claimed? It was nonsense. Almost as quickly as the thought had entered my head I dismissed it as I stood with Izzy and our cousins in the temple.

Then I was taken by surprise and grabbed by a rough pair of hands. I tried to see who it was that had seized me. The light was continuing to fade, but it didn't take me long to realise in horror that I was looking straight into the face of the young temple guard I had attacked three days ago when I stole the jar of nard. My shouting at Izzy had drawn more attention to us than I had realised and, unfortunately, the guard with a score to settle was back on duty.

Unlike the last time we had encountered each other, though, it was the guard who had the upper hand. He had two colleagues with him. Bigger, older and more experienced colleagues and it was them who had grabbed me. I tried to wriggle free, but it was useless and brought only more attention to the scene. I saw Caiaphas look over and then move on away from the scuffle; the High Priest obviously deciding it was of no interest to him. Fortunately, no one had taken any notice of Izzy who was still holding the bag of silver coins. In the melee I was relieved to see him smartly turn away from the arrest and walk out of the temple. I didn't trust Izzy completely, but I would rather have the coins outside of the jurisdiction of the temple.

However, Josh and Dan were not so fortunate. They also made to leave the scene, but the young temple guard drew his sword.

'You're not going anywhere. At least one of you was with him the other day.'

'I don't know what you're talking about,' I tried to bluff my way out of the situation. 'This is the first time I've been to the temple for years.'

More guards were descending even as I spoke. I knew there was no way the three of us could fight our way out of this problem, but it looked as if talking my way out of it would fail as well.

'Don't lie to me,' the guard crowed, buoyed by the increasing number of guards. 'I remember you very well. You tried to tell me you had bought that jar. I only gave your story any credence because you look so much like the High Priest I thought you might have been a relative of his.'

I thought I had been angry before but a whole new level of fury raged through me at the guard's words. I had spent too many sleepless nights wondering who my father was, wanting to avenge Mother's rape. Now I had it confirmed that my biological father was living in luxury in Jerusalem untouched by the scandal of an illegitimate son who had spent years in poverty. With a roar I ripped myself free of the two guards who had been restraining me as the red mist descended and bestowed on me some sort of additional strength which I used to fly at the young guard.

The two of us fell to the floor. His sword fell from his hand and clattered loudly on the temple's floor. In an instant I had straddled the guard, using my knees to pin him to the ground as I sat on his stomach. Before anyone else could react, I picked up the sword and repeatedly thrust it into the guard's chest. Blood spurted everywhere, I couldn't see where I was plunging the blade. Hands grabbed at me, trying to force me to stop, but I shook free of their grasps and continued the frenzied stabbing.

'No! No! No!' I screamed with every thrust of the sword.

I could feel blood spraying up as an army of unfamiliar hands tried to move me. As my fury subsided I allowed them to pull me off of the lifeless body below me. It dawned on me that before the end of the week I would be joining that guard in the land of the dead as my sentence to execution could only be a formality.

I felt surprisingly calm at the prospect of my death. My life had not amounted to very much and, of late, I had grown tired of my hopes being raised only for them to be smashed to pieces. There had been the release from my debts, the encounter with Naomi, the jar of nard, even the thirty silver coins, but still I was no more than a common thief and murderer. I was the scum of the earth and the earth would be better off without me. There was nothing in life I would miss. It was sad to think how pathetic my life had become.

I noticed that one of the prison guards holding me had blood pouring down his arm. I looked at the wound on his bicep in confusion. I had attacked only the young guard, I could not see how this other one had been injured in that way. Dragging myself back from my own self-pity, I looked around the temple court and saw that both Dan and Josh had joined in the fight. Josh had already been restrained but Dan was still wildly lashing out at the guards even though he was hopelessly outnumbered.

A lump formed in my throat. My stupid, pain-in-the-backside cousins had joined in my fight. They had no idea what had caused my blind rage, but, when it came to the crunch, they had backed me up. They had fought in my corner regardless of the odds stacked against them. I wondered why it had taken me to the eve of my death to realise that, despite their lack of brainpower, my cousins were fiercely loyal. But now that loyalty needed to be reined in.

'Dan, it's over,' I called to him as he fought like a cornered rat. 'Put the sword down before they kill you.'

When he looked over at me I could see the fear in his eyes. There was a look of doubt on Dan's face, but the sword was laid down and six or seven guards bundled him to the ground before he, his brother, and me were led out of the magnificence of the temple courts and away to the rat-infested pit of the city jail.

* * * * * *

This was not the first cell I had dwelt in. Chained to the wall, the darkness, stench, and damp were nothing new, but never had I shared an incarceration with so many rats. I gave up trying to keep them off my body. I had only so much energy to keep kicking out at them, keeping them at bay. Eventually fatigue had beaten me, and the vile rodents gained their revenge for every kick they had suffered as they ran all over my body sinking their teeth in to every part of me. I was surprised when, after what seemed like a frenzied attack, the rats dispersed and left me alone. I could only assume they had satisfied themselves that I tasted bad and was of no use to them.

As I listened to them scurrying around the cell I wondered how my cousins were faring. After we had been thrown into separate areas of the jail, I fell to sleep in the pitch dark. When I awoke, I had no idea how long I had slept or what the time was. What I did know was that I was hungry, although the stench of the drying blood on my clothing was making me feel sick at the same time.

'Of course,' I said aloud to the rats shocking them so much I could hear them scurrying even further me, 'that's why you fellas were so interested in me – you thought I was a rotting carcass.'

It wasn't only my biting cell mates who reacted to the sound of my voice. I heard my prison door being unlocked and then it creaked on its hinges as it opened.

'On your feet, pig.'

The stiffness in my joints told me I had been in the cell for longer than I had imagined. I struggled to keep my balance. As I stood I reached back to the wall with one hand to steady myself. The guards walked across from the door and one of them drew his sword, placing the tip of the blade at my throat.

'One false move and you're dead.'

I knew that the guards would not take any chances with a murderer. The other guard knelt down to unchain my ankles and I kept my hand on the wall, knowing the slightest stumble could be enough for my throat to be cut. The guard at my feet stood up and grabbed my other arm.

'Let's go.'

The guard with the drawn sword stood back to allow his colleague to pull me towards the door. The movement was disorientating, and I fell over my own feet. It was only the firm grip on my arm that stopped me from falling to the ground. The guards laughed; this was obviously normal behaviour from one of their prisoners.

'Can't find your feet?' one of them chuckled. 'Don't worry, you'll know exactly where they are once we've nailed them to a cross.'

I remained silent because I was afraid that if I said anything it would betray the fear which had gripped me. I had not expected the execution to come so soon. I thought there would at least be a trial, an opportunity for me to plead my case. But now it appeared that this was to be my final few moments before the agony of execution made death a welcome visitor.

I had seen crucifixions before. The nail wounds, although excruciatingly painful, were not enough to kill. With outstretched arms, the whole weight of the body seemed to rest on the person's rib cage and it took monumental effort to keep breathing. In the end, exhaustion would kick in and the man would gasp for breath until he could breathe no more. It was like drowning outside of water. It was a slow death. I had heard of one man who lasted an entire day before he finally died.

My legs still felt weak as I was led up the passageway from my cell towards the main door of the prison. Another guard was opening it and I was aware that my breathing had already become very short and shallow. My mouth was dry but my hands damp and clammy. Instinctively I tried to slow down the speed of my journey into the outside world and towards the horrors it held.

The cold metal blade in the small of my back convinced me to keep up with my escorts. Briefly it flashed through my mind that death could come far quicker and less painfully from the guard's sword than from a cross, but I knew it was only wishful thinking. There was no way any guard would kill a prisoner destined for crucifixion. They would know exactly how to cut me to maximise the pain but keep me alive in the process.

As I walked out of the prison building I was surprised at how fresh the air smelt. At first, I thought it was the contrast with the putrid atmosphere of my cell but then I also noticed the wetness on my face from the rain that was falling as a persistent drizzle. I wondered if this was how a person's body reacted to its imminent death: becoming more aware of the sensory nature of life. The quietness of the early morning hurt my ears as much as any loud noise would, the smell of the wet earth was as aromatic as any perfume, and the first hint of morning light as bright as any candle flame.

As I continued my route march the guards said nothing, either to me or each other as we made our way into the city and around its narrow streets. I had no idea where they were going to execute me, but I found that it mattered very little. I was surprised to find that even my initial fear had abated, but was sorry to find that, in its place, I felt an over-riding feeling of regret.

I regretted almost every aspect of my sorry existence. I had been conceived in the hatred and violence of rape and I had never escaped from them. Mine was a life of one series of disappointments after another. The worst times were when hope seemed so close, only for it to be snatched away at the last moment. But more than anything else I found I regretted my first murder of the man I had thought was my father. The man had stood by Mother after the rape and had raised me as his son. His only 'crime' was to accept Izzy back into the family fold after he had bankrupted us all. As the drizzle began to clear and the early morning sun started to break through the clouds, I realised how many times I too had taken Izzy back after he had messed up and needed help. I knew I would go to my grave realising it should have been Izzy I killed that night. My anger had clouded my judgement, as it had done time and time again since.

Now judgement had been brought to pass on me and I had, quite rightly, been found guilty.

CHAPTER THIRTY-TWO

MY THOUGHTS WERE ABRUPTLY INTERRUPTED as the guards stopped outside an ornate building I had not seen before.

'Where do we go in?' the one with the sword asked the other. 'I've not been to Pilate's palace before. I don't know the way.'

'Pilate's palace?' I was incredulous. 'You mean I'm not being killed now?'

The words tumbled out in relief, but I immediately regretted them.

'You thought we were going to crucify you now?' smirked the guard holding my arm. 'I thought you were quiet. Most prisoners spend their time pleading their innocence with us on the way to the trial – not that it does them any good. But you thought we were taking you out to die – that won't happen till later today.'

The guard lost himself in laughter as he thought of me being a dead man walking twice in one day. He looked up at his fellow guard.

'We've got a right stupid one here.'

'And you're stupid if you think he'll get killed today. The prison is over-run with thieves and murderers who thought they'd get away with it over Passover. He won't get executed until tomorrow at the earliest. Now shut up and show me where we need to take him.'

With his bubble burst, the first guard sullenly swung around and dragged me towards the side entrance of the building. The other guard followed on in silence.

The entrance for prisoners was down some stone steps. The guard pulled me so hard I almost fell down them but instead I collided with him. He fell down the last couple of steps and twisted his ankle. Roaring with pain I thought he was going to retaliate, but before he could, the doorkeeper, alerted by his cry, opened the door.

'What's going on?' he lisped through a mouth which was missing at least half of its teeth.

'Prisoner for you,' replied the uninjured guard as his colleague cursed me and hopped about on one foot.

'Bit early ain't it?'

The doorkeeper rubbed the grey stubble on his chin. The man's bleary eyes made it clear that the guards had woken him.

'We've got a load of them to get through today, so we started early. Now are you going to keep us out here all day or can we come in?'

Without saying another word, the old man opened the door wide enough to let us enter the basement of Pilate's city palace. My arm was now grabbed by the guard who had drawn his sword earlier because the one I fell on could barely walk. Hope sprang up deep within me. If I was escorted back to the city jail later on by just one guard I stood a chance of escape.

'What's he done then?' the doorkeeper asked.

'Murdered a temple guard.'

'Any witnesses?'

'Yeah, about eight of us saw the attack.'

'And not one of you could stop him?' The doorkeeper seemed to eye me with a newfound respect. 'Your dead colleague can't have been too popular.'

'Shut up and just tell us where to take him.'

'If you're looking for a death penalty you'll need to go down the corridor and then to your right. And get your prisoner to duck down, that passageway weren't built for tall beggars like him.'

The three of us must have made an interesting sight as we made our way into the depths of the palace. I had to bend from the waist as the ceiling was so low. Even then I was aware of my hair brushing against mildew and the creatures that made their home in it. Meanwhile, as one guard pushed me with his sword still raised, the other hobbled along behind complaining with every step. There was no way the injured guard could accompany us back and I was certain that I could overpower the other one and get out of Jerusalem. I had a new determination that this was not going to be the week that I died.

The thought gave me renewed courage and I was surprised at how calm I felt as we made our way around to the right and to a Roman official. Despite the early hour, the official was already at his desk, using the light of two candles to read through some scrolls. Only the smallest amount of sun came in through a tiny window located high up in the corner of the room.

'Name?'

The official's eyes remained fixed on the parchments on his desk and I wondered if the man had actually spoken or merely cleared his throat. A shove in the back from one of the guards soon clarified the situation.

'He's talking to you, pig.'

I had to fight the urge to swing around and let fly at the guard. It was only the thought of how I would make him suffer when we were alone on the return journey that made me fight the urge.

'Barabbas Iscariot.'

'What's the charge?' Still the official did not look up.

'Murder of a temple guard,' my escort spat the words out with venom this time.

'Witnesses?'

'Eight temple guards and some of the High Priest's party saw the incident.'

'In the name of the Emperor and acting in the place of Pilate, the governor of Judea, I sentence you to death by crucifixion.'

I was stunned, during the whole exchange the official had never once looked up from his work.

'Don't I get the chance to say something in my defence?' I asked.

'Do you have a defence?' the official asked his eyes still focused on the parchments on his desk. 'Do you claim it was self-defence?'

'No . . .'

'Then the conviction stands. Now take the stinking oaf away. He's making it smell in here.'

I was about to scream at the man behind the desk to look at me when the uninjured guard spoke.

'We need him to stay here. My colleague's injured and I can't risk taking him back alone.'

Immediately the official looked up. He had only one eye, the other had been lost years ago in a fight judging by the vicious scars around the empty eye socket. The disfigured face looked eerily sinister in the candle light of the room and I recoiled at the sight. The official noticed my reaction and immediately lowered his head and returned to the work on his desk. In that moment I realised why the man had not previously looked up.

'We've got no room here.'

'But I can't take him back alone.'

The official sighed. He clearly did not want another prisoner and he had no sympathy for the temple guards. I silently willed him to insist that the guard return me to the cell in the city temple. It was my only hope.

'All right.' Another sigh came from the direction of the desk. 'Take him up to the next floor and a guard will find somewhere to put him. Now get that stench out of here.'

The guard pulled my arm and shoved me out of the room. And in that moment, I knew my life was as good as over – but the thought left me untroubled. This was yet another example of my hopes being raised only for them to be crushed completely. I was sick of it. I had had enough. Death would be a welcome relief from the torment of life. The regrets I had felt earlier had disappeared, it was time to get out. I had never been a religious man and I did not know what to expect on the other side of the grave. But I was sure it could be no worse than the thirty-three years of misery my life among the living had amounted to.

Without any hesitation I followed the guard back down the corridor and towards the door where we had entered the building, the steps to the next floor were just by it. The doorkeeper was sleeping so soundly at his post that he did not register our return. He barely stirred when the injured guard spoke up.

'I'll wait for you here. I'm not going to try those steps with my foot.'

The other guard grunted in response. I was not sure whether it was in agreement or contempt, but he went on without his colleague, pushing me up in front of him, encouraging me on my way with the tip of his sword. I wanted to tell him there was no need to force me up to the cell, but I decided the words would be wasted so I continued on in silence.

We were met at the top of the stairs by a jailor who looked irritated to have a new inmate to keep an eye on.

'Who's he?'

'Murderer called Iscariot. Due to be crucified for killing a temple guard so you'll have him only for a day at most.'

'Why aren't you taking him back with you?' Clearly the jailor thought, correctly, that I was being dumped on him.

'My companion has hurt his foot and is hobbling round like a cripple. It's too risky for just one of us to accompany him back so the guy downstairs said to bring the prisoner to you.'

The jailor spat on the floor near enough to the guard's foot to make him move it out of the way. It was enough to make the jailor smirk and encourage him to think he had scored some sort of minor victory. He turned around and walked away from us. The guard and I stood still not sure if we should be following.

'Well, are you bringing him down here or not?' the jailor called back.

We set off after him, catching him up as he stood opening a door which clearly was going to be my last resting place before my death. The guard propelled me towards the open doorway.

'The guy downstairs said you were full,' the guard exclaimed as he pushed me into an empty room.

'This is the last cell available and it's Passover, it'll soon fill up,' the jailor replied unapologetically. 'Does he need feeding?'

'If you want, I don't care.'

The guard left the room and I could hear his footsteps heading back towards the stairs. The jailor was still standing by the door. Once he had watched the guard walk away he turned to face his newest prisoner.

'So, what's all the blood on you?' he asked.

'The guy I killed.'

'Well you stink, take it off.'

'I've nothing else to wear.'

The door slammed shut. I could hear the jailor muttering to himself as he shuffled away from the door. I looked down at my clothes. The blood was drying out but I looked and smelt like a slaughterhouse. A few moments later the door opened again.

'You still not taken it off?' my jailor asked as he threw me a garment of some sort.

I reluctantly began to disrobe in front of him, throwing my bloody garment towards the jailor and hurriedly putting on the new clothing. Almost at once I could sense the fleas and lice living in it, but it was better than being naked. I still remembered my humiliation as Jericho Zac's prisoner. The jailor gathered up the discarded clothing.

'Breakfast?'

I gave a slight nod of my head waiting for the sarcastic comment or the put down. The jailor left the room again, slamming the door behind him. He was gone for slightly longer this time. When he returned he had with him some barley bread and a jug which, as he handed it to me, I saw contained cheap ale.

'Thank you.'

'No, thank you. If you've killed one of those jumped-up temple guards and rid the world of one more arrogant git you're all right by me.'

I think my eyes must have widened in disbelief.

'Don't look so surprised,' the jailor continued. 'Do you know anyone who likes those guards at the temple? Right pain, every single one. Shame you've got to die when as far as I can see you've done everyone a favour.'

As he spoke he picked up a leg iron from the floor. One end was attached to the wall behind me and before I realised what was happening, the other was clasped around my ankle.

'Least I can do while you're here is look after you properly.'

With that he turned and left the cell, slamming the door for a third time.

I had not realised how hungry I was until I started eating. The bread was dry and stale but washed down with the ale it was like manna from heaven. I was sorry when it was all gone. I drank down the last of the ale and belched loudly wondering if this was going to prove to be my last meal. If the guards were right and my execution was not going to be until the next day, I hoped that I would be given more to eat before then.

I looked around the room and decided I had spent time in worse places. The dungeon at Jericho Zac's place came to mind, so did some of the caves I had slept in while travelling between Bethany and Galilee. I thought about Capernaum and the Sea of Galilee which I had left a few weeks ago and as I did I remembered the reason for the journey. I had wanted to discover who my father was and, if possible, make him pay for attacking my mother.

She, of course, had tried to discourage me. She had not wanted me to make the trip but I had ignored her. I wished now she had succeeded. It had done me no good to discover my father was the High Priest.

My stomach churned as I remembered the previous evening and seeing Caiaphas' blue eyes. Yet at that moment I had still doubted. That was until the guard had spoken of the family resemblance I had to the most powerful Jew in Jerusalem. That chance remark had tipped me, confused and angry as I was, over the edge and cost both of us our lives.

'Poor beggar,' I said aloud despite being utterly alone.

Perhaps the young guard had lost his life for nothing. With time to reflect it seemed impossible to think that Caiaphas could have raped a woman, fathered an illegitimate son, and still gone on to be High Priest.

I lost all track of time as my head swam with thoughts and counter-thoughts. Finally, I decided for certain I was wrong. There was no connection between me and Caiaphas – that had been an assumption I had jumped to which had cost the guard his life and, in the not too distant future, was going to cost me mine.

I was distracted from my thoughts by the sound of the door reopening. I looked up expectantly hoping that this meant I was going to be given some more food.

Instead Mother walked through the door.

CHAPTER THIRTY-THREE

I'M NOT SURE WHY I ever thought I knew my mother as she had the ability to constantly surprise me – and this prison-cell visit was not going to be any different. As she entered through the door I saw such an intense sorrow in her eyes that I was stunned into silence. Then she shocked me by rushing into the cell and throwing her arms around my neck. I felt myself reddening with embarrassment as I looked across and saw the jailor standing in the doorway.

'You can have only a few moments,' he said glancing over his shoulder to check no one was in the corridor. 'You shouldn't really be here at all. I suppose that waste of space of a door keeper just let you in without checking who you were.'

Without waiting to have his suspicions confirmed, the jailor turned and left the room, this time closing the door slowly and without any noise at all. I patted Mother's back, signalling that she could break off her embrace which she did. As she moved to sit down just a few feet away I was surprised to see tears flowing freely down her face.

'It's not so bad, Mother,' I said, struggling to find words to reassure her. 'The jailor's treating me well. He seems to think I'm some sort of hero because it was a temple guard I killed.'

'He's an idiot then!' Mother sobbed, breaking down in front of me. 'And so are you. What were you thinking of? Did you really think you'd get away with killing him?'

I had found myself touched by my mother's obvious sadness at my plight. But it did not last. Even now in her grief, and with my death just hours away, she sat in the grimy cell criticising me just as she always had. I couldn't believe it! I couldn't put up with her any more – I certainly would not miss her the other side of the grave. And, once her initial shame of having had a son executed had gone, I was fairly certain she would not miss me either.

'I killed him because he told me I looked like one of the High Priest's family.'

It couldn't have shocked her more. Her tears, her temper and whatever remained of her sorrow completely disappeared. They were replaced by shock and, I decided, guilt. In that moment I knew for certain who my father was, and it churned my stomach.

My mother bowed her head. I wanted to keep the silence between us, hoping that it would eventually force her to speak. But time was not on my side. The jailor had said that we could have only a few moments and I wanted to make sure that I made use of every single one of them.

'Well, aren't you going to say anything?'

Still Mother sat in silence opposite me. It was as if the flag stone she was staring at was the most interesting thing she had ever seen in her life and she was unable to take her eyes off it. But I knew shame when I saw it. In normal circumstances even I may have been considerate to Mother's feelings. But these were not normal circumstances, I did not have time to waste.

'By this time tomorrow I'll be dead,' I told her bluntly. 'Before that happens I want to know about my father.'

My mother looked up with a new determination in her eyes. At first, I feared it was a determination not to tell me. Then I realised it was the opposite. After years of silence about my paternal lineage, she had decided the time had come to tell me everything. She licked her lips and I could sense she was considering how best to start.

'I came to Jerusalem for one of the festivals when I was fourteen. It must have been Passover. I was so excited. It was only the second time I'd come to the city and it seemed big and bright and full of people. I was a naive girl from the country and the city was like some sort of paradise.

'I was already engaged to your father, sorry, I should say to the man I married, but we had done no more than kiss each other. I knew that was going to change soon as our wedding was just a couple of weeks away. I made the trip with my parents and this was to be the last opportunity I had to behave like a young girl rather than the responsible married woman I was soon to be.

'Obviously, as a woman I couldn't stray into much of the temple and I began to get bored. So, one time, I decided to explore more of the city. It was stupid of me to go alone, I realise that now, but it didn't occur to me that I was putting myself in danger.'

As she had sat there recalling that trip to Jerusalem, I watched her light up with enthusiasm as she remembered life before marriage and motherhood. I saw a change in her demeanour as she reached what was obviously a more painful part of her story.

'I had no idea where I was going but I ended up at the Tower of Ovens by the Valley Gate. That's where I met him. Of course, then he and his family were nobodies. The marriage into the High Priest's family wasn't until a few years later. What he was, though, was confident, arrogant but, I hate to say it, charming – at least at first.

'When I first saw him, I was awestruck. I'd met some strapping, handsome lads on the farms at home but he was on another level. He had a beautiful body and a beautiful face to go with it. And those eyes! I'd never seen anyone with blue eyes before. I was a stupid girl and he was a clever lad who decided that he could have his way with me.

'I can still remember him saying hello. I couldn't believe that a city lad like him would show any interest in a simple country girl like me. He made me laugh at first. I thought he was lovely even though we spoke only for a few moments. When he suggested going round the back of the tower to get out of the hot sun I didn't think twice about going with him . . .'

Her voice trailed off and she sat in silence. I looked away – how many times as a youngster had I used my charm to seduce a young girl? I really was my father's son.

'It's okay.' I looked towards her. 'You don't have to tell me what happened. I understand.'

'I thought it was my fault.' She looked at me with new tears of sorrow in her eyes. 'I thought I had led him on and that he was just doing what any man would do.'

The tears flowed freely down her face. Despite everything that had happened between us, she was still my mother and I wanted to comfort her. But the truth was I didn't know how.

'What happened when you got home?'

'I was too full of shame to tell anyone and it never dawned on me that I would get pregnant. So, I got married and when I found out I was expecting I assumed it was through my husband. It wasn't until you were born with blue eyes that I realised who your father was.'

'And so, presumably, did everyone else.'

'No, only my mother. When she looked at you she told me I was a whore. But she told everyone else that she had had an uncle with blue eyes and that I must have passed the family trait on to you.'

'And everyone believed her?' I was incredulous.

'Everyone chose to believe her because they didn't want a scandal in their community. But I know the man who brought you up never really thought of you as his son.'

I nodded. It made sense of my unhappy childhood and the difficult relationship with the head of the family.

'But what did you do? Why didn't you confront him?' he asked.

'Because I didn't know who he was,' she replied exasperated. 'When he attacked me he was a nobody. I never thought I would see him again. And

I didn't for the next fifteen years. Then, when we were at the temple for another festival, I came face to face with him.

'By then the marriage into the High Priest's family had happened. I still had no idea who he was until one day, as I was sat on the temple step, he walked past me and our party. One of the men said something to him and he stopped and replied. I knew him at once.'

'What did he do when he saw you?'

His mother surprised me by laughing bitterly.

'Absolutely nothing. He didn't remember me. I was probably one of hundreds of girls he had been with.'

I was shocked.

'So, he doesn't even know I exist.'

'Not for most of your life, no. But he knows now.'

The door opening interrupted our conversation just when I was desperate to hear more. Both of us looked up to see the jailor come into the cell.

'You need to go now,' he ordered.

'Please, just a few more moments.' I think the desperation in my voice made him hesitate before he answered. He looked behind him, down the corridor, before turning his attention back to us.

'If I'm caught letting her in your cell I'll be done for – so make it quick.'

With that he turned and left the cell. I didn't want to waste a second of the remaining time with Mother.

'How does he know about me?'

'It was when Jericho Zac wanted his debts repaid.' It was clear mother wanted to get the whole story out before the jailor came back. I wondered if it made her feel better to get the story out in the open.

'I knew the sort of things Zac would do to you and I was desperate to do something to help. Like I've told you before, I went to Jerusalem and I went to the temple. I don't know how I managed to bluff my way past the guards, but I got to see Caiaphas. I told him who I was, who you were, and the circumstances you were in at that time.

'What did he say?' I asked eager to find out how such an influential man had reacted to the news.

'At first he didn't believe me. But when I told him you looked just like him, including your eyes, he started to waver. Then I told him that if he didn't get you free from Jericho Zac I would tell his father-in-law Annas about the rape and about you. He couldn't risk upsetting him by bringing shame and scandal to the temple. That Annas is still the power behind the High Priest. It didn't take him long to promise to sort it out.'

As I listened to Mother's story the whole encounter with Jericho Zac came back to me. The mystery man on a horse must have been one of the Caiaphas' officials. The High Priest sent him to Jericho to negotiate my release. It would have taken only one question from the official to confirm that story: *What colour are your prisoner's eyes?* He need not even ask Zac who may have realised the significance of the question, either of the thugs who brought me in would have noticed.

'There was one stipulation to your release,' Mother said interrupting my thoughts. 'You were never to go to Jerusalem.

'That's why I tried to dissuade you from making the journey. You were determined to find your father, but I knew discovering him would be no good for anyone. And I've been proved right.'

When the door to the cell opened again I wondered if the jailor had been standing outside the door listening. There had not been enough time for him to make his way down the corridor and back. Whether he had heard what had been said was irrelevant though, because I knew Mother would have to leave straight away. So, it appeared, did she. Before the jailor said anything, she struggled to her feet. After straightening her clothes she paused to look at me one last time.

'Well, son,' she said, 'I'm sorry this is how it's ending. But I don't think either of us are really surprised that your life is ending up like this, are we? I did warn you.'

I looked up at her and wondered, if I had lived beyond today, if she would ever have stopped telling me how she was always right.

'No, I guess you were right. I should've listened.'

'It doesn't mean that I'm not sorry. It'll break my heart to see you on a cross. I wish there was something I could do.'

With that she bent forward and kissed me.

'This is all very touching,' the jailor snapped, 'but I've got more prisoners to bring up from downstairs and I can't do that with you here. It's time to leave.'

I was determined to hold back my tears as I watched Mother wipe away hers and turn towards the door. I desperately wanted to say something but was at a loss to know what.

'Goodbye, Mother,' was the best I could do.

CHAPTER THIRTY-FOUR

I DIDN'T HAVE LONG TO reflect on what Mother had said before the new prisoners were brought into the cell. I noticed that it was a different jailor to the one who had allowed my visitor, but I just assumed it was the end of his shift as he didn't return again that day.

All through the day a sizeable number of prisoners were taken in and out. I soon discovered I was the only one under a death sentence, the others had all been condemned to a flogging and the cell was merely a holding pen until their time to receive the whip had arrived.

At the start of the afternoon when the jailor opened the cell door, I looked up terrified that my name was going to be called and I would be led away to my death. But as the afternoon progressed, though, I realised that it was too late for any more crucifixions that day which meant that, as the light of day dimmed, I had found myself alone in the cell again. I settled down to spend at least one more night on the earth. However, I didn't expect to sleep well considering the horrors that were waiting for me the next day.

It was the sound of yet another jailor opening the cell door to bring in my breakfast that had woken me. Wiping the sleep from my eyes I realised that I had actually slept incredibly well. I was amazed, but also somewhat disappointed – I had only hours left to live and yet I had wasted them sleeping. It was not as if I was going to need my energy for a long day ahead.

As I stirred and sat up I discovered that, while sleep may not have deserted me, my appetite certainly had. I could only pick at the dry bread, and the ale tasted cheaper and more bitter than it had the previous day. I pushed the breakfast away wondering if my appetite might return later, though, I doubted it. Then I heard the key turn in the lock and looked up to see the jailor returning to the room.

'Not hungry?' he asked, although his tone suggested that he had no interest in the answer. 'Well, I've got to clear this away, we've got another cell mate coming in to join you.'

I said nothing. I had not been interested in the other prisoners yesterday and I could see no reason to be interested in any of them today. My concern was that, as the jailor picked up my barely touched breakfast and walked out of the cell with it, my appetite immediately returned. I was about to call out to ask for it back when a guard appeared at the door with the new prisoner. At first, I was not going to let that get in the way of my food until I saw who my new cell mate was.

Jesus stood in the doorway.

'What are you doing here?' My hunger was instantly forgotten, as my blood ran cold.

Jesus said nothing but allowed himself to be pushed into the cell by his guard. He stumbled towards the wall to the left of me but regained his footing, standing stock still as the guard took the chain attached to the wall and clasped the other end around Jesus' ankle.

'He's said nothing for hours.' The guard looked across from him as he locked the shackle. 'I shouldn't think he'd have anything to say to a murderer like you.'

The guard straightened up, spat in Jesus' face and turned and left the room, slamming the door behind him. My gaze never left Jesus who made no effort to wipe away the guard's phlegm that was trickling down his cheek. That was when I noticed that the cheek also had a fresh bruise on it. As I looked more closely I could see that Jesus had taken quite a bruising since I had last seen him – obviously the guards had regarded him as an easy target for their abuse.

Still he said nothing. His eyes never left the door.

'What happened?' I asked. I felt uncomfortable as I was certain that Izzy must have had a hand in Jesus' arrest and the other man's silence was unnerving me.

Jesus turned his head away from the door and looked at me as if he hadn't realised I was in the room with him. The look in his eyes was one of abject sorrow, but his face was set determinedly. I wasn't really expecting a reply and was startled when Jesus spoke.

'I was arrested after your brother betrayed me.'

I could think of nothing to say. I knew Jesus would have guessed my part in the plot to betray him. I desperately wished I had never asked the question and hoped Jesus would say something else. I was not bothered whether it was a tirade of abuse or the pitiful wailing of a man betrayed. But he just continued to stand, looking directly at me, as if waiting for a response. I struggled to think of something to say.

'You might as well sit down. You'll be here ages before they decide what to do with you,' was the best I could manage.

'They've already decided to kill me.' Jesus sat down on the floor, resting his back against the hard stone wall.

'Kill you?' I was amazed. I had expected Jesus to receive a flogging, perhaps a night or two in prison while the Passover was on, but I had not expected him to be crucified. 'What can they charge you with that means the Romans want you dead?'

'The High Priest and his family have told Pilate that I've claimed to be the new King of the Jews.'

There was a resignation in his voice, almost as if Jesus had expected this moment to come. But, for me, there was a macabre irony in all of it. It had been my father, the High Priest, who had schemed to see Jesus executed and it was his illegitimate son who had unknowingly helped by arranging to have Jesus betrayed in the first place. I had played a part in the family's plans, but they would be totally unaware of it.

'Sorry.' It sounded pathetic, but I knew I should accept some blame for the position Jesus found himself in.

'Why are you sorry?' Jesus seemed genuinely surprised.

'I put my brother up to betraying you to the High Priest. But I never expected–'

Jesus raised his hand.

'It's all right,' he reassured me. 'You didn't know what you were doing.'

In the silence that followed I slowly shook my head in disbelief.

'I don't understand why they would want to kill you.'

'I'm a threat to them and all that they stand for,' Jesus replied. 'I'm making people realise that the priests have taken the good things God gave and turned it to their own advantage and into something bad. They want to use religion to keep people in their place, which as far as they are concerned, is subservient to them. But God wants people to enjoy their life and to be blessed by Him, not weighed down with harsh rules and regulations.'

'But is it your job to tell people that?' I was incredulous. 'Is it really for you to tell the High Priest and his lot that they've got it all wrong?'

'Yes, it is.' The passion stirred within him as he spoke. 'And not just them but everyone else as well.'

Despite the situation we were in, I found myself chuckling.

'Well, Jesus,' I said with my smile never really reaching my eyes, 'I wished you'd said God wanted to bless me. If you had I might never have ended up in the mess I'm in now.'

'Your trouble was you never listened.'

I sat up straight. Was that a rebuke? I had felt sorry for the position Jesus was in and, to a lesser extent, guilty for my part in it. But the tone of his words had carried a measure of accusation within them. Had this deluded odd-job man from Nazareth ever said anything worthwhile to me? The smile dropped from my face.

'What do you mean by that?' I shot back, my temper rising. 'What could I have ever heard from you that was worth listening to? All you did was tell stories about my life when they were nothing to do with you.'

Despite my imminent death, I was ready for a fight. I jumped up, straining at my chain hoping I could reach Jesus and add considerably more bruises to his face and elsewhere on his body. But the jail had been well constructed, the chains had been designed to prevent the prisoners, even those with as long a reach as I had, from hitting one another. In sheer frustration I turned around and slammed my fist against the wall. I roared as my frustration and rage was replaced by the searing pain travelling from hands up my arms. I sunk back to the floor.

Jesus remained sitting against his wall, unmoved by my reaction.

'Wasn't it good for you when Jericho Zac and Jairus cancelled your debts?'

Jesus spoke in a voice of such calm authority that, despite my anger and pain, I found I had no choice but to listen attentively to every word.

'Didn't that tell you,' Jesus continued, 'that God was blessing you? And when I told the story of the man you attacked on the Jericho road and of your brother going off and wasting his inheritance I was telling everyone, including you, about the way God cares for you – even if you don't deserve it.'

As I sat silently my fist throbbed. But it was the words of Jesus which captured my attention rather than any pain. I realised he was right. It had been Jesus' intervention with both Jericho Zac and Jairus that had cleared my debts once and for all and Izzy had told me how Jesus had used the story of a father's love for his wayward son as an example of God's love for people. I shook my head.

'I haven't been able to see what's been right under my nose.'

I looked up at Jesus.

'I can see what you were trying to do now. But it's too late, isn't it? We'll both be dead before today ends.'

Before Jesus could reply the cell door opened. I expected the jailor to enter but, instead, the one-eyed Roman official bounded into the room. Gone was his self-consciousness at his deformity. In its place was an overabundance of excitement.

'This is quite a day!' he exclaimed before hurriedly continuing before either of us could interrupt him. 'I have never known anything like it in all my years of working for Rome.

'One of you is going to be a free man in just a few moments.'

I looked at the official. He was obviously excited, but he looked just as sane – and disfigured – as he had when I had first encountered him the previous day. But what the man was saying was totally insane. Both Jesus and I had been sentenced to death by the authority of the Romans who governed the land. A death sentence was never waived. In fact, I knew I was an exceptional case in that I was still alive a whole day after the sentence had been passed. Yet now this very excited official was saying I had a chance of avoiding the torture of the cross and being released. It made no sense at all. Somewhere deep within the darker side of my personality I convinced myself this was some malicious prank designed to give a condemned prisoner false hope just before his death. I looked across to Jesus to see his reaction, but my cell mate's face was unreadable.

'What do you mean?' I cautiously asked the official not wanting to appear too hopeful in case this was all a ruse.

'I mean one of you is going to have his sentence squashed.'

I wondered how much the man could see out of his only eye as, in his excitement, he was blinking at a rapid rate.

'Pilate has been reminded of a custom that I've never come across before which says that one prisoner facing death can be released at Passover. And it's going to be one of you two.'

Still Jesus remained silent.

'So how will Pilate decide which of us is to be released?' Despite my best efforts I could hear both excitement and hope rising in my voice.

'Pilate won't decide. The crowd will. Whoever they choose to be executed will be executed and whoever they decide to release will be released. They'll shout for the person they want to die'

I was astounded. I had never known a situation before when the people would decide something such as this en mass. This was an amazing turn of events in my life – however much longer it lasted for.

'When do they decide?' I asked trying to calculate if I could contact my family and make sure they were shouting for Jesus to go to the cross.

'Any moment now,' the official replied as he made for the cell door. 'I'm just about to record the result.'

With that he was gone. I looked across at Jesus who still said nothing. Given the circumstances, I judged there was nothing to say between us and so I strained to listen for any noise coming into the cell from the outside world.

As I listened I realised how desperate I was to hear Jesus' name being shouted as the man the crowd wanted to see executed. I felt a new wave of passion for life surge through my body. I wanted to live, I wanted another chance. With an enthusiasm I would have thought impossible to feel just a few moments ago, I realised I was desperate to see the next day, next week, next year. I did not want to die.

I could just make out the distinctive sound of a crowd of people. The murmurings of lots of different conversations all going on at the same time. I had been so caught up in the previous conversation with Jesus that I hadn't noticed the build-up of noise from the world outside of the prison. I wondered if I would be able to hear the crowd's verdict. Then the shouting of one name swamped the silence of the cell.

'Barabbas! Barabbas!'

CHAPTER THIRTY-FIVE

FOR A FLEETING MOMENT I felt a tinge of regret that I had never married and had children. But it was only fleetingly. I had never been husband or father material and I knew it. So, did every woman I had ever met. No, it was better that I had not inflicted myself on a wife or a child. I had made enough of a mess of my own life, and that of the family I did have, to regret not adding to the number of lives I'd ruined. But I was sorry that my life was going to end before I had reclaimed my family's farm or avenged my mother's rape. But who was I kidding, I had never had it in me to do those things either.

My thoughts were disturbed by the sound of the cell door opening.

'On your feet. You're free to go.'

I couldn't bring myself to look up and see the guard lead Jesus out of the cell. It was not so much disappointment of the outcome of the crowd's decision, but more the ridiculousness that I had allowed myself to hope that they may have picked me. Jesus was a celebrity figure among the people – of course they were going to choose him to live. I was a nobody from nowhere why should anyone be bothered whether I lived or died?

However, watching Jesus leave the cell would be too much to bear. That man's freedom sealed my own doom and so I sat against the wall not lifting my eyes, I would hear the door slam once Jesus had gone and know that I was on my own again. It would give me a few moments of solitude before the torture began. I wondered idly if the crucifixion would hurt all the more because of the damage I had done to my hand.

'Come on, don't you want to go?'

I wondered why Jesus had not sprung to his feet ready for freedom. Curiosity got the better of me and I looked up. Sure enough, Jesus was still slumped against the wall with a look of resignation on his face. I turned towards the guard wondering what he would do next. As I turned my head I realised that the man was looking directly at me.

'Didn't you hear them calling your name?' he asked. 'They were shouting for you to be released, though God only knows why.'

'Me?' I was bewildered. 'I'm to be freed? But the official said the crowd would shout for the man they wanted to be killed.'

'Don't take any notice of him. He went mad after he lost his eye as a youngster. Pilate told them to shout the name of the man they wanted to be released and they chose you. Now, stand up so I can get that chain off you before they change their minds.'

I struggled to my feet barely able to take on board what had happened. For the first time in my life things had gone my way. No, I knew that wasn't true. This was another occasion when Jesus had helped things go my way. He had done it with Jericho Zac and Jairus, and now, because the crowd had chosen me over him, Jesus had turned events in my favour again. This time I was not going to let it go to waste.

Lost in my thoughts, I barely realised that the guard had undone my chain. Suddenly the one-eyed official entered the cell. His excitement was still very clear.

'Barabbas Iscariot,' his voice was high-pitched with emotion. 'By the power invested in me by Pontius Pilate, Governor of Judea, I declare you acquitted of any and all charges brought against you. You are free to go.'

'What does that mean exactly?' I was struggling to keep up.

'It means that you are free and that no charges can be brought against you unless they relate to instances from this moment on.'

The official's excitement was already dimming. Explaining the legal technicalities to someone he evidently saw as an uneducated oaf was irritating for him. However, as his excitement waned so mine grew. No charges could be brought against me for anything in the past. Not the attacks, the murders, the muggings, nothing. I couldn't even be charged for the theft of the alabaster jar from the temple at the beginning of the week. The slate had been totally wiped clean. It was as if, in that moment, I had become a totally new me.

'Don't waste it, Barabbas. It's a new start for you.'

Jesus' voice surprised all of us. What shocked me more was the way it appeared that Jesus had been reading my thoughts.

'I'm not going to,' I replied, stepping towards the man who was going to die in my place. 'Thank you.'

I put my hands out towards him as he still sat with his back against the prison wall. Looking up, Jesus responded by taking hold of my hands. As our fingers touched a surge of warmth radiated out of Jesus onto my hands and up my arms. Immediately the pain I had been in from punching the wall went. Jesus smiled.

'Come on, this is all very touching, but I've got other work to do.'

The connection between us was broken by the guard's sarcastic words as he pulled on my arm. I decided not to protest but allowed him to usher me out of the cell and down the corridor, away from the most remarkable man I had ever met. As we walked towards freedom I wriggled my fingers and stretched out my palms. The pain was gone completely. In fact, both my hands felt better now than at any time I could remember. It seemed as if Jesus' healing claims had been genuine after all.

By the time we reached the stairs that led to the entrance, the doorman had disappeared completely. By now I had had enough of being man-handled by the guard and so I shrugged free of his grasp. I was a free man now and no one was going to push me around ever again. I decided that things were going to be different from now on as I walked away from the stairs and out of the side door of the building. Looking back, it is incredible how confident I was that everything was going be better right from that moment. I didn't realise that there were still more horrors to come.

As I stepped out into the world free and looked up, it struck me how the overcast sky was in complete contrast to my mood. And at that moment, I was grabbed by the jailor who first locked me in the cell. Panic seared through me. Was I about to be locked up again? Then I saw Mother standing there, too.

'Barabbas, you're free!' She beamed.

'But you need to get out of the city now,' the jailor added anxiously looking around him.

Without having time to respond, I was being escorted away from Pilate's palace and towards the outer edges of the Jerusalem. I guessed I was heading towards one of the smaller, less used gates that populated the city's wall.

'Don't I at least get the chance to have something to eat and drink?' I asked, pulling myself free.

The three of us stopped. Mother looked at the other man, a pleading look on her face. The jailor looked from her to me and then back again.

'No,' he said with an air of authority. 'We were told to get him out of the city straight away.'

With that he continued his march towards the city wall. With my mother obediently following on, I appeared to have no option but to continue with them in heading out of Jerusalem. We were walking through an area of the city I did not recognise. It contained some of the smallest and poorest houses I had seen in the capital. At the end of one particularly narrow and cramped street we reached a small gate in the city wall. The jailor heaved it opened and walked out of the confines of Jerusalem.

He turned around and watched us follow him into the open space. A look of relief spread across his face now that we were no longer in the city. He sat down and rummaged in a bag he had concealed under his cloak. He brought out three small fishes and a small bottle. He threw them at me. Fortunately I caught them cleanly and then sat down on the dirt by the wall to eat and drink.

'I wasn't sure you'd have had breakfast,' the jailor explained. 'I thought you'd want something to eat and drink before you start your journey away from here.'

'What makes you think I'm going away?'

'You've got to. It was part of the deal.'

'And when did you start making deals on my behalf?' I was growing irritated with this pompous man who had started to give me orders. But then Mother reached out and put her hand on my shoulder.

'Don't get angry, son. If it wasn't for Bartholomew you'd be carrying your cross for execution later this morning.'

'How? What did he do?' I asked wolfing back the fish.

'He heard what we spoke about in the cell yesterday and suggested I go back to Caiaphas to see if he would help you again.'

I put down my drink.

'That was a risky thing to do.'

'Yes, it was. But I was willing to try anything to save my son.'

Mother sat down beside me, linked her arm through mine and smiled. I tried to take on board what she was saying. As I did, I realised that I had completely misunderstood her. I had always thought the bitterness and resentment in her was as a result of me. But now I could see that it was her life she resented. Her motherly instinct to love and protect her child was strong.

'What happened?'

'He was not pleased to see me.' She sighed. 'He tried to get rid of me but when Bartholomew told him the two of you looked alike, he had to do something.'

'So, you went as well?' I was surprised that the jailor had taken such an interest.

'I told you,' the man replied, 'I hate temple guards and anything to do with the temple, so I was only too happy to stir it up for the High Priest.'

'In fact, it was Bartholomew who came up with the idea of how Caiaphas could help you. He dreamt up the long-lost custom of releasing a prisoner at Passover time.'

'You mean there is no custom?' I was confused by the story I was hearing.

'Oh, there is a custom,' Bartholomew pronounced proudly. 'But it hadn't been called upon for some years. When I reminded Caiaphas of it, he was only too happy to mention it to Pilate. But it was on the condition that you leave Jerusalem today and never return. He could do without having a criminal walking around the city who looks just like him.'

'But how could you be certain Pilate would accept the idea or even that I would win the public vote?'

Bartholomew shrugged his shoulders.

'When has a High Priest ever lost a vote?' he said dismissively. 'The only risk was Pilate not agreeing, but apparently he was very keen. I think he was hoping that Jesus of Nazareth would go free.'

'What matters is that you are free and can get on with your life again,' Mother said, giving my arm squeeze.

I surprised her by pulling it free and getting to my feet. I shook my head as I rubbed my dirty, tired face. I could not lose the thought that I should not be a free man. It should have been Jesus who was released. It was disconcerting that I was now developing a conscience – a few days ago I would have happily watched another man die in my place. But not any longer.

'I don't deserve this. Jesus should be the one to go free.'

'And he will,' his mother replied. 'They'll change their minds, give him a flogging and let him go. Give him a month to recover and he'll be fine and back to his old self.'

Mother's naivety took me by surprise. "The Romans won't let two condemned men free on the same day – or even the same week. Jesus will be crucified today.'

Mother gasped. Her shock was evident. She really had believed that Jesus wouldn't die.

'That can't be right.'

I could hear the uncertainty in her voice. She looked over at Bartholomew.

'Will they kill him?' she asked.

Bartholomew gave only the briefest of nods in answer.

'Thank goodness my youngest is laying low, then.'

'Where is Izzy?' I had almost forgotten my brother. Then I realised I had completely forgotten about two other members of the family.

'And what about Josh and Dan?'

'No one knows where Izzy is.' I could hear the concern in Mother's voice. 'No one's seen him since he handed Jesus over to the authorities. And I've been too busy trying to save you to worry about your cousins. But you know what they're like, they'll be all right. They always are.'

The shock of Jesus' impending crucifixion had evidently not knocked my mother's optimism for her nephews. But I was inclined to agree with her. Josh and Dan were like cats. It didn't matter what height they were dropped from, they always ended up on their feet. But I was concerned about Izzy. I wanted to find my younger brother as I knew he would be vulnerable to the fury of Jesus' followers.

'I'm going to find Izzy,' I told the other two. Something within me told me that he needed me. At that moment I just did not realise how much.

CHAPTER THIRTY-SIX

AS I STARTED TO WALK away, Bartholomew reached out and took my arm.

'Just make sure that you look for him outside of the city.'

I had already decided the best places to look for someone in hiding was outside of Jerusalem, but it annoyed me that this stranger should think he could give me orders.

'What has any of this got to do with you?'

As I moved to square up to him Mother stepped in between us.

'Barabbas, Bartholomew has been good to you. It was his plan that got you out of that jail.' She hesitated for a moment before adding, 'He's been good to me as well. He's going to take me on as his housekeeper, and, if that works out, we may even get married.'

I had so much wanted to be a different person once I had been released from prison. Jesus had shown me how life could be different if only I would grab the opportunity. But that was before my mother had shown up. At that moment I could feel a familiar fury rising up again. I grabbed the front of Mother's dress and pulled her off the ground so that our faces were level.

'So, your son has gone missing, your nephews are languishing in prison, and you're moving in with a man you hardly know like some cheap woman?'

The words were accompanied by a spray of spittle Mother tried to blink away while trying to disguise her fear.

'Anyway,' I continued, 'how can any man marry a woman who continually bleeds?'

'Jesus healed me.' The words were said in no more than a whisper.

With a snort of contempt, I dropped Mother who staggered back into Bartholomew. It struck me that the man had done nothing to come to the defence of his 'housekeeper'. I decided that a man like that was exactly what she deserved.

I turned and walked away from the pair of them and away from Jerusalem. They did not try to stop me. As I put some distance between us, I could feel my temper coming back under control with every step I took. Striding off, I decided that Bartholomew was doing me a favour. If the jailor and Mother were married it would relieve me of the responsibility I had carried for what had seemed like an eternity. Bartholomew would have to cope with the woman.

Jesus had told me this was my opportunity to start something new and I was not going to let the chance slip through my fingers. But first I was going to find Izzy. He may have been a pain, but he was my brother and with Mother starting a new life there was an opportunity for us to do the same ourselves. Two brothers, buying back our family home with the money Izzy had got from the temple authorities. At that point I thought, mistakenly, that the two of us had a future together.

Then I heard an unfamiliar voice call out my name. I turned instinctively and saw the diminutive figure of Jericho Zac bustling his way over to me. I knew that the little man had hated me and the fact that I had twice avoided paying back my debts to him. I had no idea why he hated me as much as he did, but I was convinced that, at that precise moment, Zac was going to make it the third time lucky for him and would settle his score with me. That only meant trouble and so I turned back around and began to run.

As I ran off, I heard my enemy curse and begin to run himself. That gave me some hope, he hadn't called to any hired muscle which meant he was intending to confront me on his own. I was twice his size; I was at least twice as strong. If it was just me and him, he didn't stand a chance. I stopped running, turned, and waited for him to catch up to me. I was ready for the fight.

'Barabbas, finally you stopped; I would never have caught you.'

His friendly tone was almost more unsettling than the times when he had flown at me in a rage. Feeling particularly unnerved, I clenched my fist, ready to strike out if necessary.

'I've been looking for you for days,' he continued as he walked towards me. 'We have matters that need to be settled between us.'

So, I thought, this was to do with the debts. I knew I owed him more than I could ever repay and more than he would be able to sell me for as a slave. I shuddered as I considered how the little runt may intend for me to make any payments. But it didn't make any sense. He was alone, he did not stand a chance against me. What could he do?

'What matters?' I asked, trying to make sense of this confrontation.

He stopped where he was, just a few yards from me. He sighed and appeared to be considering what to say next.

'You really don't know, do you?' he shook his head.

'Know what?'

'Sit down,' he instructed as he settled himself on the ground. 'There's so much you need to know.'

Despite who this man was, I sat down. I was curious to know what he had to say. What didn't I know? Was it how much I owed him? Somehow, I didn't think that was what he was talking about.

'You don't remember me, do you?'

I was about to answer when he interrupted.

'Not from a few years ago, but from when we were younger.'

I knew I was looking at him blankly.

'No, I didn't think you did. That was one of the things that really annoyed me and drove me on. I worked with you and your family on the farm.'

Realisation started to dawn. It had never crossed my mind that we may have known each other in the past, but now my memories were stirring and it was all coming back to me.

'Yes,' I replied. 'Yes, I do remember now . . . hang on, it was you who told me that Izzy was back.'

'Yes,' he replied. 'Although he was Judas to me, only the family called him by his nickname. But, yes, I told you he was back, and you nearly killed me for it.'

I wasn't sure what to say. So, I said nothing and allowed him to continue.

'But I survived, although it didn't do me any good. Your father died, and your mother sacked me. She had always had it in for me. She treated me like I was pure rubbish. I hated her and her entire family for that. And so, I worked to destroy you all.'

I was shocked. 'To destroy us? How?'

'I stirred up problems with the people who traded with you. I besmeared your family's name. I made it so that no one would do business with you.'

I could see a fear taking over him. Here we were, sitting miles from anything and anybody and he was telling me that he had played a part in destroying the family business. I could hear the blood starting to pump in my ears and felt the red mist begin to descend.

'Wait, wait,' he pleaded as I shifted my position and began to get to my feet. 'There's more I have to tell you. You'll want to hear it. I guarantee it.'

I paused for a moment. My anger was telling me to react there and then, but I was also curious. I wanted to know what else Jericho Zac had to say. Looking back, I can't remember what I was expecting, but it certainly wasn't what I heard next. I settled myself back on the ground and he took that as his cue to resume his story.

The story he told me left me dumbfounded. I was amazed that I had been a victim of one man's hatred and been absolutely unaware of it. However, the whole situation with Reuben that now seemed so long ago finally made some sense. I had been set up, duped, and all because Zac had been badly treated by my family. If I hadn't felt enraged by his actions, I would almost have felt sorry for him carrying around so much hatred and living his life merely to try to take his revenge on someone who had completely forgotten he even existed.

I might have felt sorry for him, but I was too angry, too engulfed with fury. As soon as he finished describing his scheme, I lunged at him. I had wanted to be a different person after being with Jesus in that prison cell but that was before.

Now I wanted to kill the pathetic little man in front me and there was nothing and nobody that would stop me.

CHAPTER THIRTY-SEVEN

MY ENCOUNTER WITH JERICHO ZAC had left me shaken. When he had first caught up with me I could not have imagined how our conversation was going to end and now that it had ended I was desperate to find Izzy. It was the only thing that mattered.

As I trudged over the uneven ground I wished I hadn't been so hasty in leaving Jerusalem. After all that had happened, I really did not feel like eating but my stomach was growling with hunger. Three small fishes had hardly constituted a big enough breakfast that morning and the weight of my legs as I walked told me I could have done with the energy more food would have brought me. If I had stayed in the city I could have gotten some food before leaving. As it was, I faced about an hour's walk to the nearest village on an empty stomach although that could prove to be longer if I didn't manage to avoid twisting an ankle in the divots which I was struggling to see in the gloom.

I suddenly stopped walking. My mother, Jericho Zac, my desperation to find Izzy, and my complete confusion about the future had dulled my common sense. It was gloomy. I couldn't be sure of the time, but I knew breakfast had passed, that the day had progressed enough for there to be a crowd outside of Pilate's palace, and that time had moved on since then. I reckoned it could not be far off noon. With it being spring, the day should be bright and light. So why was it dark like late evening?

The only thing I could think of to explain it at the time was that it signalled the start of a huge storm. I set off again, wanting to get to a village and shelter before it started so that I could organise my search for Izzy without being soaked to the skin. I found my way onto a road hoping the village it led to would have hospitable residents. As I walked, the need to relieve myself had me searching for an area to do so. I came upon a row of bushes that appeared to mark out a privately-owned field. I wasn't bothered that I was probably trespassing, so I went around behind one of the bushes.

Once I had finished I turned around wondering what field I was in. It was not agricultural; the ground was no more than a waste land with a couple of trees in the far corner. I looked at the trees and squinted. In the unnatural darkness of the day it was hard to be certain, but it looked like something was suspended from one the branches. I knew I should make my way to the nearest village before the inevitable rain came, but I thought it would not take me long to see what the shape was.

I walked across the field trying to make out what was hanging there. I was less than half way across before I was certain it was the body of a man. With each following step the hairs on the back of my neck started to rise. My stomach churned, and, although I dreaded what I was going to encounter, I broke into a run across the final few yards.

Even in the gloom I could make out the body of my brother hanging from one of the branches. There was a bloody mess on his clothing and a pile of gore on the ground a few inches below Izzy's dangling feet. The smell, as I half ran and half stumbled towards the scene, was worse than any prison cell I had ever been in. My brother had always been shorter than me, but now, as Izzy hung from the tree, our eyes were level. Mine were full of misery and sorrow, only death stared back from his.

I untied him and gently lowered him onto the floor. Sitting down I cradled my brother's head in my arms and softly sobbed.

I looked at Izzy's face which was frozen in a look of hopelessness and pain. The body was icy cold and smelt of rotting flesh, but I did not care. I had a pain in my chest and I could hardly catch my breath. Tears flowed as my sobbing became uncontrollable. This was not how it was meant to be. Yesterday I had convinced myself that I should have killed Izzy all those years ago, but the reality of my pain-in-the-neck-brother's death put all such thoughts out of my mind. This was a sadness I had never experienced before and, in amongst the grief, it frightened me. This was my fault. For me it was inconceivable that I should live and my poor hapless brother should die.

As my initial raw emotions began to ebb I knew I would have to return to Jerusalem to tell Mother. The thought terrified me – it was not something I felt qualified to do. Instinctively my mind began to think of things to do before going back. First of all, I had to decide what to do with Izzy's body.

I stood up and looked around. The ground was pitted but soft enough to dig a grave for Izzy but I had nothing to dig with. Interment was out of the question, so I had to think of something else. I knew I had to act quickly because the smell of Izzy's rotting body would soon attract wild animals who would devour it. That would have solved the problem of what to do with the corpse, but I was determined my brother's mortal remains would not finish as wild dog meat.

Then I remembered a place called Golgotha. It was a rock face not far from where I was which the locals said looked like a skull. Consequently, the small caves within it were often used as tombs by the people in the area who could not afford their own private resting places. Izzy, as a suicidal death, should not be buried with those who had died of natural causes, but I was certain I could carry the body up to Golgotha and not be spotted by anyone – especially with the unnatural gloom which was shrouding the entire day.

I gently picked up the body and began walking unsteadily over the uneven terrain. I looked back at the spot where Izzy had killed himself. There was still the blood and gore on ground and it irked me that the animals would feast even on that, but I knew there was nothing I could do about it.

My initial sorrow had receded. Now I had a sense of purpose in laying Izzy to rest. Everything I had ever done for him in the past had always been done grudgingly but not this. If I allowed myself, I knew I could be overcome with a sense of guilt that all this was my fault. But that would do no good.

What was done was done and now I had to ensure my brother's remains were looked after.

As I made my way towards Golgotha I was aware of a crowd of people a little way on gathering around a crucifixion site. There were three crosses as far as I could see, and I wondered if one of them had Jesus nailed to it. Izzy would have been distraught if he had thought his betrayal would lead to his hero's death. In that respect it was as well that he had not lived to see the outcome of his actions.

As I carried Izzy's body my body grew steadily weaker. The dead weight in my arms was getting harder to carry and a couple of times I almost dropped him. But sheer grit and a brotherly determination drove me on until at last I reached one of the public tombs. I put Izzy down in front of a cave whose entrance had been sealed by a large stone. I sat down and rested, exhaustion and hunger had left me sapped of any strength. I knew I needed to eat but there was nothing edible in this place and so I decided to get this job done and then find something to eat.

I used the last of my remaining strength by putting my shoulder to the stone and pushing it out of the way. It took several attempts before it finally shifted and, when it did, I was almost knocked over by the stench that assaulted my nostrils. Some of the bodies in the cave had obviously been there only a few days and their putrid stink was at its worst. I gagged as I picked up my brother and carried him into the blackness of a cave engulfed by death.

There was nowhere specific to lay his body, so I laid him in a small nook near the entrance. Ideally, I would have liked to have placed the body further back in the cave to avoid the likelihood of the grave interloper being discovered, but the smell and atmosphere of the place meant that was never going to happen.

As quickly as I could I stepped back outside and struggled to put the stone back across the entrance. Once it was in place, I sat with my back against it. I had never given God much of a thought in my life and I was surprised to find that it crossed my mind to offer up a prayer, but I did not know any and the inclination soon passed.

Instead I stood up and set off away from the caves hoping that eventually I would lose the stench of death that had seemed to engulf me.

The gloom of the afternoon continued to perplex me. However, the darkness meant people still had candles burning in their homes and I could see a small hamlet of houses within walking distance of Golgotha. The only problem was the most direct route to it, and, in my drained condition, the only one I was going to take, took me right past the crucifixion site I had seen earlier.

If one of the victims was Jesus I knew I would rather not see the man suffering the agonies of death when it should have been happening to me. So I headed off with my head down, hoping the three crosses I could see held complete strangers.

There was the usual gaggle of onlookers which any execution generates. I had never understood the fascination in watching men die and, no matter what crime they had committed, I thought the people who stood around, drawn by their death, committed an offence far worse than any which were criminalised by the law.

However, this crowd looked different from the usual motley crew. There were representatives from the temple dressed in their finery as well as poor peasants, both men and women. As I got nearer I was able to make out the people's faces in the gloom that had gradually developed into a darkness like night.

As the women's faces came into focus my stomach lurched. Mother was among the group. Tears stained her cheeks and sorrow pierced her eyes. This was not what I wanted. I was certain now that I was approaching a cross which held Jesus, but I was more concerned at encountering my mother at this moment. She was clearly already distraught at what she was witnessing, so how would she react to the additional news that her youngest son was dead?

I had wanted to put this moment off, but I was going to have to face it sooner than I wanted to. But I wasn't ready and for a fleeting moment I wondered if it might have been easier to have been crucified myself. But that was nonsense. The wailing of the men on the crosses told me they were experiencing an agony I couldn't have begun to imagine.

I slowed my walk, hoping that it would give me time to compose my thoughts before I got to Mother. Then my attention was taken by the woman standing next to her. It was Naomi. A rush of emotions coursed through me. Despite everything I was going through, I was delighted to see her but mortified as well. It was too much, this encounter was not going to happen. I would find another path to take and somewhere else to get some food. I turned to walk away.

'Barabbas!'

It was Mother's voice, and it pinned me to the spot.

'Barabbas, isn't it awful when it's family.'

Relief swept through me. I was not going to have to tell her about Izzy. Someone else had obviously done the job for me. This was still going to be bad – I knew I would still have to face the recriminations and accusations and I needed to speak to her about Jericho Zac – but at least it would not be my job to tell Mother that Izzy was dead.

'Yes, Mother, it is,' I said before realising she was no longer looking at me.

Her attention had turned towards the three crosses. They stood just a little higher than an average man which meant that, for someone as tall as me, my eyes were level with the crosses' victims, just as Izzy's had been as he hung from the tree. On the middle cross, which was made of rough wood and soaked in blood, was Jesus. His eyes met mine. I looked deep into those eyes and saw such sorrow and pain that I could almost feel it myself. Jesus' drawn face seemed to change slightly as if to acknowledge my presence. Overcome with guilt, I looked away and glanced at the two crosses on either side.

My breath caught in my throat at what I saw.

CHAPTER THIRTY-EIGHT

HIS ENCOUNTER WITH BARABBAS DID not go the way Zacchaeus had thought it would.

He was amazed when the big guy had run away when he had called out to him. Zacchaeus had spent a lot of his adult life knowing that he was feared by people, but it had only been since his encounter with Jesus that he really noticed it. He had decided that it was utterly ridiculous, he was just a small man, living a small life chasing money. However, at the point that he called out to Barabbas, he could still invoke that fear in people and the man he was after had turned tail and run.

It had infuriated him. Didn't the man realise that he had the strength to beat him to a pulp? But then that realisation had obviously dawned on Barabbas as he suddenly stopped running and turned to face Zacchaeus and allowed his pursuer to speak.

That was when Zacchaeus got his second surprise. Barabbas really had not realised who he was. It had taken far more explaining than he had expected for Barabbas to remember him from their time together on the farm all those years ago. But eventually recognition had come, and, as Zacchaeus continued his story, he began to realise the danger he had placed himself in. He could see the red mist descending on the other man as he described how he had destroyed the family by ruining their business, conning them of money, and leaving them saddled with debts they could never pay.

At the moment Barabbas lunged for him with his face a mask of fury, Zacchaeus was certain he was going to die. He felt the colour draining from his face as two huge hands connected around his throat. He had only one last hope, so he struggled to free his wind pipe enough to call out.

'We're related!'

Time froze. Zacchaeus could only hear his pulse beating as the world stood still. Barabbas seemed to be looking at him but there was a blankness in his eyes.

'How?' he asked as he released Zacchaeus from his grip.

Rubbing his neck as his struggled to take back control of his breathing, Zacchaeus backed away from his assailant, looking to put some space between him and Barabbas. He knew that what he had said was not completely accurate but wanting to save his life had made him desperate.

'I swear, I did not know,' he said. 'It was Jesus who told me.'

To Zacchaeus' amazement Barabbas laughed.

'Of course, he did.'

With that Barabbas sat back down again. 'Well, you'd better tell me what he said.'

Zacchaeus was uncertain what this reaction signalled, but he decided to follow the instructions he had been given and hoped that he would get away with his stretching of the truth.

'One of the things that made me follow Jesus was the fact that He told me things about me that I didn't even know myself. I had never known who my parents were, but Jesus was able to tell me and what He said made so much sense that my life started to take a new shape.'

Zacchaeus could sense Barabbas getting impatient, so he decided to cut to the main details that would be of interest to his listener.

'My mother was your father's sister.'

'My father's sister? Who was that?'

As Jesus had also told him about Barabbas' parentage, Zacchaeus knew that he was on shaky ground here, but he decided to push ahead with his explanation.

'I'm talking about Simon, the owner of your family's farm. His sister was my mother.'

'He wasn't my father. We're not related at all.' Barabbas' tone made it difficult to tell whether this was going to be a problem. Zacchaeus decided to continue and adopted a conciliatory tone.

'Okay, but you can't dispute that I am your half-brother's cousin.'

Zacchaeus paused. Barabbas said nothing and sat where he was.

'So, we may not be blood relations,' Zacchaeus continued, 'but we do have family connections. Close family connections.'

Barabbas grunted, which Zacchaeus took to be an agreement and a prompt for him to carry on with his story.

'So, my mother was Simon's sister. While her brother, the man who raised you, was seen as a pillar of the community and a man of upstanding morals, my mother was a woman of ill repute. She was after almost any man she saw, and she got most of them it would appear. My father was the son of a merchant who stopped to do business with my grandfather. The two slept together and I was the result, although by the time my mother knew she was pregnant the man was miles away and never heard of again.

'At first your mother was good to mine. She thought that my mother had been raped and told her about her own attack. Of course, she had no idea what sort of a woman she was. When she discovered that my mother had been a willing participant she was horrified at the shame my birth would bring to the family. But my mother told Simon about how you had been conceived. Before that he had no idea. Jesus said, it was at that point his feelings towards you changed. From then on your mother hated mine.'

Zacchaeus paused for breath.

'So, Jesus knew about me and my mother's rape?' Barabbas asked bewildered by this deluge of information.

'Jesus knows so much,' Zacchaeus confirmed. 'He knew that my mother had been sent away to stay with a distant cousin before her pregnancy became obvious to the outside world. He also knew that she died shortly after I was born.

'At that point, your mother was all for me staying far away and being forgotten about. But Simon would not hear of it. He insisted that I be brought back to the farm and raised there. He agreed that my identity would be kept secret, even from me, but he was determined to play a part in raising me.'

Zacchaeus saw the realisation dawn in Barabbas' eyes. Suddenly the harsh treatment Barabbas had received from Simon made sense, as did Simon's preferential treatment of Zacchaeus.

'When you father died,' Zacchaeus added, 'your mother wanted me off the farm as soon as possible. I guess I was a reminder of the shame my mother had brought to the family and to the revealing of her attack that had soured her relationship with her husband. Now, looking back and with the benefit of this knowledge, I can understand it. But at the time I was enraged and spent too many subsequent years trying to exact my revenge. I realise now what a waste of a life that has been. It's why I wanted to start to change, to focus my life on helping others rather than destroying them for my own amusement – which never amused me in the end anyway.'

Barabbas put his head in his hands, and, with the tips of his fingers, began massaging his forehead. After a few moments, he took his hands away and looked Zacchaeus directly in the eyes and all the fury and impatience he had felt was gone.

'What a pointless mess,' he said. 'It's all so pointless.'

'You're right,' Zacchaeus had agreed. 'It is. But, Barabbas, I want to put things right. I want people to live full lives. That's why I gave away so much money after Jesus' visit. That's why I wanted to find you. I want to put things right.'

'But how?' Barabbas asked. 'How can we put things right after so many years?'

'I can start by giving you back your farm.'

'The farm?'

'Yes, part of my plan to ruin you included me buying the old farm. It was a waste of money, but I could afford it and I had plenty of bigger estates in my ownership. So, I bought it and then forgot I even had it. It's not been farmed for years and has just laid there as waste ground, but it's yours again. I've done all the necessary legal work to put it in your name. All you have to do is go and claim it.'

Barabbas was dumbstruck. So much of his life had been spent wanting to get the farm back. To make amends for the wrong he had done in killing the man who raised him. All of those efforts had been in vain as he failed time and again to bring any sort of redemption for his actions. And now he had been offered all that he had ever wanted from a man who had previously only been his enemy.

'Well,' Zacchaeus asked, 'do you want it?'

Barabbas didn't initially know what to say.

'Yes, yes I do,' he managed after a couple of moments. 'Thank you.'

CHAPTER THIRTY-NINE

I STRUGGLED TO TAKE IN the scene in front of me. Jesus was nailed to the central cross with Josh and Dan on their own crosses on either side. I could not believe that they were there enduring their own agony for the crimes they had committed with me as I stood there a free man. All I could do was stare.

Earlier that day, after my encounter with Jericho Zac, I had plans for me, for Izzy and for my two cousins. Izzy was already dead, and Josh and Dan would be joining him once their agony was over. I knew that could take a long time. I also knew I should be with them. I knew I should have been on that central cross, but Jesus was there instead. And at that moment I realised that he had chosen to be there. I know my mother thought that she and her new man had planned it, but Jesus was clever enough to have gotten himself off any charges that had been brought against him. But he hadn't and, for reasons that I could not understand as I stood there, I realised that he had chosen to die.

My attention was taken by the sound of Josh speaking. Any words spoken while on a cross increased the pain the man suffered, but Josh was managing to speak through his pain and, even in the darkness, I could see anger etched into his face.

'What a scumbag! You can't even save yourself. We wouldn't even be in Jerusalem if it wasn't for you, Jesus.'

'Will you shut up.' I was surprised when Dan interrupted the verbal onslaught. 'We've been evil all our lives, but Jesus has done nothing to deserve this.'

I watched mesmerised as Dan struggled to catch his breath. Every movement he made brought with it new levels of pain to his tortured body, but it appeared that he was determined to say more.

'Jesus, remember me when You get Your kingdom.'

I wasn't sure if Dan's words were meant sarcastically or if he had become delirious in his agony. There was not going to be any kingdom for Jesus, the man looked even closer to his final breath than Dan, but then he looked up and turned his head to face Dan. With a supreme effort Jesus spoke.

'I tell you the truth,' he gasped, his voice no more than a whisper, 'today you'll be with Me in paradise.'

'You lying pig,' Josh's voice sounded out with far more strength than the other two had spoken. That was not good for him, it meant he was taking longer to die. 'If this is paradise I'm not looking forward to hell.'

This time it was Josh's turn to wriggle his body to try and take in more air. As he did so he turned and saw me.

'You're a piece of work, aren't you?' he spat, still consumed by hatred. 'Me and Dan are nailed here and you're walking around free.' He shook his head. 'How do you live with yourself, Barabbas? It's your fault we're here. You're to blame for all of this.'

A sudden intake of breath stopped Josh's outburst as his pain ratcheted up to a new level. He panted like a woman in labour as he sought to bring the agonies he was experiencing back under control. With a scream he let rip a string of obscenities aimed at me as I stood just a few feet away. I did not know how to respond.

Looking away I realised that all the people who had gathered to witness the execution had turned their attention towards me – Mother, Naomi, Mary and Martha, and other women I recognised as followers of Jesus. Standing just behind them was one of Zebedee's sons. Was it John? I found it hard to make out his face in the pitch darkness that seemed to have replaced the previous gloom. The Roman guards, sensing the potential for trouble took a few paces towards me and I recognised one of the soldiers who had taken me to Pilate's palace the previous day.

Still the screaming insults were being hurled at me by Josh. As the Romans approached, I glanced over the soldier's shoulder and found myself looking Jesus straight in the eye. Ironically, I struggled to breath as I looked at the man who was dying in my place. Fatigue, hunger, and panic took over. I turned to run away but my head started buzzing and the world around me swam. I think I lost consciousness before I even hit the ground.

The impact of the fall roused me from my faint, although nausea and dizziness left me feeling disorientated and only vaguely aware of what was happening.

Two pairs of hands reached down to help me up. I was grateful for their assistance and pleased when I realised they belonged not to Roman soldiers but, instead, to Mother and Naomi.

The next few minutes were a blur as I was gently shepherded away from the verbal abuse raining down on me from one of the crosses and towards the wall that surrounded Jerusalem. I wanted to protest and take control of myself, but all my strength had drained away. I meekly allowed the two women to lead me into the city and to a house in the poor part of town.

As Naomi guided me towards some bedding on the floor, I was vaguely aware of Mother arguing with a man who was already in the house. I could not make out the words that were being shouted and, at that point, I was not interested in what the row was about. I was only gratefully that I could lay my head down and go to sleep.

* * * * * *

The sunshine was struggling through the shutters that covered a small window telling me I had slept through the night as well as the previous day's afternoon. I stretched as I woke and looked around. I heard my mother's snores before I saw her sleeping across the room in the far corner. Between the two of us there was another sleeping body, but I couldn't make out who it was. Looking closer I could see I was in a house that belonged to someone with very little money. It was a typical pauper's home, one room for sleeping, living, and eating in and its condition left much to be desired. As I was assessing the house my stomach started growling, prompting me to sit up and look for any signs of food.

My movement disturbed the sleeping body on the floor and I was surprised to see the familiar face – and body – of Naomi. She threw off her bed clothes as she registered that I was awake and came straight over to me. I admit to being disappointed that she was fully dressed. I still smiled as she approached and was about to say something when her own words cut across mine.

'Be quiet, your mother only got to sleep a little while ago.'

I raised my hands palms outwards in a gesture of surrender.

'I was surprised she didn't disturb you with her sobbing,' Naomi added in hushed tones.

'Was she crying over Izzy?' My intended whisper came out as a croak.

'Oh, so you know already. Yes, someone discovered his body in one of the communal graves.'

I cursed inwardly. I thought I had hidden Izzy's body well enough that it would not have been discovered so soon. I had even botched up my own brother's burial. Embarrassed, I looked away from Naomi.

'Had you put it there?' she guessed.

I nodded.

'I found him in a field. He had hung himself, poor sod, his bowels had dropped out of his body,' I whispered in reply, not wanting to chance my mother overhearing this part of the conversation.

'I'm sorry.'

We stood in silence for a moment. It was awkward, and I wanted to change the subject and stop thinking about my dead brother.

'Is this your house?' I asked.

'No, this is Bartholomew's house. Your mother and I brought you back here after you collapsed at the cross yesterday. He wasn't impressed – he kept saying you should be out of Jerusalem – but your mother insisted you had to stay here until you got your strength back.'

'Where is he now?'

'He went to work last night. Poor man, I think he was pleased to get away from your mother's grief.'

I had wanted to move the conversation on from Izzy's death, but curiosity got the better of me.

'Does she know it was suicide?'

'Yes. She didn't see his body, but she was told his injuries made it obvious what had happened. I guess the guilt of betraying Jesus was too much for him. Did you know he was going to do that?'

I so desperately wanted to lie, but I also knew that Izzy deserved some honesty. I silent nodded my head.

'But why did he do it?' There was pain and confusion behind the dark brown eyes that were looking so intently at me.

'The High Priest paid thirty silver coins–'

'Thirty?' Naomi was stunned.

'Yes, only thirty. I'd wanted sixty.'

As I spoke I realised that I had no idea what had happened to that money. Before I could give it any more thought, Naomi slapped me. I wasn't hurt, but I was stunned. Naomi stood before me, it seemed as if she was waiting for me to strike her back. When I didn't, she let out a barely audible sigh which sounded like the saddest noise I had ever heard.

'Why?' she asked as tears ran unrestrained down her cheeks.

'We lost a fortune when you poured that oil over Jesus and we wanted to get it back.' I paused waiting to see if Naomi would react to her part in the chain of events. When she remained silent I added, 'We never expected them to kill him, though.'

'No, but they did. A good man, a very good man died yesterday because of you.'

'You should have done more to get him set free.'

I hoped the rebuke would stop Naomi's accusations and deflect some of the blame away from me. However, I immediately saw that I had missed the mark as I was greeted only by a confused look.

'What do you mean?' she asked. 'How could we have got Jesus set free?'

'With the ceremony they held yesterday morning.'

Even as I said the words, I could see that Naomi had no idea what I was talking about. I sighed as I realised that the whole public vote had been a sham and that the followers of Jesus had not been told about it.

'The High Priest got Pilate to agree to release either me or Jesus depending on who the crowd shouted they wanted to be released. And they shouted for me. The stupid thing is I was as guilty as sin and Jesus was completely blameless.'

'But why would the High Priest want you to go free rather than Jesus?'

It was obvious that Naomi had no idea of my mother's history with Caiaphas. The question was whether I should tell her or not. I desperately wanted to. I wanted this woman to know who I was, why I behaved as I did, and how life had dealt me such a bad hand. But I also knew that if I did it could endanger her. The High Priest would not want his past sins known by others and if he thought some poverty stricken woman was aware of the type of person he was he would not hesitate to have her killed.

'Because he hated Jesus, I guess.'

I surprised myself by putting Naomi's welfare before my own preferences. Could this be what it meant to love someone? If it was, it was soon thrown back in my face.

'So, Jesus died in your place,' Naomi hissed in accusation still not wanting to wake Mother who was continuing to sleep across the room from us.

'But you can't blame me for that,' I insisted. 'He didn't say anything to defend himself. For someone who was so good with words, I don't understand it. He could easily have talked himself out of the trouble he was in. It was almost as if he chose to die.'

'Whomever's fault it was, it seems such a waste that He died. Let's be honest, how long will it be before you get arrested for one of the many other crimes you've committed in the past?'

'But that's the crazy thing, Naomi. When I was spared I was told that my whole slate had been wiped clean. No charges can be brought against me for anything I've done in the past.'

Suddenly the look on her face changed. All through our conversation she had been looking at me, but now it seemed as if she was looking into me – into my eyes and through on to my soul.

'So, Jesus died and as a result you get a whole new start in life.'

I didn't respond. What was there to say. Even to my selfish way of thinking I knew it was not fair. Jesus had infuriated me in the past, but he had done nothing that deserved the death penalty – unlike me. Naomi was right, yesterday had seen the end for Jesus and yet the start of something completely new for me and, of all the men Jesus had ever met, I was the least worthy to deserve this outcome. I still could not work out why Jesus had allowed it to happen, a few well-chosen words would have been all he would have needed for him to go free and for me to be nailed to a cross.

The thought of having nails driven through my hands and wrists caused me to remember again the healing Jesus had carried out on my injured hand. I could still remember the warmth that flowed from Jesus' touch. I wanted to tell Naomi about the experience, but the look of sorrow on her face told me now was not the time. I could not think of anything to say to the woman and so I looked away, my guilt and shame leaving me mute.

'Don't waste it, Barabbas. It's a new start for you.'

Those words again. It had been the last thing Jesus had said to me, and now Naomi was unknowingly echoing his words. This time, though, they were said with bitterness and recrimination.

Before I had the opportunity to reply, the front door opened and the owner of the house walked in, his night shift over.

'What are you still doing here?' Bartholomew asked.

A murmur from Mother took everyone's attention. The three of us glanced over to where she slept, each one of us holding our breath to see if Bartholomew's entrance had woken her. We each had our own reason to hope that she would not wake and we all let out a sigh of relief as, after a couple of lip smacks, the gentle snoring resumed.

Bartholomew slowly turned and quietly shut the front door. He softly stepped over to Naomi and me and resumed his conversation in a whisper.

'So? Why are you still here?'

'I've only just woken.'

'Well, now that you have you can get out – of this house and the city. I told you what Caiaphas said.'

'Caiaphas?' Both of us turned to Naomi who was evidently startled by the fact that the High Priest had any interest in a low-life criminal.

I didn't want her to know about my connection to the top man at the temple and I spoke quickly to avoid Bartholomew saying more than was necessary.

'Part of the terms of my release. I'm banished from the city. But I don't feel well enough to leave now Bartholomew. Let me stay for today and I'll leave at first light tomorrow. Don't worry I'll keep out of the way. No one will know that I'm here.'

But Bartholomew was not willing to play host to me.

'No, you go, and you go now.'

He moved back towards the door and opened it for his unwanted guest. I knew that I would now be fine to make the journey out of the city, but I was hungry and not as energetic as normal. The strain of the last few days had taken their toll, both emotionally and physically. I really did not want to leave the house at that moment. Then I was struck with inspiration which I knew would buy me some more time.

'Just let me wake my mother and say goodbye.'

CHAPTER FORTY

IT WAS VERY EARLY THE next morning when I wiped the sleep out of my eyes and left the house.

After I woke my mother the previous day she had cried some more over the death of her youngest son. I had wanted to tell her that I knew about Zacchaeus, that I had discovered more of our family's secrets, but it didn't seem to be the right time to do that. I surprised myself with my show of compassion, but I wasn't surprised when Mother didn't seem at all concerned about my impending departure. That evening we said our farewells with the understanding that I wouldn't wake her when I left.

Naomi was also sound asleep as I took a swig of ale just before opening the front door to the outside world. I would have liked to have woken her to say goodbye so that we could part as good friends at least. But I knew that was never going to happen.

I had been given a new start, but it was to be a new start without Naomi, without Mother, and without the brother and cousins I had entered Jerusalem with just one week earlier. I was amazed at how dramatically and permanently my life had changed in those seven days. As well as not telling Mother about Zacchaeus I also didn't tell her about the farm. I was looking forward to rebuilding it without her interference, but I desperately wished the others were there to share it with me. I shook my head as I silently closed the door of the house behind me – who would have thought I would miss Izzy, Josh, and Dan.

I was pleased I had woken and left before Bartholomew returned from his shift at the prison. He struck me as an odious creep, but if he was thinking of marrying my mother, I reckoned he also deserved some of my sympathy as well. But that sympathy did not extend to saying a final farewell to the man.

That was not the only reason I left the house so early. Before I made my way out of Jerusalem for the last time there was one other person I was desperate to see. And from the knowledge I had gained since being in the city, early in the morning was the time to meet him. I really did not know why I wanted to have this final confrontation. There was no need for it and, if it went dreadfully wrong I knew I could potentially face prison again. But I needed some form of closure and I was determined to get it regardless of the risks that I was only too aware of.

And so, as the sun was still only a hint on the horizon, I looked up again at the magnificent architecture of the temple with clammy hands and my heart in my throat. I joined a reasonably small queue of people who were also waiting to see the High Priest that morning. The sacrifices had not begun so the air was free of the smell of animal dung and cooking meat. The money changers were setting up their tables and life was just beginning to stir within the huge, ornate building.

There was a murmur of idle conversation within the queue and from what I could make out, none of it was about Jesus. I thought it was amazing that within such a short space of time the man who had caused such a scene within the temple just one week ago had been so quickly forgotten. I guessed that was only to be expected given that the man the people had hoped was going to be their new leader was now dead. Even to the most loyal of Jesus' followers it had to be obvious that he was not God's chosen one and that it was time to move on and look for the next would-be Messiah.

I still felt guilty about my part in the death of Jesus. I had never imagined betraying him to the temple authorities would result in his death. Or in the death of my brother and our cousins. Without realising what I was doing, I started rubbing my hands together as if I washing them; I think it must have been the growing tension I was experiencing as I reflected on all that had happened. Nothing had turned out as I expected and now I knew that I had no way of knowing how this morning's encounter with my biological father would turn out, but I knew that I would never forgive myself if I didn't at least try to see. I would face any consequences, even if it meant losing the farm or even my life. Only two days ago I had been given a new life. Now that life was on the line, but this was a meeting I had to have.

As well as being unable to keep my hands still, I was also struggling to keep my breathing even. I tried to convince myself that the risks I was taking were the sole cause of my nervousness. But I could not fool myself. For the first time in my life I was going to meet my biological father more than three decades after my birth. That doesn't happen to many people.

I was so lost in my thoughts that I barely noticed the progress I had made through the temple courtyards and into the room where the High Priest held his audiences. My attention returned to my surroundings, though, as the large door opposite where I was standing with the rest of the crowd opened and the High Priest and his entourage entered the room.

I could not take my eyes off the tall man who was the centre of everyone's attention. I was shocked at how similar we looked; it was no wonder he wanted me to leave the city. It would not take much for anyone to see the family resemblance. However, despite my stares, Caiaphas had not noticed me. He continued to make his way towards his chair, or should it be called his throne? Then, for a fleeting moment, his eyes met mine and my heart stopped as I waited to see what his reaction would be.

But there was none. There didn't appear to be any flicker of realisation. Caiaphas appeared to pay me no more attention than any other of the assembled crowd there. Then, much to the surprise of his attendants, he changed direction and walked towards a smaller door in the far corner of the room. He opened it himself, walked through and closed it firmly behind him.

The entourage who had entered into the room with him could not hide their surprise and confusion at the High Priest's actions. They stood, rooted to the spot, unsure how to respond to this unexpected change in the daily routine.

In what I could only describe later as a moment of madness, I decided to grasp the opportunity the indecision had created. I dashed towards the smaller door and, finding it unlocked, followed Caiaphas through it. I had taken only two steps before the temple guards sprang into action, but I had already slammed the door shut before they could catch up. I was grateful to find that I was able to secure the door from inside, preventing my pursuers from following me into the room. I continued to face the door as they hammered on the other side of it and I started to panic, wondering how easily they would be able to break it open.

Without any warning I felt a strong hand on my shoulder pulling me away from the door. I sprang around in surprise, only to be pushed to one side by Caiaphas who had obviously retained his strength despite his age and undoubtedly pampered life-style.

'Go away, I am safe!' the High Priest called out through the shut door.

The hammering stopped immediately.

'I will be out shortly,' Caiaphas continued. 'The people are to wait, and I will see them soon.'

The room we were in was small and poorly lit by a tiny window high up on the only external wall. The poor lighting only seemed to enforce an intimacy between us that I didn't think either of us wanted. Judging by its size, I guessed it had originally been built as a large store room but now it was empty. Caiaphas moved away from me and stood in the corner. It seemed to me that he was trying to put as much space between us as he could. But then I realised he expected me to follow him away from the door.

I followed my father wondering what was going to happen next and how much I would come to regret my impulsive action. As I came close to him, the High Priest gripped my shoulder, demonstrating that he was still a strong man. I knew that I was stronger than him but if he was armed, I knew I wouldn't stand a chance in any fight between us. Unsure what I should do next, I did nothing but wait for the older man to take the initiative.

'Why are you here?'

The question was whispered. Clearly Caiaphas did not want our conversation to be overheard by anyone else.

'I wanted to see my father.'

'I am not your father.'

I was about to contradict him but there was something in his tone that convinced me that he was telling the truth. As I tried to gather my thoughts together we stood in silence. Caiaphas was obviously waiting for me to respond before he went any further.

'Then who is?'

It came out as a whisper.

'I thought your mother would have told you.'

That was when it dawned on me. In any conversation I had had with my mother about my father she had never actually confirmed that it was the High Priest and I had never pressed her to confirm it. I had assumed we had been talking about Caiaphas in every conversation we had, but now I realised that she had been talking about someone else. But who?

Caiaphas smirked as he realised that he had the upper hand in this conversation.

'Well, well,' he said. 'So, you really don't know.'

His blue eyes seemed to sparkle in amusement. And that was when I realised that I had the opportunity to take control.

'No, I don't,' I answered. 'I thought it was you because we look so similar. Now, if you don't tell me, I will leave this room and announce to everyone outside that door that you are my father and with our resemblances in build and eyes, who is not going to believe me?'

'No one will when I instruct them to disregard your lies.' The response came with a lot of bravado, but I could tell he was rattled.

'You can tell them what you like, but once I've planted the seed of the idea in people's minds it will never go away. Your reputation will be ruined.'

I thought he was going to kill me. He lunged towards me and I thought I saw his hand reach for a weapon under his outer cloak. I stepped away and he missed me but I knew I had no chance against him if he was armed. I cursed my stupidity for not being better prepared. But then I realised that his arm had not gone for a weapon but that he was gathering up his robes to make sure he didn't trip over them. As the younger man, that gave me a chance. I stepped back towards him and wrapped my arm around his neck, crushing his wind pipe and preventing him from calling out to his guards outside.

'Now, you will tell me who my father is or, so help me, I will kill you.'

'My brother, my bother. My brother is your father,' he gasped as he struggled for air.

I let go and Caiaphas sunk to his knees panting for breath.

'Tell me,' I instructed him.

He looked at me and knew he was beaten. Rather than standing again, he turned around from his kneeling position and sat on the floor.

'It was my brother who attacked your mother,' he said. 'It brought shame to our family, but we thought that we had got away with it when your mother returned home from Jerusalem and my brother died shortly afterwards of a breathing disorder.

'But your mother never forgot and when you were arrested for your debts she came to see me. She told me that you bore such a family resemblance that if I didn't step in to save you she would reveal the shame and tell everyone about your parentage. That's why I acted. That's why I saved you again when you should have been crucified. I couldn't take the risk. The real power in Jerusalem rests with my father-in-law, Annas, and he would have removed me from my position for the disgrace.'

I looked at the man in front of me and instead of seeing the powerful high priest, I saw a man well past his prime, worn out with the effort of trying to keep his position. I almost pitied him. I knew what it was to suffer as a result of my brother's actions. And I also knew my brother had suffered even worse as a result of mine. Thinking of Izzy and his death spurred me on to try to make some atonement for his death.

'My brother, Izzy, well, you'd know him as Judas, killed himself.'

'I'm sorry to hear that,' Caiaphas replied as he rose to his feet. 'It must have been after he returned the silver coins to me.'

So that was what had happened to the money. Izzy's guilt must have led him to return it and Caiaphas had accepted the money back and allowed Izzy to go to his death. Now I wanted Caiaphas to die. I thought again about Jesus and the new start his death had given me. I was not going to waste it on this contemptible excuse for a man. The anger abated.

'I want the money Judas returned to you.'

I surprised myself at my response. Getting the money back had never been part of the plan. However, this was clearly what Caiaphas had been expecting and he chuckled.

'I should have realised, people like you are all the same. You face prison and execution, you see your hero and your brother die, and all you want is money.'

The High Priest continued to chuckle as he reached for a money bag which had been hidden from view under his cloak. But he abruptly stopped his laughter when I grabbed the bag and tore it from the belt it was attached to.

'I'll have it all,' I hissed. 'And then I'll keep out of Jerusalem and I'll never let on that I'm a child from your family.' Caiaphas opened his mouth to reply but I didn't give him the chance. 'And, believe me, if enough people saw us together they wouldn't need much convincing of my parentage.'

Caiaphas sighed in resignation and I could tell that he knew that the two of us looked too similar, especially with our matching blue eyes, for anyone to doubt any claims I could make.

'Make sure you stay out of this city. If I see you anywhere in its boundaries I will make sure that you are killed.'

Before I could answer both of us jumped as someone started hammering on the other side of the door. Caiaphas pushed past me and unlocked the door.

'What is it?' he asked, the authority and volume returning instantly to his voice. 'What do you want?'

A dishevelled temple guard stood on the other side of the door, panting hard having evidently run quite a distance to find the High Priest.

'It's Jesus,' he gasped, trying to catch his breath. 'His body's gone from the tomb and there are some people saying they've seen him alive!'

The temple descended into uproar. The name which nobody had been mentioning just a few minutes ago was now on everyone's lips again.

'What nonsense!' Caiaphas declared as he swept into the audience room and beckoned to his entourage to follow him through the other door into his private chambers.

'You come with me,' he bellowed at the messenger. 'And keep your mouth shut if you want to live. I won't have these kinds of lies spread around.'

As I watched him walk away, I took the opportunity to make my way out from the room and towards the temple's front door. I slipped the money bag under my clothing. I had no idea how much money was in it but, judging by its weight, it was considerably more than thirty pieces of silver.

I smiled as I encountered the sunshine outside and felt the warmth on my face. I wondered what the story was with Jesus. I knew he was dead and, despite what some people said, dead people did not come back to life. I also knew that Jesus' death had given me a new start in life that had been helped by Zacchaeus returning the family farm to me. It dawned on me that I actually didn't need all the money I had taken. I decided I would find the man who owned the field Izzy had died in. I would buy and keep it as a memorial to my brother.

I made my way towards the main gate of Jerusalem wondering how I would locate the field's current owner. Before I left the city, I briefly looked around, knowing that I would never return. Perhaps I might eventually hear on the grapevine who had taken Jesus' body, but I would not be holding my breath waiting to hear. A new and better life was there to be lived, away from the memories of the last week.

I laughed out loud. I had a feeling today was not going to be a good day for Caiaphas, but it was only what the scumbag deserved.

EPILOGUE

It was an unusual view which greeted me as I made my way down to the shore of the Sea of Galilee.

Rubbing the sleep out of my eyes, I watched the boat change direction, setting back out to sea as the sun rose over the picturesque seaside scene. I was going down to the water's edge to meet the boat's exhausted crew and help them bring their nets in after a night of fishing. I had never known a time when a boat's route back to the shore had been cut short because the boat had set out again for the deeper water. Even when nothing had been caught, the crew would curse their bad luck but still head back to their homes and some sleep.

Personally, I was never bothered whether the fishermen had enjoyed any success as there were still bound to be nets to mend and other work to do to prepare the boat for the next fishing expedition. When I had left Jerusalem, I went back to the old family farm, but, without my family there, it was just another plot of land. I realised that my wanting the farm in order to put things right with my family only worked if my family were with me – and they, much to my sorrow, were not with me.

So, I sold the land and returned to Capernaum with the money. I was rich enough to be able to buy a home and still had enough money that I did not have to work full time. I went back to working casually for Zebedee on his fishing boats.

I probably could have gotten by without the work but needed the activity in order to deal with the loneliness I felt. I was amazed at how much I missed Izzy, Josh, and Dan considering how often I had complained about them. I even had times when I missed Mother, but that never lasted long. Perhaps I felt differently because she was still alive in Jerusalem. But the loss I still felt for the other three was enough to keep me awake at night when guilt and recriminations took siege of my thoughts.

Fortunately, there was no one in the village who knew in any great detail what had happened during the Passover. That was until two weeks earlier when Zebedee's sons, James and John, had themselves returned from Jerusalem. They had been very close followers of Jesus and I had been concerned that they would cause me trouble given the involvement Izzy and I had in their friend's death. But as I braced myself for my luck to turn bad again, I was amazed to find the two brothers were not in the slightest bit interested in me or what I was doing.

My surprise at their behaviour turned to amazement when I heard the story they had come back with from the city. James and John, and other Jesus followers, were telling everyone that Jesus had returned from the dead and was fit and alive! I had been at the temple when the guard had brought that news to the authorities, but I had thought it was just a piece of wild gossip that would be forgotten after a couple of days.

At first everyone in the village had been excited by the incredible news, but over the past few days the yarn was wearing thin. The brothers and the rest of them had returned, but there was no sign of Jesus. In fact, there had been only a few of his most loyal friends who claimed to have seen him. There was no doubt Jesus' body was missing, but for a man who had made a point of speaking to thousands of people while he was alive, it did not make any sense that since his return from the grave he had made himself known to only a handful of people.

There was no animosity towards those who had made the claim. People pitied their obvious grief-fuelled delusions. I had been surprised to find I shared that feeling of pity. It was not an emotion I could remember feeling in the past. A few weeks ago, I would have been annoyed and irritated by the ridiculous words of James and John but now I felt I understood their grief and hoped that their imaginations were helping them to cope.

My attention was caught by the sight of a fire burning just along the beach. The morning air was still fresh, so I made my way towards it hoping that it would help to keep me warm while I worked out what was happening with the boats. As I approached the fire, though, I realised that it was a small affair, but as it was the boat belonging to James and John which had set out to sea again, I thought the fire's meagre heat was better than nothing while I waited for its return.

There was no one tending to the flames. I guessed that its maker must have gone looking for some more driftwood to build it up. I hoped the wood would prove to be drier than that which was currently burning as it was generating a disproportionate amount of smoke for such a small bundle of sticks.

Coughing as I inhaled another lungful of smoke, I turned away from the fire, rubbing the ash out of my eyes. I looked across the water and saw the boat putting its nets out again.

'What are they doing?' I spoke aloud, but only to myself. 'Why are they fishing now when they've been out all night?'

'They didn't catch anything.'

The voice took me by surprise. The fire's owner had returned. I turned to look at him, but I couldn't see past the plumes of smoke. The new driftwood was obviously no drier than the original.

'How do you know that?' I asked as my eyes began to stream. I took a step back from the heat I had desired just a few moments before.

'They told me as they were approaching the shore. So, I told them to go out and have another go.'

I was suddenly aware of the smell of cooking fish. I guessed they must have been put into the flames. Obviously my newly found companion had enjoyed more success in catching some fish than those men on the boat. I wondered who the man on the other side of the smoke and flames was. His voice sounded familiar, the accent was certainly local, but I could not work out who could convince a tired crew of disappointed and fishless fishermen to go back out to sea at the end of their shift. Perhaps it was another of Zebedee's relatives, someone whose word carried authority.

The smoke was beginning to clear, but before I had the chance to look across and see who the voice belonged to, my attention was taken by movement from the boat. Even from a distance, I could see the crew frantically signalling to the other boats which Zebedee owned to come over and help them. Their luck must have changed; they had evidently caught such a huge haul of fish that they couldn't handle it all.

'Looks like they've got a good catch,' I said turning to look at the man who was bending over towards the flames, tending to the fish he was cooking. 'You were right.'

'I always am.'

Jesus straightened up and looked directly at me.

My stomach somersaulted, and the blood drained from my face. I stood, opened-mouthed struggling to put some order to my thoughts.

'It's normally at this point that you ask if I'm a ghost.' Jesus smiled and pronged a fish with a stick. He pulled it out of the fire and took a bite. 'But, as you can see,' he said between chews, 'I've too much of an appetite to be a ghost.'

I was unable to say anything. I had heard James and John and the others insisting that Jesus had come back from the dead, but I had put it down to a mixture of grief and wishful thinking. But now the reality was standing opposite me eating his breakfast. As I watched him, Jesus stretched his arm out over the fire and offered me the stick with the fish on the end of it.

'Do you want any?' Jesus asked.

I could do no more than shake my head in disbelief. Finally, my thoughts and emotions calmed down enough for me to ask a single word question.

'How?'

In reply Jesus did no more than raise a quizzical eyebrow.

'How are you alive?' I was starting to raise my voice in a combination of anger and confusion. 'I saw you die. How can you be alive?'

'The simple answer is God raised me back to life,' Jesus replied.

'But why?' My initial fear was giving way to confusion as I struggled to take in the reality of what my eyes were seeing.

'So that I can do for other people what I did for you.'

I knew my mouth was opening and closing but not a sound was coming out. Jesus appeared to take this reaction as his cue to continue his explanation.

'You see,' he continued, 'you were given a brand-new start in life because of me, Barabbas. You had all your debts with Zacchaeus and Jairus cancelled because of what I did and, because I died in your place, you escaped the punishment you deserved and could start your life all over again as if you had never done anything wrong.

'Now that I have come back from death, I can offer that new start to everyone. If people believe in me, they have a new opportunity in life, just like you've had.'

I couldn't understand how Jesus could do for everyone what he had done for me. But I guessed that, if Jesus could come back from the dead then anything was possible. Then I remembered Jesus' words as I had left our shared prison cell.

'You told me not to waste the new start you'd given me.'

'And I hope you haven't,' Jesus replied. 'Now take the fish and have something to eat.'

I realised that Jesus' arm was still outstretched, offering me the fish on a stick. Without really wanting it, I took the offered food and put it in my mouth.

'So,' said Jesus as I chewed on my mouthful, 'what have you done with yourself since you left Jerusalem?'

'I've bought myself a new home and have tried to settle down.'

'I had hoped for so much more for you.'

I was stunned. Jesus knew the part I had played in his agony and death. Surely, he should have wanted only bad luck and misery to befall me. But I could see in Jesus' eyes the sincerity of his words. This man really did want the best for me.

'What else can I do?' I asked wondering what those hopes of Jesus were.

'Sell your home and leave here. Go back to Bethany and to Lazarus and his sisters' house. Tell them you've seen me and that I've told you to stay with them.

'It won't be long now before my followers are going to be joining together and letting everyone know what happened at Passover and about the teaching that I've given. Once that process starts people like you are going to be travelling all over the world spreading the good news of what I can do for people. I want you to be a part of that.'

Excitement started to build within me. This was going to be something exciting, worthwhile, and new to do. But then reality hit.

'Me?' I questioned. 'I've never brought anything but fear, horror, and regret to other people. How can you expect me to know how to tell people your good news?'

'Because all you'll have to do is tell them what I did for you – you'll be speaking from first-hand experience.'

I could hardly believe my life could change so dramatically, yet again, in such a brief period of time. But that always had been my experience whenever I had encountered Jesus. So perhaps this born-again man had a point. Perhaps all I had to do was tell people about what had happened to me.

'Are you going to have breakfast with the others?'

Jesus interrupted my thoughts and I saw that the boat had made it to shore and that some of Jesus' followers were speedily making their way up the beach towards us.

I looked at the approaching group. Then I looked at Jesus.

'No thanks,' I said. 'I've got a house to sell and somewhere else to be.'

AUTHOR'S NOTE

SON OF THE FATHER IS a work of fiction based around real people and biblical events from 2,000 years ago. It is not, though, an historical record. I have utilised a novelist's artistic licence to create fictional events as well as relationships, conversations, and back stories for individuals who may only feature in one or two Bible verses.

However, there is one truth that runs throughout the fiction. It is that, regardless of what a person may have done, how many mistakes they may have made, and how many times they tried to put things right, they can always be saved from their situation, and if necessary themselves, by Jesus Christ. No one is beyond His redeeming grace.

I am very grateful that the team at Ambassador International have allowed me to tell that truth and this story through them. I'd particularly like to thank my editor, Daphne Self, for all the work she has done in improving my initial manuscript and Hannah Nichols who was so diligent and accommodating in the design of the book.

I also want to thank my wife, Alison, for the encouragement she gave me and the suggestions she made when I first started to create this story. I should also mention my sons Matt, Luke, and Ben, who, throughout the time it has taken me to complete this project, would regularly prompt me with the question: 'Dad, how's your book coming along?' Boys, you now have your answer.

For more information about
Andrew Stone
and
Son of the Father
please visit:

www.facebook.com/author.andrewstone

For more information about
AMBASSADOR INTERNATIONAL
please visit:

www.ambassador-international.com
@AmbassadorIntl
www.facebook.com/AmbassadorIntl

If you enjoyed this book, please consider leaving us a review on Amazon, Goodreads, or our website.

CPSIA information can be obtained
at www.ICGtesting.com
Printed in the USA
LVHW011528010620
657133LV00033B/2003